CAMBIUM
and the life of
Lanagan Murphy

Chris Grayling

PublishingWorks, Inc.
Exeter, NH
2008

Copyright © 2008 by Chris Grayling.

All rights reserved. No part of this book may be reproduced or transmitted in any form or by any means, electronic or mechanical, including photocopying, recording, or by an information storage and retrieval system—except by a reviewer who may quote brief passages in a review to be printed in a magazine or newspaper—without permission in writing from the publisher.

PublishingWorks, Inc.,
60 Winter Street
Exeter, NH 03833
603-778-9883
For Sales and Orders:
1-800-738-6603 or 603-772-7200

Designed by: K. Mack
LCCN: 2008925795
ISBN: 1-933002-79-4
ISBN-13: 978-1-933002-79-8

This book is
DEDICATED
To

All the animals who have enriched my life
by sharing their lessons, their lives,
and their love with me.

And To

My parents, who always welcomed these
precious creatures into our home when
I was a child (and even therafter).

CHAPTER ONE

"Come on, come on," she urged, as she looked back over her shoulder. "We'll be starting in two minutes. You mustn't be late! Don't dilly-dally! Come on, come on. Hurry."

"What a worry wart, that one," whispered a calmer onlooker under her breath. "Hasn't she realized by now that all her fussing won't make us walk any faster? Most of us totally ignore her."

Some, however, did walk more hurriedly than others. They had all attended meetings like this before, countless times, and all would attend countless more in the future, without question.

It was a diverse crowd, as would be expected. Some were tall and stood heads above the others and some were quite tiny. Some were muscular and rugged, with broad shoulders and square jaws. Others were lanky and lean, with very delicate, tapered features. Some were fair, some were dark, and many showed mixtures of two or more colors. There were certainly many shades represented in the large group, as well as several countries of origin. Yes, it was a diverse crowd indeed.

They arrived from the snow-covered territories and they arrived from the hot, dry regions. Some traveled in groups, some traveled in pairs, and others walked alone. Actually, no one was really alone here. Still, they all came. From far and wide and from nearby, they came.

It was common to see the small ones and young ones being carried by the larger, older ones. Here, all were welcome and every age was represented—age in a very unique sense of the word. Here, age did not really exist. Here, things were quite different.

Everyone moved forward in an orderly fashion, never complaining if the group in front of him or her was walking slowly or if an older one stopped to lift a younger one. Everyone was patient and kind, which was highly out of the ordinary when one considered the sheer size of the crowd. But, everyone in this place was very different than those in other places. Different indeed.

When they arrived at the meeting place, some sat and others stood. Little ones sat on the shoulders of taller ones. All talking ceased and all eyes focused straight ahead. Every eye remained fixed on the enormous peculiarity that stood before them.

None of them knew exactly how it had come to be here, but they and others like them had been gathering here for centuries, and as far as they were concerned, it had always been here and always would be.

"Come on, come on. Gather around, gather around," bellowed the red head. She pushed her way through the crowd, leaping over the small ones and jostling around the large ones. Finally, she stood at the foot of the gigantic curiosity. Tilting her head upwards, she looked up, twenty or thirty feet above her small frame. "Everyone is here, Cambium, everyone is here. I've made sure of it. Let's get started."

Everyone stared at the gigantic Tree, heavily branched, thickly leafed, and broadly rooted. Although they had seen it innumerable times, the fascination and awe never seemed to diminish and always returned anew at every meeting.

The trunk seemed endless in circumference; its surface was deep and creviced, and rich silvery white and gray in color. As everyone stared in anticipation, loud cracking sounds began to reverberate from the Tree, like the sound of stentorian lightning during a severe storm. Everyone listened and watched, as high above them the ashen bark on the Tree split sideways forming two horizontal slits, each three feet across. The cracks widened and separated, and massive green eyes appeared beneath them. It was as if the Tree had awakened.

Then, several feet below the eyes, the bark in the center of the Tree groaned and stretched outward. The sound of splintering wood echoed throughout the landscape, and soon, a nose appeared. Each nostril was as wide as a cannon ball. After the nose was fully formed, another horizontal crack appeared, this one as wide as the nose was long. The slit opened, and then above and below, rugged lips pushed out from the bark. With a final cracking noise, the mouth was complete. The crowd cheered. The Gathering had begun.

"Welcome, welcome to this most sacred of celebrations," came a voice from deep within the Tree. It sounded ancient, yet pristine. It carried to the farthest reaches of the grounds without diminishing in volume or clarity. Ears perked and all eyes focused on the Tree. Total attention was given to each word and no one stirred.

"As always, we will begin our Gathering today by welcoming home those who have completed recent assignments. Miss Mallory, will you please escort the procession forward?"

On cue, the red hen fluttered and jumped and skirted to the group of animals to the right of the massive Tree. There, red velvet rope hung from golden posts and corralled a very large group of dogs and cats. The crimson ropes met in the front of the fenced area and were tied into a beautiful large bow. With a look of privilege on her tiny face, Miss Mallory reached upward with her outstretched wings and unfastened it, allowing the sanguine rope to fall to the ground. With one wing across her chest and the other out to the side, she bowed and waved the group forward.

The long line of animals was varied and well mannered. Some small critters rode on the backs of larger ones. Every so often there was a cat or a dog with a silken scarf draped around their neck. Some of these ascots were white with gold trim and others were red trimmed with silver.

All of the animals passed in front of Cambium in single file and he crossed a branch over his trunk in a bow of thanks. When the occasional neckerchiefed critter walked by the Tree, their cravat vanished instantly.

One by one, each animal made their way past the Tree and proudly looked into the faces of those in the audience. The crowd cheered. Then, each walked into the drove and sat among the thousands and thousands of other animals in attendance. The procession was long and took several minutes. When everyone was seated, the Great Tree spoke.

"It is always a joy and a privilege to welcome back home our family and friends from their recent journeys. They are journeys you all have taken many times, and which you will take many times again. With each new journey comes not only adventure, but also responsibility. We each have been given unique gifts and obligations, and it is up to us to fulfill our destiny and the destiny of those around us, both here and elsewhere. We must always remember our purpose. We must always keep our objective in the foreground of our mind and actions. We must always remember that we are each a part of the whole, that everyone is a component to the ensemble, and also to each other. All are equally important. All are equally vital. All are necessary. All have a purpose."

The Tree paused, perhaps for emphasis, and then a sudden, warm breeze blew in from the west and the massive Tree began bending and swaying. Branches listed this way and that; leaves rustled as they rubbed and slid across each other. No leaf was lost and no branch was broken. The Tree moved with the wind like a dancer at a masquerade ball. The animals closest to the Tree felt the tepid breeze and their fur was flattened by the air as it blew. Some turned toward the zephyr, enjoying the warm wind as it drifted over their face. As the wind dispersed, all eyes once again faced forward as the tree limbs slowed and came to a resting-place, once again standing motionless.

One by one, white dots began appearing amidst the branches and leaves. The tiny white spots shone like Christmas lights and slowly grew in size. Each flicker of light flattened and spread, until each was wafer thin and the size of a bear paw. Then the flickering ceased, and all that remained were shining sheets of pearl-white hanging from the limbs like huge, snow-covered leaves.

"There are many assignments to be distributed today. As you know, some will be very brief and many of you will return before our next Gathering. Other assignments will be lengthy and difficult, filled with trial and pain. To those of you assigned to one of these more difficult tasks, remember that no suffering is ever permanent and all suffering always serves a purpose. Remember that every one of you will return here again at the completion of your assignment, with increased wisdom to share with us all."

"Some of the assignments distributed today call for volunteers. Others have been designated towards some of you specifically. I reviewed your requests for specific locations and specialized tasks, and after sorting through both your prior assignments and your own personal needs, I have composed a list of appointments that will greatly influence both this place and the place to where you will be once again traveling. As always, if you are not comfortable with the task for which you have been assigned, I will postpone your task until a later date. But rest assured, you will eventually need to face the challenges you are putting off. Shall we begin?" Cambium queried to the crowd.

A murmur and consensus of nodding prodded him to continue.

Using one of his lower branches like an arm, the Great Tree reached upward and grabbed one of the shiny sheets. Another branch met the first and he unfolded the first piece of glowing paper and spoke.

"The first assignment is for a feline. If you are not currently in feline form, this assignment does allow for canine modification, providing you have had past experience as a cat."

A bull dog in the front row lowered his head in disappointment and was comforted by the dog to his left.

"This task will require past experience with suffering and with children," continued Cambium.

A cat in the crowd bellowed out, "Yeah, and sometimes those go hand in hand!"

The crowd chuckled in understanding.

"Previous experience with abandonment and hunger are required as well. How many of you are ready for possible consideration for this assignment?"

The crowd shifted and separated, allowing dogs and cats to move forward. After several minutes, eighty-four volunteers stood in front of Cambium, some standing bravely and others cowering somewhat, with their heads hung low.

The Great Tree continued, "Very good, very good. I know all of you and I know the places and the faces you have been. I believe that some of you are perhaps better prepared for this particular assignment than others, so I will rely on my instincts to make a final decision."

"Collier, please step forward."

A black and tan Doberman left the small crowd and took a few steps forward.

"Elgin, please step forward."

A shorthaired gray cat looked at those to his left and right and then walked ahead.

Far back in the large crowd, a small group of animals began talking amongst themselves. "I'm relieved I didn't get called up for that assignment," whispered a large white dog. "In my last assignment I was not in this form but I was still a dog. I was kept outside in a concrete pen in the rain and snow for six long years. I was never allowed in the house. Of course I have no memory of the pain and anguish I must have experienced, but I clearly remember what happened."

A large calico cat shook her head compassionately and whispered, "I know what you mean. Next time I want to be appreciated and respected."

A small Abyssinian to her left remarked, "Cats were treated like royalty in ancient Egypt. They were pampered and fed the richest delicacies. They were even given silken beds and collars made of precious gems."

The large white dog leaned downward and snickered, "Yeah, and when the king or queen passed through, the cats were turned into mummies and put right next to the humans in a box. Real nice, huh?"

When the chatting ceased, they looked up to discover that the small group near Cambium had dispersed and only one animal was left before the huge Tree: the shorthaired gray cat. Once again, all ears were perked.

"Elgin has agreed to accept this assignment. He will be departing later this week and will be back in four months. He will be teaching someone about choices. Elgin will be traveling to a dreary inner city tenement district and is being assigned to a two-walker who will soon be homeless. When the man awakens in the morning three days from now, he will find Elgin by his side. Over the next four months, the man will be presented with opportunities to learn about responsibility as well as compassion for others. Elgin will be instrumental in his decision making process. Our friend will return to us in four months and we will hear then what became of the man and what Elgin has come back to teach us."

The dogs and cats at the Gathering sat back on their hind quarters and raised their arms in applause. The clapping was muffled of course, but jubilant. Dogs howled and cheered, cats meowed loudly and lauded with furry paws. Everyone applauded as the gray cat took the pearl white paper in his mouth and sat to the side of the enormous Tree.

Cambium lifted an arm and pulled down another folded paper. "This will be a Level IV assignment. Your Earth form will be canine. Species modification is permissible. Your stay below will be long term and divided into two segments, the first with a family of five two-walkers and the second with a solitary human named Bethany. Your personal lessons will be training and dedication. Bethany's lessons will be acceptance and determination. Who is interested in this assignment?"

A hundred or more animals walked forward. He handed the paper to the dog to his far left and as the sheet left his wooden hand, a duplicate sheet appeared. In like fashion, he distributed the multiplying sheet to the other animals, who huddled in small groups to read the specifics about the assignment.

After everyone thoroughly read about the upcoming journey, the sheets disappeared. All but three of the animals had returned to their places in the audience. Cambium selected one from the abiding group and handed him the only remaining sheet of shiny paper. The brown and gray mixed breed took the parchment in his mouth and sat proudly.

"Thank you, Gentry. You will be leaving in six days. Your assignment form will be a brown Labrador. Go in peace. We will see you again in nine years."

The dog walked away to the cheers of the crowd. Once again, Cambium spoke.

"Gentry's assignment also calls for five littermates. Three of these siblings will have Level III journeys, one will have a Level IV and the last assignment will be very brief, but necessary. If you are interested in this assignment, please step forward for consideration."

Perhaps two-dozen animals walked forward. Cambium provided assignment details, and in the end, five cats sat before the Tree and made their individual journey selections. Cambium smiled and bid them adieu.

When the last of the shiny white papers had been assigned, the large group of departing animals sat facing the huge Tree, which gently bowed and said to them, "You have all been given an assignment and have agreed to perform the task to the best of your ability. As always, once you enter the portal, you will forget this place and you will find yourself in the other world. You will not remember your task in full detail, but most of you will know to whom you have been assigned. The habits and instincts associated with your assignment form will return to you there, and your true nature will remain inside you. When you return to Everlife, you will report to me on the success of your journey and the progress of your human. If, during the course of your assignment, it becomes necessary for us to relay additional information or guidance to you, you will be directed to the following meeting places which have been arranged for your support."

Instantly, a holographic globe of the Earth emerged from beneath the leaves and branches of the Great Tree. It spun gently on its axis for several revolutions, displaying the names of each country when the appropriate continent faced the crowd.

The Tree continued. "The first Meeting of the Full Moon will take place three weeks from now. If you are called, you will feel a strong desire to leave your human and travel to the meeting location."

The globe flattened and one by one, countries sprung upward from the map. Individual states and provinces from the various countries were highlighted and raised farther upward. Then one or more cities or towns in the state were labeled in light and pulled even higher above the map, leaving a trail like the tail of a comet. Then the state was pulled back onto the map and the next state was enlarged and highlighted with the brilliant colors and lights.

"If you are unable to attend due to fences or other restraints, you will be prompted again sometime in the future to another Meeting of the Full Moon that will be in your area. Those of you leaving immediately, go now to the Portal. Check out at a Green Departure Post and leave your Everlife identification tag on the pegs there. Go in peace. We will see you all again."

The animals departed to the applause of the crowd.

CHAPTER TWO

William Colbert walked towards his car with a briefcase in one hand and his eyes looking down at the pavement. He came close to pinching himself, to test whether he was dreaming or maybe even sleepwalking. Ten days ago, if anyone had suggested where he would be going this morning, he would have assuredly informed him or her that they were crazy. But, since he was unfortunately wide-awake, the only test he needed today was one to determine his sanity.

The elevator ride to the top floor seemed to take much longer than it should have. William stared upward at the floor numbers as they sequentially lit and paused, while passengers entered and exited. Some carried files or stacks of documents, and others pulled boxes behind them in stainless steel carts that were once reserved for little old ladies walking to the corner grocer.

William watched them all come and go. Each was groomed and dressed in the finest executive ware imaginable. He suspected that most had spent as much on today's suit as they had on two month's mortgage.

Finally the doors slid open onto the marble and mahogany expanse of the 9th floor, the offices of Hillman, Mottler & Greggors, Attorneys at Law.

There was a lengthy history between the Colberts and the Hillmans; a history that William chose to suppress, recalling only in rare moments of necessity ... such as today.

William stood in the elevator wondering if he was really going to exit. He regretted being here and honestly did not want to go through with this, but he knew he had exhausted every other option. When the doors began closing again, someone muttered and he woke from his brief mental lapse and took an arduous step out of the elevator.

"Good Day, Sir. With whom do you have an appointment this morning?" said a woman at the reception area.

Clearing his throat and gathering his thoughts, William replied, "My name is William Colbert, with ColPro. I'm here for a 9:20 meeting with Mr. Hillman."

"Oh yes," she spouted. Getting up from her seat and walking around the enormous reception desk, her heels clicked together so loudly that William's attention was drawn to her shiny red high-heeled shoes. He smiled and chuckled silently, wondering if this polished up-town receptionist had once been a farm girl with a little dog named Toto. After a second thought, he decided that there was no way.

And his smile faded.

He was escorted to a large conference room where a twelve-foot table sat, surrounded by burgundy leather chairs. The table was designed more for intimidation than for necessity. William was accustomed to offices reeking of money and supposed prestige. There was a time in his younger days when he would have been intimidated by this bold display of extravagance. Not anymore.

Once in a while, maybe once in a law firm's history, a case would come along that brought in settlement shares of seven figures and made front-page news. Of course those settlements occurred most often in the daydreams of attorneys whose abilities were as miniscule as the cases they settled. But once in a while that big settlement did come along, and such was the case several years ago with Hillman, Mottler & Greggors, Attorneys at Law.

The red-shoed receptionist pointed to the corner of the room and William was instructed to help himself to a cup of coffee or a glass of freshly squeezed juice. He could easily imagine this woman in the aisle of an airplane pointing to the emergency exits at the middle and ends of the aircraft. He poured himself a cup of coffee and sat down. He wished he were in his own office, sipping coffee from his own mug, instead of where he was now. He considered getting up and walking out, but realized that his need was stronger than his pride.

His cup had been emptied for a good twenty minutes before Sherman Hillman Jr. opened the conference door, walking into the room with an entrance he had surely practiced endlessly during his senior year of law school. William stood and smiled politely, knowing that the pompous man entering the room was the best chance he had for making his "little problem" go away.

Reaching out his ring clad hand and exposing his gold watch, Sherman Hillman Jr. smiled with perfectly veneered teeth and offered William a firm handshake and a generic greeting. With the other equally ring clad hand, he motioned William to sit down. Sherman took the seat at the head of the table, of course.

"William. It's been a long time. How are the folks?"

William smiled with a courteous smile reserved for times such as these, when he knew the conversation was obligatory with no sense of sincerity or genuine concern.

"They're well, thank you."

"Good, good," smiled Sherman, leaning back in his chair and folding his hands on his ample stomach. "Well William, what can I do for you?"

This was it. This was the moment William had been dreading. He had known Sherman since childhood but never liked him. As adults, they saw each other occasionally at civic functions and fundraisers, but they never intentionally socialized.

The aversion between the two families began when William's father and Sherman Hillman, Sr. were in college. They had been placed together as dormitory roommates their freshman year and although their friendship could never have been considered a close one, they got along decently enough. Following the end of the term, they decided to room again in the fall, most likely due to convenience rather than mutual esteem.

Their sophomore year progressed uneventfully until the week of midterms when Thomas discovered that the money he kept in his desk drawer was missing.

He had been saving for months, putting a dollar or two into the envelope whenever he could and keeping it taped securely to the back of the bottom drawer. Only one other person knew about the money; his roommate Sherman.

It took Thomas three days to make his formal accusation. His stomach had been tight with emotion and disgust for several hours preceding the dreaded confrontation. $224 was a lot of money back then, but the missing cash did not bother Thomas nearly as much as the thought of his friend being a thief.

Sherman denied the allegations and seemed genuinely offended by them. However, as the days passed, Thomas began to notice how Sherman could change the tone of his voice and manipulate his facial expressions, seemingly at will. These subtleties, Thomas had previously overlooked, and before long, Thomas was quite adept at determining when Sherman was lying. Unfortunately, Thomas discovered that his roommate was very comfortable with dishonesty, a trait that served him well in his following years as a practicing attorney at law.

Thomas never mentioned the missing money to Sherman again and maintained a cordial environment in the dormitory for the remainder of the semester. But, when the school year came to an end, neither student mentioned rooming together in the fall.

Since the irony gods often have a baneful sense of humor, William Colbert and Sherman Hillman, Jr. found themselves as classmates throughout grade school and again in high school. Thomas mentioned nothing to his son about Sherman, Sr. and simply sat back and watched how things played out with the two boys. It was no surprise that William developed a strong dislike for Sherman, Jr. by the time they were eight years old. The aversion grew proportionally, as did they.

William took a deep breath and looked at his own folded hands, which rested on the massive mahogany table. After exhaling, he looked up at Sherman and spoke.

"As you know, I run the company my Dad founded many years ago. I keep my eye mostly on research and development, but I am also involved in production and purchasing. We're still a relatively small company compared to some, but we are a healthy little fish in the big sea of corporate America.

"One of our newest products was set for production this month, and based on preliminary sales of the item, it was probably going to be our best seller to date. We bought a building here in town to serve as our manufacturing facility. All the machinery needed for production was installed and we hired almost a hundred people from the community as full time employees. Everything was set to go and then I got a phone call."

"What kind of phone call?"

"The kind of call that you never want to get. The kind of call informing you that the U.S. Patent office made a little mistake and is revoking your patent. It seems that someone else developed the product four years earlier and applied for a patent, which was granted. Then, we submitted ours and let's just say there were apparently some loose ends and some oversights at the Patent office. We were granted a patent seven months ago and it was rescinded ten days ago."

"Ouch," sighed Sherman.

"Ouch is an understatement. I'm in the hole for two million in pre-production costs. Stores that have been buying from us for years were promised they would have the product on their shelves before anyone else. We have orders scheduled to be filled by Christmas, and now we can't produce anything because of my little 'ouch.'"

Interlocking his hands behind his head, Sherman leaned farther back in his leather chair and looked at the ceiling. "Have your company attorneys contacted the other company?"

"There is no other 'company.' There is one guy, just one stubborn man named Eugene Morgan in Fargo, North Dakota, who refuses to sell his patent. We offered him six figures. He is adamant about not selling. He said he worked on the idea with his father for years, and it was the old man's greatest accomplishment to own a patent with the family name on it. The father since passed away, but the son has no desire to sell it for any price."

Sherman smiled a reckless, sinister smile. "There's always a price, William, always. It just depends on what you're willing to pay."

"You mean your retainer? How much are we talking about?"

Settling his chair back down to its normal position and leaning forward on the grand table, he looked straight into William's eyes and all sense of concern and warmth left the face of Sherman Hillman, Jr.

"No, I'm not talking about my fee. You have no legal options, William. The U.S. Patent office simply made a mistake, that's all. They have no obligation to compensate you for your losses."

William was speechless.

"Your situation does not involve State Law and it does not involve Federal Law. What you *are* dealing with my friend, is 'Murphy's

Law'," continued Sherman as he pointed to a large framed document on the wall."

William's blank expression revealed his naiveté.

"Murphy's Law," explained Sherman. "Anything that *can* go wrong, *will* go wrong."

"So you're saying there's nothing I can do?"

"Not at all. You have many options to pursue with Mr. Morgan."

"I'm not talking about breaking his legs or doing anything illegal," said William defensively.

"The practice of law does not deal with legalities, William. It deals only with winning. It involves strategy and manipulation. Our great legal system allows us to accuse anyone of anything, without any basis in fact or truth whatsoever. The Court system and due process of law can make someone's life so miserable that they ultimately agree to give us what we want. What are you willing to pay to have Mr. Morgan sign over his patent? How far are you willing to go? How much pressure are you willing to put on this guy? Is slander acceptable? What about intimidation? How about trumped up charges of one thing or another? What exactly are you willing to do to get what you want?"

"I'm not willing to do anything wrong," explained William.

"If you want to talk to someone about right and wrong, go talk to your Minister. In a court of law, the concept of right and wrong is extremely relative and interpretive. Nothing is black or white, William. The Judicial System sees only shades of gray."

William listened in disbelief.

Sherman got up from his chair and started walking away from the table. As he grabbed the doorknob he turned back toward William.

"If you want the rights to your patent back, just let me know. I'll need five grand up front."

Then he opened the door and left.

William sat there in quiet reflection for several minutes. When he finally got up from his chair, the large document on the wall caught his eye and he walked over to it.

"Murphy's Law," he read aloud softly. "Anything that can go wrong, will go wrong."

After another minute or two of self-pity, he picked up his briefcase and walked out of the conference room. The meeting had not gone as he had expected. But then again, what was he expecting to hear from the mouth of Sherman Hillman, Jr.? Surely nothing virtuous or ethical. In that regard, Sherman had lived up to William's expectations fully.

The front door opened and an elderly woman bounced into the farmhouse with youthful energy, kicking the door closed with her right foot behind her. Her arms were heavily laden with brown paper sacks and a large covered basket, and as always, her face was full of joy.

"Katie, it's me. Where are you, Dear Heart?" she bellowed as she walked down the hall towards the kitchen.

Katie responded with a less boisterous bellow. "I'm in the kitchen as usual."

"My word, woman. Do you ever leave the kitchen? Did you actually make it to bed last night or did you just take a seat at the table and drop your head for a few minutes before dawn?"

"Ha ha ha," sneered Katie as she continued stirring the pot on the stove.

Millie set the basket and paper bags on the table and pulled out a chair.

"What did you bring me?" asked Katie. "Have you been up to the farmer's market already?"

"Oh yes, I have," answered Millie, reaching into the first bag and taking out a jar of honey.

Scowling at her, Katie retorted, "I thought we were going to go to the farmer's market together today."

"I thought so too," replied Millie, "until I remembered that today was the day of the huge estate sale up at the McNammara place."

With eyes widening to the size of saucers, Katie screamed a muffled childish scream of delight.

"I forgot all about the estate sale!" uttered Katie happily, setting down the wooden spoon and turning off the stove. "What on earth would I do without you?" she asked, looking at Millie with sisterly love and appreciation.

Untying her apron and sitting down at the table, Katie pulled back the red and white check fabric from the basket and moaned with delight at the sight of fresh blueberry muffins. Millie pushed back her chair and headed for the kitchen windows. "Maybe if you let some light in here, you'd be able to see what I brought you." Millie then reached up and pulled the curtain string, allowing the morning sun to fill the entire room with warm, golden light.

Then, walking over to the cupboard to the left of the stove and taking out two small plates, she turned towards the table and added, "I bought you another present at the farmer's market but you won't get it for about four months. Sandy and Ted Ellis ordered a flat bed of South Carolina peaches and I ordered you a bushel. Sandy's even going to deliver them this year." Opening a drawer, Millie grabbed two butter knives; she spent just as much time in Katie's kitchen as she did in her own and knew exactly where everything was kept.

With a mouth full of fresh muffin, Katie mumbled, "How 'bout you make us a pot of tea while you're over there." Smiling with love for her friend, Millie said she'd be happy to.

The phone rang, and Millie, being closest to it, picked it up and pushed a button. "Hello?" The phone rang again. "I hate this phone," she said as she pushed another button and tried again. "Hello, Colbert residence. Millie the maid speaking."

"Hi, Aunt Millie" said William as he leaned back in his own office chair behind his own desk.

"How's my favorite Nephew?" asked Millie, smiling from ear to ear and turning towards the table to look at Katie.

"Just fine, Millie. Is my Dad around?"

"He's outside putzing around in the yard. I'd give the phone to your Mom, but she has a face full of blueberry muffin at the moment. Let me get your Dad."

Placing the phone on the counter, Millie opened the kitchen door to holler for Thomas. William pulled the phone away from his ear, amazed at the bellow he heard coming through the telephone line. The holler that came out of Aunt Millie sounded like it came from a woman three times her size and half her age.

Thomas walked in wiping his hands on his pants and picked up the phone. "Hello, Son, what's up?"

"Hey, Dad. How are the hens?"

"You know darn well they're fine. Stop with the small talk and tell me what's been bothering you for the past few days."

"How do you always know, Dad?"

"Because I'm your father. What's going on?"

"Well, Dad, I have a problem but I really don't want to talk about it over the phone. How about I drive out there and spend a few days?"

"Sounds great Will, but why don't you just hop on a plane?"

"I thought it'd be good to do some thinking before I got there, to try to work things out in my head."

"I don't want your head too full while you're driving. We heard that some nasty weather might be blowing in. How 'bout you give me the abridged version right now?"

"Well, remember that new patent R&D was so excited about?"

"Yeah, you told me we'd be going into production any time."

"Well, legal got a call last week from the Patent Office attorney saying there was a problem."

"What kind of problem?"

"Well, the patent was posted for objection eight months ago and there was none. We got our official patent papers a month later and started pre-production."

"This is all old news," said Thomas as he paced the kitchen floor.

"Well, a few days ago the Patent Office called saying the attorney handling our application made a mistake. Dad, they rescinded our patent."

Pulling a chair out from the kitchen table, Thomas sat down and rubbed the back of his head, gently pulling at his hair, something his wife and son knew he only did when he was very upset or highly concerned. "Why didn't you tell me sooner?"

"I was hoping things would work out by now."

"Oh, Will, how did this happen? I know you put a lot of money into pre-production already."

"I know Dad, that's the problem. Our legal department contacted the other party ten days ago and they just heard back on Friday. He said he wouldn't sell."

"What are you going to do?"

"I uh ... I went to see Sherman Hillman Jr. today to get his opinion."

The older man groaned so loudly that it carried over the telephone line.

William continued, "I know. Things had to be pretty bad for me to go see him."

"What did he say? He's a real horse's back end, but he and his father have a way of getting things done."

"He basically told me he could get us what we wanted, but that it would take some underhandedness."

"What did you tell him, Will?

"Well, Dad, I haven't made up my mind yet. I'm seriously thinking of letting him do whatever it takes to make this problem go away."

"Don't call him back until you've come out here and we talk about it some more, OK? Things will look better in the morning."

"Dad, you've been saying that ever since I was little. I'm not sure this problem will look better in the morning."

"Now, Son. We'll talk about it when you get here and fully consider our options. We'll be looking forward to having you home for a few days. Drive safely and call us when you get on the road."

After their good-byes, Thomas placed the tiny telephone into the base and looked at his wife. William had given the phone to them the previous Christmas, saying it was high time they threw away their old wall phone and replaced it with a modern, compact cordless model. He gleamed with pride as he explained the features and conveniences of the new phone, and told his mother she could keep it in her pocket when she walked out to the garden or to the mailbox. She had in fact done that one day, only to have it fall out and remain lost for the next two days. She and her husband had heard it ring twice from somewhere in the tall grass, but by the time they made it outside, the ringing had stopped. It was strictly by chance that Thomas saw it reflecting the sun one afternoon just before running over it with the lawnmower.

"I hate this phone," said Thomas. Do you think he'll notice if it's gone when he gets here?"

Katie smiled and said, "I could lose it in the yard again if you want me to."

William hung up the phone and sat with his head in his hands. It would be good getting away for a while, having time to think. After all, wasn't thinking his specialty? Wasn't thinking what R&D was all about? Wasn't thinking the one thing that William considered the most important aspect of staying atop of your competition and keeping your company moving in the right direction? William excelled at thinking; that is why he was so good at his job and at running his father's company. Why then was he having such an unbelievably difficult time thinking right now?

In retrospect, it was not that he was having a difficult time thinking. He was thinking more than he wanted to, actually. What troubled him was the nature of his thoughts. Different scenarios ran through his mind, all involving his ultimate victory over Eugene Morgan. Every scenario had the same final scene: Sherman Hillman had made William's "little problem" go away. Every thought resulted in ColPro owning the patent again and carrying on with business as usual. The thoughts he was having all revolved around Eugene Morgan being broken and signing over his rights to the patent to William's company. But these thoughts were troubling him more than he could imagine, and he wanted them to stop.

He reached for his phone and pushed the button for his secretary.

"Yes, Mr. Colbert."

"Liz, I'm taking the rest of the week off. If anyone calls, just take a message. If I have any appointments scheduled, reschedule them. I'll have my cell phone with me, but don't call for anything except an emergency, and I'm talking blood or fire."

"Yes, Mr. Colbert," came the voice from the speaker.

William pressed the button again to turn off the intercom and pushed his chair back from the desk. A minute later his secretary walked in holding a large manila envelope.

"Betty just brought this up from HR," she explained.

William thanked her as he placed the envelope in his brief case. He grabbed his jacket from the seat back, grabbed the attaché, and headed home to pack for his trip.

William placed a suitcase in the trunk of his car and walked around to the driver's side door. He had so much work to do at the office that he could not afford the time away, but he knew he needed to think this situation through. Taking a long drive and having a change of scenery would help him think more clearly.

He had inherited his Dad's temperament and it suited him well. He rarely lost his temper and always considered situations thoroughly before making important decisions. And even though he was a grown man, he most often called his Dad prior to making any big decision. Thomas had made it clear when he left ColPro that William was now in charge and did not need his Dad's approval or even consideration on company matters. Thomas trusted his son and knew that the mistakes William would make were the same mistakes he himself made as a younger man. Hindsight was always 20/20, but Thomas was a wise father and knew that his son would have to experience the lessons first hand. Consequently, he kept out of company matters for the most part, but did welcome the times when his son asked for his opinion or advice.

William set his briefcase on the empty passenger seat, leaned back in the driver's seat, took a deep breath, and reached forward to turn the key in the ignition. Talking to no one but himself, he said, "I hope things are a lot different when I get back here in a week."

William had been driving for nine hours and both his stomach and the gas tank required filling. He had been lost in thought for most of the drive: thoughts of the pending problem with the patent; thoughts of Eugene Morgan who owned the patent rights; thoughts of what Sherman Hillman could or would do in order to get Morgan to relinquish the rights to the patent; thoughts of what would happen in the worst case scenario. That latter possibility occupied most of his thoughts.

He had used his condo as collateral to secure the loan for the manufacturing equipment. If the deal went sour, he would be forced to sell it to pay off the debt. He had used his entire savings as a down payment on the building where the machines were sitting idly. Since he had advance orders on the product, he used some of that money for raw materials. His accountants had assured him that his investment capital would be returned in 2-3 months once production was underway and orders had been filled. The company had expected to see a sizeable profit shortly after that, and if sales exceeded conservative predictions, William would easily triple the size and profit of the company his father had started thirty-five years previously.

He pulled into a filling station just off the highway and scanned his credit card at the pump. Leaving the handle in the gas tank, he walked into the adjacent convenience store for a bite to eat.

There he saw an entire section of souvenirs: display after display of magnets, back scratchers, shot glasses, and post cards, each darning the brightly decorated icons of the Land of Lincoln. One postcard in particular caught his eye and he lifted it from the wire rack and read the front of it. "We enforce Murphy's Law in Illinois. Anything that can go wrong, will go wrong." Returning the card to the rack after significant hesitation, he walked past the remaining souvenirs and over to the counter to peruse his dinner options.

There were hotdogs and smoked sausages, gently turning over and over and over on heated stainless steel rods, each row carrying a slightly different variety of product. Row one carried pure beef hotdogs; row two carried turkey hotdogs; row three carried beef smoked sausage; row four carried spicy smoked sausage, but did not mention the kind of meat; and row five carried corn dogs, which were the only items on the rolling display that wobbled slightly every time they rolled over. William wished that instead of the little cards telling you what kind of hot dog was on each row, that someone had the courtesy to tell you what day of the week the hot dogs had been placed on this horizontal merry-go-round.

He turned towards the back of the store and the frozen drink machine. The flavors and colors looked appealing, but he knew if he drank something that cold and big, he would be stopping a lot sooner than nine hours from now. So he passed the frozen beverage machine and headed toward the refrigerator and the small commercial microwave.

After much deliberation, he purchased a small order of nachos, three sticks of mild beef jerky, a package of white powdered donuts, a bottle of iced tea, and a chocolate candy bar.

He returned to his car and set the nachos on his briefcase and rested the ice tea in a cup holder. The other goodies were in his coat pocket. He removed the gas nozzle from the tank and documented his fuel purchase and odometer reading in a small journal. After turning the key in the ignition and buckling his seat belt, he shifted into drive. As he drove away from the pump, a polite signal bell toned from the dashboard and the red "check engine" light turned on.

William stopped the car and tapped the glass above the display. The light did not change. He turned back toward the store and parked.

Walking up to the counter again he asked the distance to the nearest town. Twenty-seven miles. He asked the distance to the nearest mechanic. Twenty-seven miles. He asked the distance of the closest towing facility. He should have guessed the answer to that last question.

He got back into his car and took out his cell phone. Just before dialing, it dawned on him that his parents would be sound asleep by now. He would assume the engine light was a sensor malfunction and would continue driving.

The road was dark and few vehicles passed him in either direction. The engine light remained lit. William paid close attention to the temperature gauges and his speed. Oh how he wished that light would go off.

After several miles he pulled off the highway onto the shoulder of the road, remaining prudent enough to keep the engine running while he opened the glove box. Underneath the ketchup packages, the plastic spoons and forks, the straws and taco sauce, he finally found the owner's manual. Running his finger down the Troubleshooting guide, he flipped to the section on warning lights. Unfortunately, the only information written was to consult a factory-authorized mechanic as soon as possible.

While returning the manual to the glove box, William noticed a small first aid kit and got an idea. Opening the kit, he removed an item and unwrapped it. He peeled back the protective coverings and with the precision of a surgeon, he leaned forward and placed the Band-Aid over the illuminated "check engine" light. With a sense of resolute pride, he smiled and once again pulled out onto the highway.

CHAPTER THREE

There was a crowd around the black metal post. There were many posts, all exactly the same, but each surrounded by a different crowd. Near the top of the post was a metal sign that read "ARRIVALS." A large Saint Bernard with black canvas saddlebags on his back walked with an orange and white cat sitting atop him. The cat reached down into one of the bags and grabbed a scroll every time they approached a post. Then the cat stood on his hind legs and hung one of the two-sided parchment rolls on a peg high on the black pole. On the top of each scroll, a letter of the alphabet was written in large bold print. Beneath each letter on every banner was a list of names.

"Let me through, let me through," pleaded the white furry dog as he pushed his way forward from the back of the crowd.

"Patience, patience, Lanagan," said the orange cat, looking at the dog in rebuke.

"Is he coming back today, Fluff Stuff?" Lanagan asked the cat pleadingly.

"The name is Cimmaron, and if you want information from me Lanagan, I suggest you call me by my given name."

"Yes, Ginger Snap," said Lanagan as he got closer to the pole and glanced up to read the names listed under the large "F" on the scroll that the large orange cat had just hung.

"Yes, he's coming back today," said the cat, as he got back on all fours. The Saint Bernard turned and headed toward the next post. "And the name is *Cimmaron*," added the cat.

The large white dog was not about to take the cat's word on the matter, and read down the long list of names until he found the one he wanted to see.

"Flanders! Ah, yes! My dearest friend is coming home!" He looked across the page to the right hand column to see what time he would be arriving. His eyes widened and a smile stretched across his face. "NOW!" he shouted. "He's coming home NOW!"

He muscled his way through the crowd and around to the area behind the post, which bordered a very strange but wonderful place called "Passage Wall."

The wall was not an ocean and it did not lie horizontally, but it looked like water when you stood in front of it. It flowed, yet remained motionless; was fluid, yet solid; was clear, yet blue—blue, yet silver and metallic. It was a magical portal between the worlds: a place where friends said good-bye and hello over and over again, forever. When someone left this place, they always returned. And they always returned better than when they left. The same, but better. The same, but different. The same, but improved. And at any second, Lanagan's best friend would be returning to this wondrous place.

The white bear of a dog sat staring at Passage Wall. It extended far to the left and far to the right, but this section of the portal was designated only for canine and feline use. Lanagan knew it must actually begin and end somewhere, but he was not exactly sure where and the matter was never much of a concern to him anyway. There were other areas of the Wall used by other animals, but the dogs and cats in this part of Everlife never traveled to the distant parts of the portal.

To his left, the Wall fluttered and its surface gently shook, as if somewhere farther down the Wall, an elephant had stuck his massive foot into the fluid and caused a rippling effect. Through the liquid came a small brown and white dog. First her nose poked through and then came her face and ears. Her eyes were closed as her neck and shoulders came through, then her front limbs. The rest of her body emerged and finally her eyes opened. Others were there to welcome her home with smiles, kisses, and wagging tails.

The small dog took a few steps forward and placed her front paw on a transparent box. A red light scanned her paw and a voice came from the post above the box saying, "Welcome back, Keo. You have successfully completed your Level III assignment. Please place the collar on your neck prior to leaving this area."

Lanagan watched as an opaque collar appeared on a peg and an orange tag bearing the designation "Level III" hung from it. The dog lifted the collar with her nose and slid it over her head. When it settled around her neck, it disappeared.

Lanagan faced forward again and the portal began to gently wave in front of him. A black nose appeared, then a dark fuzzy muzzle and face. Soon, an entire enormous, shaggy black dog emerged from the passage.

"Flanders! It's so good to have you back!" Lanagan said as he approached and rubbed his face and neck into his friend's. The big black dog brushed his whole body up against Lanagan, nearly knocking him over. "Let me check in and then I'll tell you all about my trip!"

"It's a deal!" agreed Lanagan.

Flanders approached the check-in station and placed a front paw on the clear box. A single red line scanned his paw and a voice came from the post above the box saying, "Welcome back, Flanders. You have successfully completed your Level VI assignment. Please place the collar on your neck prior to leaving this area."

A semitransparent collar appeared on a peg, and hanging from it was a light blue tag that read "Level VI." Flanders stuck his face into the collar and it slid onto his neck and disappeared.

The two dogs left the Passage Wall area, and Flanders suggested that he give his report to Cambium now so he and Lanagan could spend some uninterrupted time together later. Lanagan stayed in the distance while Flanders approached the Tree.

Cambium's eyes were hidden beneath the bark and there was no one sitting at his roots. The animals had never heard any snoring sounds coming from the Tree, but everyone assumed he was sleeping when his eyes were hidden. However, he always seemed to know when someone was coming to give their report, and when Flanders heard the first loud creaking sound, he knew that Cambium had awakened.

Lanagan curled up into a large white ball and slept while his friend sat at the roots of the enormous Tree.

He had no idea how long he had been sleeping, but was awakened by a big black paw some time thereafter, and the two dogs set off to talk and play.

"Tell me about your assignment," Lanagan said.

"It was a Level VI."

"And how was it?"

"It was great. My human was a real gentle soul. He treated me like one of his children and even the kids were awesome. I slept in their bed, took vacations with them; it was like a storybook. I laid by the fire in the winter and rode in the back seat of the car with my face out of the window when we drove somewhere. I was never happier during an assignment."

"How long were you there?"

"Eleven years, seven months, and twelve days."

"Not that you were counting, huh?" smiled Lanagan.

"I loved those two-walkers. When Cambium gave me the assignment, he told me that I would learn a special lesson this time, but I honestly didn't think it would be so intense, so real, so powerful. But it was. It changed me. And Cambium just told me it changed them too."

"What do you think a Level VII assignment would be like?" asked Lanagan.

"I have no idea. I can't imagine getting any more love than I got this last time. They made me feel so special. Cambium told me that I taught the children how to give love unselfishly and that because of my life there, the kids will be more likely to give love to other humans when they get older."

"I wonder what kind of assignment I'll get next time around," wondered Lanagan aloud.

"What qualification are you now?" asked Flanders.

"After my last assignment, I was officially classified as Level VII qualified."

"Wow. Did you submit a request for a Level VII assignment for the next Gathering?"

"No, I didn't request anything special at all. I figured Cambium would put me somewhere when he thought I was ready."

Looking around to make sure no one was within earshot, Flanders lowered his head and his voice and whispered, "When you're down there, on an assignment, how much of Everlife do you remember?"

"Most of the time I don't remember anything. But sometimes … sometimes there are these flashes of memory and awareness that I get. Sometimes everything makes perfect sense and I feel total accord. But most of the time, I don't remember Everlife or even have any awareness of it. I seem to remember it mostly in dreams."

"There were a few times during this last assignment when I was really connected," said Flanders, "when I sort of knew why I was there. I had never experienced those feelings before on any other assignment, so it was totally new for me. I don't think that happens in the lower Levels."

"Do you know anyone who ever completed a Level VII assignment?" asked Lanagan.

"There are only a couple hundred animals in our section of Everlife who have; they're split just about 50/50 dogs to cats. Of course each of those groups will argue there are more of their species in the total percent than the other," Flanders smiled.

"What happens after you complete a Level VII assignment?"

"I'm not really sure. I've never met anyone personally who returned from a Level VII assignment while I was here. No one talks much about it. And since the only time our tags are visible is when we're either coming or going, I guess no one pays it much mind."

None of the animals ever really considered the specifics about how things were in Everlife. Cambium sometimes used the phrase "in the time before days," but no one really knew what he meant by that, and no one ever asked him to elaborate. As far as the animals were concerned, they had always been there and always would return there, and that was just how things were and would always be.

It was a magical place, but not in an enchanted kind of way. Everlife was a peaceful place, although far from calm. At any given moment, you might see a group of critters sitting around arguing about the relative importance of different species, or about the level of impact a certain species of animal was likely to have on a human compared to another. The dogs always felt they were more important than the cats, but the cats, of course, felt that they were the more relevant. Sometimes the debates went even further than that, discussing which breeds of dogs or cats were the most intelligent or the most significant.

Centuries ago, Cambium changed the rules a bit. Actually, he changed the rules a lot. He decided that due to these relentless debates (which he considered futile and petty), he would allow for species alteration prior to departure to Earth. He thought that once the animals experienced life as another species, the age long debate would finally cease.

Nothing could have been further from the truth, to his dismay. What actually occurred was simply a change in the debate. Cats who took canine form for an assignment returned to Everlife more convinced than ever that they were more useful as a feline. Dogs were very reluctant to even consider species alteration, and it took centuries for the first dog to actually agree to it. His name was Timber and he was a Chihuahua. The reason he decided to take the plunge was simply because he wanted to be bigger. Just a little bigger. He had never elected to change his breed (simply due to pride), and perhaps due to his adamant resolve that even a tiny dog was better than a cat on Earth.

One day, a couple hundred years after Cambium's new policy took effect, Timber agreed to change species, but only if he could be a large, male cat. He ended up being a Maine Coon, perhaps the largest of all domestic feline breeds, and he was gone for twelve years. When he returned to Everlife, he was so changed that he wanted to keep his Earth form of the cat, which of course was permissible. Soon after, other dogs took the cue from Timber and volunteered to species shift for Earth assignments. Most did want to revert back to their canine forms after returning to Everlife, but they continued to accept future assignments as cats.

Everlife was full of wonder and adventure and no human had ever laid eyes on it. The ground was a brilliant green in the area where the dogs and cats lived. It was not grass or even moss, but some kind of special creation that was always a perfect color green and always the same length. One resident had once visited Earth as a football team mascot and had walked on artificial grass in a stadium. He reported that the ground in Everlife was nothing like artificial turf either.

The ground was lush and pleasantly firm, but not difficult on which to walk. It never rained in this part of Everlife, although it did rain quite a bit in other sections of the expanse. There were no bothersome insects here either, which was a relief to the animals who had the misery of experiencing fleas and ticks on Earth.

There were large rocks on which to climb and sleep, and they were always warm and delightful. There were trees for cats to climb, and, of course, no one ever dared to climb on Cambium. Actually, someone had tried once and ended up being swatted away by one of Cambium's branches. The kitten fell painlessly to the soft ground, but word spread quickly that the unwritten rule of never climbing on Cambium must be heeded.

There were play areas for dogs and separate play areas for cats. The canine recreation areas were more rugged, as would be expected, and actually looked a lot like human children's playgrounds. There were tug of war ropes with large colorful rings on the ends for holding; the thick rope ran through a winch system that sat on a triangular shaped base. The rope was automatically measured prior to the beginning of each match, to ensure that neither participant had an advantage. Then, each dog grabbed a ring and pulled. The last twelve inches of rope leading up to the ring was painted, and when one dog managed to pull his opponent to the point where the colored part of the rope met the pulley system, a victory bell would sound. Then the machine would re-set itself.

Although there were smaller set-ups for smaller dogs, Cambium had also programmed the machines to allow for modified settings. This was done when a large dog was challenged by a much smaller dog. The machine would scan the dogs using a long yellow light and calibrate the machine to adjust for the height and weight differences. The victorious dog in these scenarios was quite often the smaller of the two dogs, who could then legitimately boast of being the stronger dog pound for pound.

There was another area in the play region where there was pile after pile of various material, some organic and some artificial. The first several piles were natural substances such as leaves, small rocks, cedar mulch, pine needles, oak bark chips, sand, and, of course, an assortment of soil types. Here the dogs could dig and dig to their heart's content. Others preferred to roll and tumble on these mounds.

Periodically, a few dogs would arrange games involving these piles. Teams would be formed and dozens of duplicate piles would be created. Various items would be hidden deep within the mounds and the dogs would compete to see who located the item first. When the first dog located the object, the second dog on the team would repeat the procedure on the next pile. The team that located the final item in the final mound first would win the event.

Some dogs preferred to keep their hands clean when they played, so they spent their recreational time with the plastic disc-throwing machine. Colorful discs were flung from the device and the dogs would catch them in mid air. There were contests for this event too, and there were times when long lines of dogs waited to use one of the machines for practicing.

There were also enormous areas for ball playing of all kinds. Although there were mechanical devices for throwing balls, some dogs preferred a greater level of participation in the throwing, so they used stationary slings to launch the balls. And because dogs can be quite mischievous at times, periodically a ball would be coated with paint or some other offensive substance prior to launching. The catching dog would ultimately grab the ball, unaware of its special added layer. When this happened, no one became angry and no one fought, however, a mental note of the prank was made and the offending party would certainly be receiving an equally special surprise sometime in the future.

The cat play area was more elaborate, to suit the more discriminating and delicate feline tastes. As in the dog playground, there was a complex section for ball playing. The balls here were lighter and often hollow, some contained bells, and others were mostly open on the outside to expose a special object within.

Extended claws were restricted in Everlife except in the feline play areas. Here razor sharp nails could grasp balls and toss stuffed toys in the air. There were trees that the cats loved to climb and they could choose a tree made from a variety of materials. Some were real wooden trees with real bark, others were fabric covered, some were carpet covered, others were blanket covered, and some were even moss covered.

There were scratching posts three stories high with large platforms every twelve feet where cats could sleep, sit, talk, rest, or eat. In between the platforms, as well as at the base of each unit, were two separate posts—one for cats climbing up and one for cats climbing down.

There were other scratching posts shaped like spiral staircases and some shaped like huge fallen logs, complete with holes on either end for entering and exiting, as well as holes on the top and sides.

There were wide padded planks covered in bright upholstery fabric, some bending and twisting like a roller coaster.

There were enormous hollow metal rings cut out in areas on the top and sides, which had noisy balls inside them. Many a furry hand would slide through the openings and push those bell laden balls around and around through the shiny colorful rings.

Often several cats would station themselves around a ring and swat the ball when it came their way. Teams of these felines would have contests to see which group could send the ball around the ring the fastest. Once in a while they would have contests playing this game blindfolded, which was always hilarious and entertaining beyond belief.

The working class dogs liked to continually exercise and stay strong, even though in Everlife no one ever got sick or tired. They just wanted to do what they had been designed and created to do. Besides, it was a lot of fun.

There were different seasons here but there was no need to wait for their cycle like you did on Earth. Spring followed winter in Everlife in a much different way. Winter was in a quadrant of its own, and there, as you walked deeper into the quadrant, the season became more intense. On the outskirts of WinterQuad, there was a gentle wind and a light snow flurry, all the time. As you walked deeper into WinterQuad, the temperature decreased and the snowfall increased. If you walked to the west, the snowfall stopped, the sun shone, and the snow was six inches deep. As you traveled farther eastward, the depth of the snow increased.

The malamutes, siberian huskies, samoyeds, and keeshonds spent most of their time here. Cambium provided sleds and harnesses on request, and although no one ever inquired as to how these items were acquired, it was assumed that Cambium did have some magical powers that he preferred to keep to himself.

Next to WinterQuad there was of course SpringQuad. Here there were warm creeks and a constant array of flowering bulbs. The smells of SpringQuad were most grand, and there the puppies and outdoor dogs spent most of their time.

There was one huge lake in SpringQuad, and although it was not permitted for one species to injure another, there were no laws against antagonism or innocent mischief. Cambium thought the latter kept everyone on their toes and amused, and in most cases this was true.

Since SpringQuad bordered the wetlands of Everlife, it was common to see waterfowl on lake Aquos. It was also common to see traditional hunting dogs sneaking up on the relaxing ducks that often dozed on the calm water or slept on the shore. Sometimes the ducks became totally annoyed and would complain to Cambium, who would enforce a period of LOSA, or "Leave Other Species Alone." When the LOSA term expired, there was sure to be a sudden increase of interspecies mischief, but in actuality, both species welcomed the fun … for a while.

SummerQuad in Everlife was different than on Earth. There was moderate humidity, maintained at a pleasant 35 percent, which kept everyone's skin and coats moist but prevented the extreme exhaustion associated with high mugginess that animals on Earth faced in certain parts of the country while on assignment. The little fuzzy dogs preferred SummerQuad and spent most of their time picnicking and discussing the different clips they had received at the groomer's during their most recent assignment.

AutumnQuad was the most popular place in Everlife, or so it seemed based on the number of animals found there on any given day. Both cats and dogs liked the perpetual hint of fall and the crispness in the air. Every time a leaf fell from a tree, another one replaced it on the branch. Purple, brilliant orange, burgundy, and deep golden leaves were always found in AutumnQuad. When they became three deep on the ground, the bottom leaf disappeared. Since it never rained there, the leaves were always deeply colored, crunchy, and never faded or dull.

Cambium arranged for one particular tree to shed leaves more quickly, which caused a large pile to accumulate beneath it. This pile remained at a constant four foot height, and with each additional layer falling on the top, the layer on the bottom disappeared. Mostly dogs, but sometimes cats, enjoyed running head long into the pile or burying their friends under the leaves.

Once a large dog with an exceptionally hard head and strong legs ran so aggressively into the pile that he struck the trunk of the tree and nearly passed out. Since there is no pain or injury in Everlife, the dog was fine, but Cambium decided to extend the length of the branches from the trunk so the pile of leaves would always remain twenty feet from the trunk, forming a deep circle around the tree. No one ever ran into that tree again.

Lanagan and Flanders made their way over to WinterQuad, talking as their paws stepped through three inches of snow, kicking the white powder playfully with each step.

"What's the hardest part for you, Lanagan?" asked Flanders.

"I guess it's knowing you're there for a reason but not quite figuring it out or not seeing the result of it while you're there," answered Lanagan.

"We've all had thousands of assignments but you know how it goes. The lower levels are easy. It's when you get up to Level VI and VII that you know you're going to be changed forever. And you know they are too. You get so attached. I guess that's why Cambium has you go through so many lower levels first; you're just not ready for those big assignments. This last one of mine, well, let's just say for the first time ever, I really miss them; I miss that family."

"Do you think they miss you too, Flanders?"

"I sure hope so. But I guess I'll never know, will I?"

"Have you ever wondered why Cambium never lets us return to the same family?"

"I never thought about it until now, since I got back this time. I'd give anything to go back to those people."

"But if you did, you wouldn't remember them the way you do now. It'd be like starting over and you wouldn't realize who they were until you got back to Everlife. Then, I think you'd regret it more."

"Maybe that's why he never lets us go back."

The two dogs sat in the snow looking into the distance. Flurries were falling and the breeze blew their long fur gently as snowflakes landed on them in silence.

CHAPTER FOUR

William passed another exit on the Interstate, the Band-Aid still covering the red "check engine" light. He smirked and felt a sense of pride and accomplishment as his odometer indicated he had driven thirty miles from the gas station where he had last filled the tank. His schedule was to spend the night somewhere over the Iowa border and he would be there in another forty minutes. Since he had made it this far, he saw no reason to think his vehicle would not make the last stretch of highway.

He had done a lot of thinking since he left his home in Canton, Ohio. He had decided to go ahead and retain Sherman Hillman, Jr. After all, Sherman knew the law better than he did, and sometimes you just needed an upper hand to make things go your way. If Eugene Morgan would not readily relinquish the rights to his father's patent, then maybe what he needed was some persuasion; some aggressive, legal persuasion. When he returned home, William would have his secretary send Mr. Hillman the $5,000 retainer. What was another $5,000 when he was already in the hole for two million?

The next forty miles passed effortlessly. William was relaxed and relieved he had decided to let Sherman handle things. He knew, however, his father would not approve of his decision.

He got to the hotel wondering how he had arrived. He had a clean driving record and had never been in even a minor accident. Sometimes, however, when he was preoccupied with a problem or situation and would drive, he would arrive at his destination with absolutely no recollection of actively driving there. He had once heard that during those instances, the subconscious mind was the one that steered and accelerated and watched the rear view mirror, while the conscious mind dwelled on the mental distraction. Whatever it was that took control of the driving duties during those times, had certainly done it again tonight, and William shook in his seat when he realized his mind had been far from the drivers seat, even though his hands had remained on the wheel.

He turned off the highway and pulled into the hotel parking lot. He peered under the Band-Aid and saw the "check engine" light still gleaming a bright, luminous red.

He grabbed his briefcase and took the overnight bag from the trunk and walked into the hotel lobby. After signing some papers at the desk, he stood at the door of his reserved room and inserted his plastic key for entry.

He dropped his attaché onto the king-size bed and hung his leather jacket over a chair, making sure the shoulders were straight and square. He was far from compulsive about his clothes, but he always made it a point to set down his slacks with the creases matched and laid over a chair back, and he did hang the shirts in his closet in a color coordinated manner. The lighter colors started at the left and the darker colors ended at the right. Inside his closet doors at home, his shirts hung neatly like slices of a rainbow. Maybe he was compulsive about his clothes after all.

His mother had taught him at an early age to do his own laundry. This he did begrudgingly. Katie decided that her son would not follow in his father's footsteps in every way, and when it came to laundry, William's path would be very different. Little William had to use a step stool to turn the knobs on the washer and dryer when he initially began his laundry duties. There were many days when he wore dirty jeans and stained shirts, simply because he had run out of clean clothes and deliberately neglected to wash his dirty ones. Katie's embarrassment at seeing her son get on the school bus with filthy wrinkled clothes was exceeded only by her resolve to teach him self-reliance. There were times when these two battles raged in the house for days at a time. When William was eleven years old, he went to school wearing the same clothes repeatedly for an entire week. Katie stood firm, however, and William finally caved in and washed his huge pile of dirty laundry. He was furious at his mother for washing his father's clothes endlessly, yet forcing him to do his own, but as he got a little older, he accepted it and never mentioned it again. Ultimately, he realized he was self-sufficient after all and that suited him very well. He would have loved to marry, but women seemed to want him for his money and social status, and nothing more. Maybe one day he would find a special woman, but until then, he was very content with his bachelor status. And with his highly organized closet.

Here in the hotel, he had a very difficult time falling asleep; his mind continued racing and running scenarios concerning ColPro. He was startled in the dark of his hotel room by the ring of his cell phone and turned the small clock radio towards his pillow and was shocked to discover it was almost one o'clock in the afternoon. Apparently, he had fallen asleep after all.

He grabbed the phone from the nightstand. "Hello, this is William," he said, leaning back onto his pillow.

"It sounds like we woke you up, Sleepyhead!"

"Hi, Mom," he said as he turned on the lamp. "I guess I did sleep in. I didn't get to the hotel until after midnight," he said, stretching one arm over his head and arching his shoulders.

"I was calling to see if you'd be home for supper, but I guess that's a definite no."

"I've got another seven hours ahead of me. If you keep the oven on warm, I can have a late supper."

"Will do. Hey, here's your dad. He wants to talk to you for a minute."

"Hi, Son. I could smell the cinders from here last night. What have you decided?"

It never ceased to amaze William that his father could sense things with him so well. He had always thought this ability was reserved for mothers, but he discovered many years ago that he and his father had a bond that was very unique.

"Well Dad, I have pretty much decided to give Sherman the go-ahead."

There was much less silence on the phone than William had expected.

"We'll talk about it further when you get home, Will. Have a safe trip. We'll see you tonight."

William said good-bye knowing full well his father did not approve of his decision. He felt that twinge of regret a child feels when he knows he has disappointed a parent. Pushing himself up in bed and propping a second pillow behind his head, William rubbed his face with his hands and silently tried to convince himself he was not feeling guilty.

After checking out at the front desk, he poured himself a cup of coffee from the lobby beverage counter and headed for his car. The afternoon was overcast and crisp and he zipped up his leather jacket, fighting the chill that had come over him.

Unlocking the car, he once again plopped his briefcase on the passenger seat and threw the overnight bag in the back. He sat down and turned the key.

Nothing. Not a sound.

He turned the key again, just in case he had somehow turned it incorrectly the first time. He had not. The engine was as still as the trees at the far end of the parking lot.

He leaned back and gripped the steering wheel tightly in his hands. In total defeat and frustration, he peeled the Band-Aid from the dashboard. Holding it in front of his face, he whispered to it, "Murphy's Law at your service. What else can possibly go wrong in my life?"

The tow truck arrived forty-five minutes later and William rode silently in the front seat of the big truck, next to the brawny man with grease-stained hands.

Standing outside of the service station an hour later, William was on his cell phone with his father.

"No, Dad. They have no idea what's wrong with it. You know how it goes: the computer says everything's fine … yeah, I know … I will … as soon as I know something … yeah, I love you too."

A taxi pulled up a few minutes later and returned William to the hotel. He dropped his suitcase on the bed once again and splashed some water on his face, thinking that perhaps it would rinse away some of his frustration and anger. It did not. He decided that perhaps a hot meal would make him feel better, so he walked across the street to the neighborhood diner.

The long Formica counter was bordered on one side by round seats that were bolted to the floor, and to the front by the cook's station. A cash register strategically sat right next to the door, obviously to discourage customers from walking away without paying.

There were two waitresses, both with blue and white pinstriped dresses and white aprons. Both looked like they had eaten their share of the homemade apple pie and a meat loaf or two—or three. Both had pencils behind their ears and both were chewing gum. Most of the customers wore baseball caps and looked like they had eaten their share of homemade apple pie and meat loaf too.

William sat at the far end of the counter, even though he passed a few empty seats on his way to the counter's end. He wiped the stool and the copper speckled counter top with a napkin before sitting down, and set his briefcase on the counter to his left. One of the waitresses walked over to him with a look of reproach on her well-worn face.

"The counter is clean, mister. I washed it after the last guy left."

Sheepishly, William glanced down at the menu and then smiled at the woman, trying to redeem himself. Folding the menu closed, he set it down and said, "Just bring me your favorite thing on the menu. Surprise me." His attempt at redemption went unrewarded. She continued chewing her gum, stopping only to move it flagrantly to the other side of her mouth. As she took his menu from the counter, she popped the gum with a loud burst and walked away.

Opening his briefcase, William removed the manila envelope that sat on top and then latched the attaché closed again. He set the folder down in front of him and stared at it.

He knew nothing about Eugene Morgan, other than he owned the patent that was supposed to belong to him and ColPro. Ten days ago, William called his HR director and asked her to run a background check on Mr. Morgan. The company always ran general checks on potential employees and even potential clients. More than once, this simple background check had prevented likely disaster. More than once it had revealed criminal records, previous fraud charges, name changes, and one time even resulted in the arrest of a man wanted in another state for embezzling from his former employer.

It was a place to start, William believed, and he had asked Betty to run the routine background check. When that came up empty, he asked her to call a friend of hers who they had retained in the past. This other chap was a private investigator and they had hired him just once to follow a potential customer who they believed was taking sample products over seas for illegal production.

William slid his thumb under a corner of the envelope flap and hesitated before opening it, as if the contents might explode when the seal was broken. He recalled a scene in a movie where a secret agent opened a seemingly innocent greeting card he found in his suit coat pocket. Assuming the card was a loving gesture from his wife, he opened the pink envelope and was ultimately exposed to a deadly toxin. As it turned out, the envelope had been slipped into the agent's pocket at the airport while he waited to board his plane.

William's daydream ended abruptly when a man sat down next to him and plopped his heavy gloves on the counter. Releasing the corner of the envelope and setting it back down, William and the man made eye contact and exchanged polite hellos. William was not in the mood for smiling, let alone conversation, and hoped this man in the adjacent seat would not start talking to him.

His hoping was in vain.

The man was as pleasant as William was frustrated and annoyed. He was a bit older than William, dressed in Carharts and wool—obviously a local. William realized his upcoming meal and his time would not be spent quietly.

The man's name was Rusty, and William looked at him thinking he had never seen a man that seemed so genuinely content and who smiled so broadly … or so often. His conversation was as light as his attitude, and was interrupted only when he turned around to look out the large diner windows. After the fourth or fifth time of turning around and looking outside, William turned with him to see what was causing this repeated inspection. Noticing William's curiosity, Rusty smiled and explained.

"My golden is in the back of my pick-up. She sits in the cab with me when I'm driving, but when I stop for errands or to eat, I let her get in the back. It's a real treat for her," he said as if he was describing his child's first steps. "Especially since she's due to have pups soon."

Rusty turned back around in his swiveling red vinyl stool and reached for the hot coffee the waitress had just dropped off for him. William wondered why he had not been brought a cup and felt like a kid whose best friend had just gotten an ice cream sundae with one spoon.

"What kind of dog do you have?" asked the pleasant stranger.

"Oh, I don't have a dog. Used to. Had one growing up and had one about ten years ago," answered William. Then after pausing for several seconds, he added, "but a woman came between him and me, and he lost."

"I bet you've regretted that move ever since."

"I did for a while. But I really don't have time for a pet right now. I work long hours and live in a condo. No yard for a dog."

"You'll come to regret that move too, I reckon. A man's got to have a dog and some property to call his own. Dogs are meant to be a man's companion and yards are meant to relax the mind and keep the soul centered. When you don't have them in your life you're out of balance."

Grimacing with taut lips, William shook his head slightly and confessed to the stranger that he was definitely out of balance. A cup of hot coffee was finally delivered to him and he was careful to move the folder farther to his left. The waitress sneered at him and clicked her gum loudly once more.

"What's with the waitress?" he asked Rusty, almost under his breath.

"Oh, ol' Thelma's OK. She's just had a hard life and is going through a tough time right now. She was born and raised in this little town and had dreams of moving on, but never made it out of the county. When she sees people passing through, especially out-of-towners dressed like you, I think it reminds her of the dream that never came true." After a lengthy pause he added, "Leave her a good tip. It'll make her day and give her hope."

William looked up from his coffee cup and said, "Why should I encourage her? She's been rude to me ever since I walked in this dump."

"That's the point. For some folks, this place isn't a dump at all. A lot of folks came here for dates back when juke boxes and Bobbie socks were in style. Some folks think it's a real treat to come in here for a hot cooked meal, especially the older folks who live alone and don't have the energy to cook a meal anymore. Yup, this place is a real palace, depending on your point of view."

"I guess my point of view is a little too pointy, then."

"Points and rough edges can always be smoothed out, William," said Rusty with a smile, and once again he turned around and looked out the window.

William was relieved when the conversation quelled. He hoped the silence would continue, but of course it did not. Rusty took a lengthy sip of coffee and then started talking again.

"Yup, she's four years old and expecting her first litter of pups. She was ten weeks old when I picked her up from the breeder. I've always had dogs and suspect I always will. When my wife Denise passed away twelve years ago, my two dogs filled a real big part of the sudden void in my life."

"Claude was a sheltie and lived to the ripe old age of twelve, three years past the time of Denise's passing. Our other dog, Carly, was a yellow lab mix that we had adopted at an animal shelter. She had been highlighted in the newspaper one Sunday and my wife saw her picture. The next morning she and I were waiting at the shelter door for them to open. Three other people were ahead of us, each planning to adopt the dog, but as fate would have it, we were the only ones who qualified to adopt her."

Pausing for another sip of coffee, he continued, "Carly was about five or six years old when we got her. Claude was seven. She lived only another two years, but we were so happy to have shared those years with her. I put a deposit on the golden retriever pup while Claude was still around. As it turned out, the sheltie passed away the day the pups were born. Ten weeks later to the day, I drove 230 miles to get her."

Feeling awkward but obligated, William asked, "What did you name her?"

"Well, she had a habit of nipping at my boots and pant legs, so I decided to name her Bootleg. Now she's four years old and ready to be a Mom. I've already got homes for four of the pups; personal friends or business associates I've known for years. All promise to alter the pups and all have had dogs in the past."

William realized that Rusty was looking forward to the litter like a man looks forward to a grandchild.

The gum clad waitress grabbed plates from the cook's station, stacked them up her left arm, and then grabbed the last one with her right hand, which she set in front of Rusty. William looked at Rusty's Salisbury steak and mashed potatoes and set his napkin down on his lap fully expecting one of the other plates to be his.

The waitress clucked her gum once more and walked out from behind the counter to the main dining area. Rusty turned to watch her. She set down a plate at the table directly behind them, then set down another at the next table. As she chewed in delight, she turned around and approached William from the back, reaching forward to set down the last plate, which she had purposely waited to deliver.

At that exact moment, a loud tractor-trailer horn hollered from the parking lot, startling everyone in the restaurant, including William. He turned around abruptly towards the sound and collided with the waitress's arm. His hot lunch turned over onto his lap.

The waitress stopped chewing her gum. William jumped up, wildly pushing the hot gravy and potatoes from his front side to the floor. Turning towards Rusty and stifling a scream, he lamented, "My life has become Murphy's Law. If something can go wrong, it will."

Rusty stood and grabbed a handful of napkins from the counter in a fruitless attempt to help.

William's fury was beyond words. He was tired, hungry, frustrated, and now covered in pot roast, mashed potatoes, and gravy. The waitress stood there in shock, glancing towards the kitchen where her boss glared at her with arms folded across his chest. She knew that the price of that meal would be taken out of her tips at the end of the day, regardless of her tenure at the restaurant. Her attitude towards customers was something her boss had been monitoring for some time.

The cook came around from the kitchen and assured William that he would take care of his dry cleaning costs and replace his meal with something else from the menu, on the house. William set the napkins on the counter, thanked the proprietor, but declined the offer. He just wanted to get out of his clothes and change into something dry.

Rusty hesitantly offered an understanding smile but knew William was in no mood for empathy. William patted him on the shoulder and wished him good luck with the upcoming litter, then picked up his briefcase and the manila envelope and headed out the door.

The wind whipped hard against his wet pants, and he flexed his head to break the gusts from his face. He held his leather jacket over his arm to keep it from getting soiled and held his briefcase in front of his body to cover the mess on his khaki pants. As he walked back across the street to the hotel, he asked himself under his breath, "What else can possibly go wrong?"

William stepped out of the hotel shower feeling much cleaner but still starving. With one towel wrapped around his waist and drying his hair with another, he walked to the small closet knowing full well there would not be a guest robe in there, but decided he needed to look, just in case. He should not have wasted the energy.

There was a knock at the door and a male voice indicated he was with room service. Cracking the door slightly and looking into the hall to make sure no one else was there, William opened the door while hiding behind it and apologized for not having a bathrobe. The waiter set the tray down on the table near the window and indicated that William could sign the guest check when it was convenient for him.

Absolutely famished by this point, William sat down at the small table near the window. Lifting the lid from his bowl of chicken and dumplings, his mouth watered in anticipation. The hotel's special of the day had actually been pot roast, but he had seen enough pot roast for one afternoon. Tearing the corner of the salad dressing packet, he poured it onto the mixed greens and lifted his fork.

The meal was far from spectacular, but it was filling and decent enough to satisfy. He grabbed the dessert from the tray and moved over to the bed and reached for the remote with his other hand. Leaning back against two propped pillows, he took a bite of fudge brownie and aimed the remote at the television.

With the push of a button, the sounds of television filled the hotel room. He channel surfed while he gobbled the last of the brownie, and after perusing sixty-eight channels of nothing, he turned off the set and grabbed some plaid flannel lounge pants and a white T-shirt from his suitcase. After dressing and hanging the bath towel neatly over the shower curtain rod, he went back to the bed and reached for the manila envelope that lay near the pillows next to his briefcase.

He returned to the propped pillows, took a long, deep breath, unsealed the envelope, and finally removed the stack of papers. The first page was the routine background check. Mr. Morgan had lived in two different states and had used the same name in each. He had no criminal record. He had excellent credit; in fact, he had no debt. He had one credit card and paid it in full every month.

Pages two through four were from the private investigator. Eugene Morgan was born in St. Thomas, North Dakota, on such and such a date and was now fifty-four years old. He and his late wife had three children, two girls and a boy. The wife had died unexpectedly, apparently from an adverse reaction to prescription medication. At the time of her death, the children were fourteen, twelve, and eight. He raised them alone and never remarried. The two older kids were college graduates and working in New York and Chicago respectively. The youngest child, a daughter, was currently in college in Davenport.

William finished reading page three of the abridged biography and set his reading glasses on the nightstand. He rubbed his tired eyes and had a sip of bottled water. After checking the time, he picked up the stack of papers again and slipped page three behind pages one and two. When he saw the photo on page four, he gasped and lunged forward toward the nightstand to grab his reading glasses, nearly falling off the bed.

Page four was an 8" x 10" black and white photograph, the first of four. It was a shot of Mr. Morgan getting into his Jeep Cherokee. The second was Mr. Morgan walking out of a grocery store. Photo number three was Mr. Morgan getting his mail from the curbside box. This photo showed his house: a large Tudor style home with an immaculate front yard. Photo number four showed Mr. Morgan lying on the manicured lawn, smiling from ear to ear, while being licked on the face by a dog.

William sat in silent shock. He leaned back into the pillows and murmured under his breath.

"It's not possible, it's simply not possible." Setting his glasses back on the nightstand, he rubbed his forehead with his hands and whispered again, "It can't be possible."

He flipped through the pages again, returning to the first page and re-read Mr. Morgan's name: Eugene Russell Morgan. The man in the photos was Rusty, the man from the diner.

CHAPTER FIVE

The animals were gathering at the Great Tree, for it was time again for The Gathering and the distribution of assignments. This time Lanagan and Flanders were on the list of dogs available for departure.

As always, Miss Mallory ran around like Chicken Little encouraging everyone to hurry along and not be late.

The animals came by the thousands. Some rode atop other creatures and some were carried by the scruff of their neck in the gentle mouths of others. For the most part, the cats traveled with other cats and likewise, the dogs. Even though all species lived peacefully together in Everlife, the animals still found that they most often preferred the company of their own kind. Those animals who had changed forms for past assignments were the ones who most often traveled in mixed company.

With the ever so familiar sounds of creaking and splitting wood, Cambium's face appeared amidst the deep bark like it had so many times before.

"Greetings, greetings creatures, one and all," he said. "Today is a glorious day in Everlife because today many of you four-walkers will be receiving new assignments. Today is also a glorious day because today we welcome back others who have returned from previous assignments within the past thirty days. Will all of you who have recently returned please come forward to be recognized?"

Miss Mallory once again untied the huge red velvet rope and the large cluster of animals formed a single line and began walking in front of the massive Tree.

As they did, applause rang out from the crowd. Paws stomped on the grass, hind legs beat on the ground, and other paws came together while the animals sat on their hind legs. As always, interspersed within the long line of animals was a dog or a cat wearing a silk scarf. Some were red with sliver trim and others were white trimmed with metallic gold. Occasionally there was a howl or a catcall from the crowd, all expressed with love and appreciation. Lanagan and Flanders bellowed out their deep "oof oof oof" wails until Cimmaron gave them a look of dismay from farther down the row.

When the procession of animals had completed their victory march and walked off to their seats, Cambium continued speaking.

"Today's assignments are all postings to the Midwest and central states of America." As he spoke, a holographic map of the United States took shape amongst his massive branches, the outline of the map lit with ropes of light that traveled around the border of the country like a shooting star. Then, one by one, the states in the center of the country became lit and lifted themselves from the flat map that lay within the mass of leaves. Each state's outline shined like two electrical currents of yellow light traveling around it, one clockwise and one counterclockwise until the two strands of light met and then reversed backwards the other way. Ohio, Illinois, Indiana, Iowa, Minnesota, Nebraska, and Iowa. City and town names from each state sprung from the map and then were pulled back downwards. Each state was highlighted in this fashion until all seven of them had been displayed on the map. When the display ended, the map disappeared and once again onlookers could see nothing but green atop the branches of the tree. Cambium raised his limb arms towards his leaves and said, "Let us begin."

Thousands of gleaming white specks appeared within the expanse of his greenery. Without losing any brilliance, every speck grew in size until each had formed a flat piece of shiny parchment. One by one, the papers folded themselves in half, still glowing with pearly white shimmers.

Cambium removed one of the shiny pieces of vellum from among his leaves. Unfolding the paper and holding it to his face, the crowd sat motionless.

"This is a Level I assignment. As you know, Level I is both the lowest Level and the most commonly misunderstood Level. Level I assignments often require the return to less domestic conditions, and often the necessity to gather your own food. Level I may or may not be easy and most often does not entail human contact. Level I assignments may consist of being a mouser or feral cat if you are a feline, or being wild or part of a pack or an abandoned litter if you are a dog. Level I assignments are important because this is how we monitor the human condition below. The data with which you provide upon your return is analyzed and adjustments to future assignments are made accordingly. Those returning from Level I assignments will have absolutely no conscious memory of their experience when they return to Everlife, because those memories are simply too painful to recall. I wish I could tell you that the number of Level I assignments is decreasing, but it is not."

Taking a deep breath, Cambium looked out onto the crowd and asked, "Who is ready for this assignment?" He reached up and gathered a hundred or more shining white squares. "All of these are Level I assignments. Please come forward."

Dogs and cats stepped from the ranks and walked towards Cambium. Those in the crowd stepped forward and others stepped backwards, as if guided by invisible escorts who guided their movements, allowing for rows and aisles to be opened and widened so the responding animals could step out and walk toward the front.

"These are the most difficult assignments to distribute. Thank you, all of you. You are sacrificial and tender beyond measure. Please step to your right and Miss Mallory will distribute your specific assignment." Applause arose from the crowd once again.

After the line of creatures had moved on, Cambium grabbed another sheet, opened it and cleared his throat to speak. "This is a Level II assignment for a feline. The location is Nebraska. This assignment is open to all felines who have successfully completed all of their Level I assignments or for those canines who have completed their Level I assignments and who wish to change form. All interested animals, please step forward."

When the lower Level assignments had all been distributed, Cambium announced a call for all Level VII candidates, the highest Level available. There was one position available and it would be long term. Lanagan and Flanders were both Level VII qualified, so they sat attentively.

"The assignment is restricted to natural canines only. This assignment will be seven years, eight months, two days, and the lessons involved deal with trust and love. Are there any volunteers?"

Lanagan looked at Flanders and cocked his head sideways. "What do you think, old friend? Should I step forward?"

"You sound perfect for the assignment, Lanagan. I think you should do it."

Lanagan nudged his friend with his snout and stepped out into the aisle and walked forward. When he made it up to the base of the huge Tree, he realized no one else had volunteered. Even considering the enormous number of animals in this section of Everlife, there was still only a small percentage who were qualified for Level VII assignments.

Cambium folded the shiny paper and handed it to Lanagan. Addressing the crowd, the Tree bellowed once again.

"Prior to Lanagan's departure in 48 hours, all of you who have had previous experience with his assignment family will be notified. Your memories of the family will be returned to you, just long enough for you to share any helpful information with Lanagan." Looking down again at the big white dog, Cambium smiled and motioned with his lower limb for him to move to the left for processing.

CHAPTER SIX

As had occurred the previous morning, the sudden ring of William's cell phone woke him. This time it was the mechanic from Larry's Garage. They had determined the problem with his vehicle and the replacement part was on back order. It would not be in until Friday morning.

"I could be the poster child for Murphy's Law," he said after ending the call.

The next two days were the longest two days of William's life. The shock of discovering that his corrival of the previous day turned out to be a kind and gentle man upset William tremendously. He had intended to purposely maltreat this man through 'legal' means prior to their kismet meeting. Why had it been so acceptable to intentionally injure a stranger? Was it a question of convenience or simply greed? Why was that option seemingly unacceptable now? Was it a question of conscience?

He stayed in his hotel room out of shame and fear that he would run into Rusty again. How would that meeting go if it were to happen? William did not even want to consider it. So instead he hid in his hotel room with the curtains drawn, flipping through the television channels endlessly. He rarely watched television at home and was amazed at the mindless array of options available atop the hotel dresser. He ultimately decided on a home improvement channel, where at least inane situational plots or vile content could be avoided. As fate would have it, a landscaping show would be airing next, and he recalled with irony Rusty's comments about the emotional necessity of a yard.

Prior to buying his condo, William owned a townhouse. He spent so many hours at the office and so much time traveling that the idea of a yard or garden never entered his mind. He knew several high-level executives who had elaborate gardens of all varieties. He had even had a psychologist suggest gardening as a means of relaxation therapy two years ago.

Two years ago. It seemed like twenty.

William had taken the company to a new level. His Dad had recently retired and his parents had moved to the country to be near Millie, his mother's childhood friend whose husband had passed away.

The first time William introduced Samantha to his parents, they were still living in the city. His Mom had an 11-year-old pomeranian named Beaumont, and he was at her side regardless of where she went or what she did. In the winter months, Katie put knitted coats and mittens on the dog, and always made sure the outfit was color coordinated. Beaumont was both affectionate and protective, barking like a guard dog every time the doorbell rang. But once the door was opened, he jumped playfully onto the newly arrived guest or repairman. Everyone loved Beaumont and he loved everyone too.

Except Samantha.

When Samantha entered the Colbert house, Beaumont immediately backed away from her and growled. Katie was more embarrassed than concerned, and picked the small dog up from the floor and held him in her arms gently reprimanding him. Still with the dog in her arms, Katie leaned forward towards William's guest to allow Beaumont a more personal introduction. At this, the dog lunged forward and snapped at Samantha's face. Everyone was stunned. Thomas considered it a sign; a sign that the woman could not be trusted. Katie put it off as perhaps a reaction to Samantha's perfume.

Thomas had been raised with a lot of animals and had been taught to always be mindful of an animal's reaction to someone. He had discovered at an early age that animals were much better judges of character than people ever were, or ever could be. Thomas rarely spoke an unkind word about anyone, but when he did, beware. He never criticized Samantha openly, even to his wife, but he never trusted her and William could sense his reticence concerning her.

William dated Samantha for three years, to his parent's dismay. They always felt she was after their son for his money and talent, not his love. Shortly after William proposed, he presented his future bride with a prenuptial agreement, which had been drawn up at his father's insistence. She was hesitant to endorse the document at first, and inevitably gave William an ultimatum to choose the marriage or the family business. William chose the company.

He never saw her again. Several months later he heard she had married the son of a prominent banker in Pittsburgh. She never returned William's engagement ring, but he felt the cost of the ring was well worth the price of the lesson learned, regardless of the pain.

Realizing his parents were right was a revelation William found difficult to accept and even harder to swallow. No one welcomes the realization that his or her discernment had been influenced by emotion or seeming adoration. When it came right down to it, William's money and position were the main attractions people found in him, not his gentle nature or normally exemplary character. Once he fully realized this, he found it more difficult to trust anyone's sincerity or motivation.

Two years ago. It seemed like decades. As he sat on the crummy hotel bed, his thoughts raced. He walked into the bathroom and stared at himself in the mirror, realizing the reflection he saw was somewhat unrecognizable.

William paid the taxi driver and walked to the counter of the mechanic's shop. He did not ask about the repair; he did not ask about a warranty; he simply handed his credit card to the greasy man behind the counter in exchange for his keys. They were handed to him complete with a cardboard ID tag; the kind that is always attached to your keys when your oil is changed, your tires rotated, or when you are stranded in Nowheresville for three days awaiting a replacement part for your engine.

He turned the key in the ignition and with a sense of relief, the engine started. The "Fasten Seat Belt" light flashed and beeped, but no engine lights remained lit. Snow began falling as he drove back to the hotel to pick up his belongings and check out.

Lanagan passed through the portal and found himself in a wooded area. It was snowing fiercely. The wind howled against his long fur, but he found it refreshing. The air was crisp and the smells of this place were exciting and invigorating. There was something about the aromas of this other world; their blending and boldness and often their harshness and pungency. They were positively delightful.

As the minutes passed, Lanagan's memory of Everlife faded. He walked in the snow, sniffing to determine where he was and to recollect any familiar odors. There were none. So, he just walked. He was no longer a dog on a mission, but merely a dog in the woods. Life was good.

William drove slowly, the windshield wipers sweeping the snow again and again off the glass. Visibility was getting worse and he wondered how much more difficult traveling would be as the day progressed. It was midafternoon and his parents had told him the forecast called for severe winter conditions. A traveler's advisory had also been issued until 6:00 p.m. He had plenty of experience with winter driving, although currently his common sense had taken a back seat to his desire to get as far away from Iowa as he could.

A tractor-trailer was up ahead, clipping along at forty-five miles per hour. William stayed behind him, close enough to see his rear lights but far enough away to be safe. Two hours later, the semi signaled that he would be exiting at the weigh station. William acknowledged with a flash of his lights and a wave that he knew the driver would never see. The snow continued to fall and once again, William was on his own.

The subtle squeal of the windshield wipers soon grew monotonous and somnolent. William reached toward his dash and selected the classical station on his satellite radio. Suddenly a Baroque piece resonated through the speakers and William settled into his seat more fully and leaned backwards against the headrest.

When flashing yellow lights suddenly appeared to his right, William sprang forward and clutched the wheel tightly, thinking that maybe he had driven off the road. The lines on the highway had disappeared at least an hour ago and visibility continued to worsen. He saw a man waving with flailing arms and he tried to stop but ended up in a sixty-foot skid that left him understandably shaken and nearly breathless.

When he regained control of the car, he decided against backing up to see what that man had wanted. It would certainly be safer to continue moving forward. Not that he knew exactly where the break down lane was anyway. He also decided to keep his speed under 30 mph.

After his heart rate returned to normal and he began to feel lucid again, another set of flashing lights appeared. He caught a brief glimpse of a man in florescent orange coveralls waving his arms wildly. The snow was so thick he could barely see the front of his hood, but he quickly looked to his right again, desperately trying to see what was going on. When he turned to face forward again, a mound of snow stood directly in front of him.

He slammed on the brakes and came within inches of the drift, where he caught a glimpse of two red eyes shining through the whiteness. His car spun and hit a patch of ice, sending it off the highway, down an embankment, and farther into white nothingness.

When it finally came to rest, the driver's side window was bloodied. William touched his head and then looked at his red-stained hand. With the other hand, he reached for his cell phone to call for help. There was no signal.

"Murphy's Law," he whispered to himself. "Murphy's Law."

His head hurt and he assumed he had at least a concussion; he also knew he needed to get help. He slowly got out of the car, walking several paces in one direction hoping to get a signal. The falling snow was thick and heavy and he could barely see six feet in front of him. He had no idea how far off the highway his vehicle had landed. He walked a few paces in another direction. Then another. Still no signal. He turned towards the wind and as the snow lashed against his blood stained face, he saw a pile of snow ahead of him. Blinking hard, he squinted and thought he saw two eyes in the midst of it. He also thought the mound was moving. Paralyzed with terror, he dropped his cell phone and collapsed.

When William regained consciousness it was daylight. He heard voices from the distance going in and out of his ears, and saw the blurred outlines of two figures approaching. He was lying under a tree and was covered with snow.

"Sir? Sir? Can you hear me? We've come to help."

William tried to lift his pounding head. His temple ached and his thoughts were unclear and confused. He tried to move but could not. He could not feel his legs.

The two men stood over him. The snow surrounding his head was reddened by blood and the only portions of his body that were visible through the snowdrifts were his head and the tip of one shoe. The snow covering his torso was at least three feet deep.

"Sir. Can you tell us your name? The registration in the glove box belongs to a William Colbert. Is that who you are, Sir?"

William struggled to raise his hand but he could not. He squinted and tried to focus his vision.

"Are you in any pain?" asked one of the paramedics.

William tried to take a deep breath, but the air was so cold that his lungs rejected it. He slipped back into semi-consciousness.

"Murph ... eeee ... aaaaawwwww.... Murphhhhhhhh ... aaaaawwwww," he said unintelligibly to the two men.

The rescue team assumed the snow under his body would be saturated with blood once they uncovered him. The top layer of snow above him was frozen; it was beyond comprehension that he had survived the frigid temperatures.

The paramedics leaned forward to brush the snow off his body. As their gloved hands cracked through the crusty top layer of snow, a growl came from beneath it. Both of the men fell backwards in alarm and fright.

The snow covering William became silent. When he opened his eyes again, the two men were staring at him. He lifted his head slightly and said, "Mur ... Mur ... ee ... aw" to the blurred figures. "Mm ... Mm ... awwww" came out and he let his head fall back onto the snowy ground.

The two EMT's called to him again, this time staying several feet away. "Sir. Sir. Can you hear me?"

William opened his eyes. "Mur ... pheeeee ... aaaawwww," and he coughed and gagged softly. "Murrphh ... Murrrpheeeeee ..." he tried to say again, while forcing a smile. "Awwwwww," he continued, but once again his coughing interrupted the syllable and added a "gggg" sound.

The two men looked at each other.

"Did he say 'dog'?" asked one of them.

"I think he did say 'dog'," answered the other.

The snow above William's torso slightly rose and the crusty upper layer cracked as two eyes glowed black as coal from beneath it.

The two men stared into the eyes and then looked back at each other in hopeful understanding. One got to his feet and quietly and questionably asked, "Murphy?"

The white monster gently raised itself off of William's body and slowly stepped away, with cakes of snow falling from it. There lay William, totally dry and warm.

The two men smiled with relief and got to their feet. "Hey boy! Hey Murph! You did it big guy! You saved him! He's gonna be fine!" and the big white dog bent down to lick William's face.

CHAPTER SEVEN

When he awakened, William was in a hospital. He had an IV in his left arm and the most horrendous headache he had ever had. He looked around and saw balloons, flowers, and stuffed animals all around his room.

His face grimaced as he lifted his head and shoulders from the bed. A nurse walked into the room bringing in more flowers and smiling. "You're a hero, Mr. Colbert. You and your dog. All these presents are from people Murphy saved. Do you realize that sixteen people would have died if your dog hadn't gotten them off the highway? No one knew that bridge went out in the storm. The highway department suspected it might and was setting up a blockade to close that stretch of highway and set up a detour. If it hadn't been for you and your dog, we wouldn't be celebrating anything today Mr. Colbert." And she took his vitals and elevated the upper part of his hospital bed.

"My dog?" was all William could manage to say.

"Murphy is just fine. One of the paramedics took him home with him after they found you this morning. Once Dr. Chandler makes her rounds later this afternoon, you'll probably be released. Don't worry, we'll get Murphy back to you as soon as you leave the hospital."

Leaning back onto the newly fluffed pillows, William closed his eyes and started putting the puzzle pieces back together, recalling the events of the snowstorm as diligently as he could. The last thing he remembered was trying to avoid a snowdrift and skidding off the road. Now, every one thought he had a dog. Since he had suffered a head injury, he realized it would be easy to play dumb and get the nurse to fill in the missing pieces.

William was told that Murphy, his dog, saved the lives of over a dozen people by barking at the cars and running across the road as they approached the bridge. When the first car stopped, the dog stood in the middle of the highway and would not let them proceed. The driver pulled off the highway and walked fifty yards up the road, discovering the fallen bridge.

When the next car approached, they saw Murphy running along the side of the highway barking and darting on and off the road. The driver then noticed the people from the first car who were jumping up and down and motioning frantically with flares for them to pull over. When they did, they learned about the collapsed bridge and the impending fifty-foot fall. All toll, five vehicles were forced to pull over and sixteen lives were saved.

After the highway department blockade and detour was finished, Murphy had gone back to William and dragged him under a tree. The storm raged but the dog had kept him covered through the night, saving him from the cold.

By 3:00 p.m., the sun was out and the streets had been plowed. William was being wheeled out of the hospital, followed by an entourage of nurses and aids carrying all the flowers, balloons, stuffed animals, and dog toys. Waiting to greet him at the exit doors was a crowd of forty-five people, including a local news reporter. It was a good thing that William noticed the red light shining on the video camera, indicating that every movement and every word was being recorded.

Among the people in the crowd were the other motorists that "his" dog had rescued. Also in the crowd was a young paramedic with a leashed samoyed in tow. The dog was sitting obediently and had a huge red ribbon around his neck that read "HERO." William maintained his composure and hoped this charade would be over with soon.

A female reporter approached him, microphone in hand, as he got up from the wheelchair.

"Mr. Colbert, what do you think about having a hero for a dog?"

Smiling and shaking his head, William honestly replied, "It sure is a shock! I had no idea yesterday morning when I woke up that in twenty-four hours, I would be leaving a hospital with a dog who had become a local hero!"

"How long have you had Murphy? Did you get him as a pup?"

Cringing at the thought of this white dog belonging to someone in the viewing audience, and dreading the idea of being later discovered as a fraud, William chose his words quickly but wisely.

"Murphy was full grown when I first saw him, but I feel like he's always been a part of my life. It sure was lucky that he saved me from dying of exposure during the storm. Maybe my luck has changed...." And he paused as he looked at the dog and remembered his conversation with Rusty in the restaurant. William added sincerely, "It's good to be alive. And it's great to know that these other people here were saved too."

The crowd applauded.

"I'd like to donate the flowers and all these wonderful gifts to the local nursing home, if that's OK with everyone. I really appreciate them and I have surely enjoyed them. Thank you all so much. I'd like to share them with some other folks now, if that's O.K. Murphy will keep the dog toys though."

The crowd applauded again.

The large white dog walked forward to the extent of the leash. William looked at him, their eyes locking and sudden silence coming over the crowd. Smiling, William said to him, "Hey Stranger. How 'ya doin?" and the dog pulled himself free from the paramedic's grasp and ran to William. The crowd exploded with cheering again, the cameraman capturing every moment of it on tape.

To say that the entire scene moved William would be an understatement.

The local towing company had donated their services to recover his car from off the highway and a local detailing company had cleaned it inside and out. Local merchants and residents filled the trunk with food and gifts. A dog groomer had shampooed and brushed Murphy and the feed store gave him food and a beautiful leather collar. The town jeweler engraved a tag for the new collar which read, "MURPHY: Life Saver" on one side, and "Best Friend to William Colbert" on the other.

After all the hugs and handshakes were given, William opened the rear door of the car, desperately hoping the dog would know to jump in. Murphy did not move. Coaxing him with his arm, William began to feel uncomfortable. Murphy did not budge.

A little girl, probably around five, pulled on William's jacket. "I think he wants to sit in the front seat." William smiled sheepishly and closed the rear door. He opened the passenger door and moved his briefcase to the back seat. Standing up and gesturing once again to the strange white dog, Murphy leapt onto the front seat, to the roar of the crowd behind him. With much relief, William closed the door and once again thanked everyone for their kindness before walking around the car and letting himself into the driver's seat.

Waving to the camera and the mass outside the hospital, William left the parking lot and headed out of town, having been given an alternate route that bypassed the fallen bridge. He could not help but notice that the dog was staring at him, seemingly waiting for William to say something.

William shook his head. "What? What do you want me to say? Thank you for saving my life? Is that what you want to hear?"

The dog sat motionless.

"I don't know what you want me to say." Then, realizing what he had just uttered, he shook his head and said aloud to himself, "Can you believe it? I'm talking to animals now. I must have gotten a really nasty bump to the head."

Turning to look at the dog again, he continued, "What do you want me to say? I already thanked you. I'm talking to you ... isn't that enough? What *is* it?"

The dog continued to stare.

William took out his cell phone and turned it over and over again in his hands.

"I imagine these teeth marks and scratches have something to do with you, but I won't ask."

He dialed his parents and his Dad picked up the phone.

"William. It's so good to hear from you, We've been worried," Thomas said as he smiled at Katie who breathed a lengthy sigh of relief.

"I know, Dad. Let's just say I got caught in that storm and didn't have any reception on my phone."

"I understand, Son."

"Tell Mom I expect to be home around 8:00 tonight, OK? ... I love you too, see you later."

The dog continued to stare at William.

"Do you need to go to the bathroom?"

The dog did not move.

The situation was starting to worry William. Sure the dog seemed friendly enough back there, but what if he had rabies or distemper or something? What if he decided to lunge across the seat and attack William while he was driving?

"Are you hungry, is that it? No, you can't be hungry, not after that send off we just had. I know they had to feed you this morning."

The dog stared.

"*What is it?* Do you want to go home? Do you miss someone?"

William then had a brainstorm. He pulled into a filling station and walked to the pay phone. Flipping through the white pages, he jotted down a number on a corner of the page and tore it off. Going back to his car he dialed the number.

"Humane Society," someone answered.

"Uh, Hi. Is this the place where someone would report a lost dog?"

"Yes, sir. We service the entire county. Did you lose your dog?"

"Well, no. I uh, I just spoke with a little boy who said he lost his big, fluffy white dog. Has anyone reported this yet?"

"No Sir, no one has reported a lost white dog. Our lists are updated every day and there's been no mention of a lost white dog. The only large fluffy white dog I know of in the entire area is the one who saved all those people during the storm. But, he wasn't from around here."

"Well, uh, on second thought, maybe it was a large fluffy cat the kid said he lost. Thank you." And he ended the call feeling like he had lied to his grandmother about peeking through the wrapping paper on his Christmas present.

"So you're not lost, huh? Don't have a home, huh? Well, join the club. I feel kind of alone right now too."

The dog continued to stare.

"Murphy," said William, and no sooner did the last syllable escape his mouth than the dog tilted his head to one side. "Murphy? Is that what you wanted to hear?"

The dog opened his mouth and William swore he saw a smile.

William smiled too, reaching his hand out hesitantly to stroke the beautiful, soft white head.

"It looks like it's me and you then, Boy. OK ... I'll keep you ... at least for now. Is that what you wanted to hear?"

The dog barked twice and leaned over to lick William's face. He then went back to his seat, curled up, and went to sleep.

The hours passed peacefully and by dusk William needed to fill the gas tank, as well as his stomach. They were almost out of Iowa by this time and after topping the tank, he opened the passenger door and grabbed Murphy's leash to take him for a walk.

He was the picture of obedience and although William had no idea as to the extent of his training, he felt it best to keep him on the leash for now.

After visiting the restroom and the dog rest area, William opened the trunk and surveyed the smorgasbord of choices. Sandwiches, casseroles, sliced fruit, Jell-O molds, cake, nut breads, and, of course, a forty pound sack of dog food. Needless to say, they rested and ate for a good half-hour.

He pulled out his cell phone and dialed his parents. His Mom answered.

"Hi Mom. Just wanted to let you guys know that I'm about two hours out. Wanted to tell you something else too." Looking over at Murphy and smiling, William added, "I'm bringing a guest with me."

"A guest? Who are you bringing? Why didn't you give me any notice? I can't believe you didn't tell me."

"Calm down, Mom. The guest I'm bringing home isn't the human kind. It's a dog."

"A dog? When did you get a dog? You never told us you had a dog?"

"Well, last time I talked to you, I didn't. It's a long story."

"How on Earth did you get a dog in the past three hours?"

"I'll tell you all about it when I see you. Tell Dad I'll be there around 8:00."

The front porch light was a welcomed sight when William arrived at his parents' house. Snow had fallen here too, but nothing like what had fallen on William the previous night. Here at the farmhouse, only a dusting covered the landscape.

The old homestead had seen its share of tornadoes and blizzards over the decades, as well as some scorching Nebraska summers. Thomas and Katie had done extensive renovating inside but their intention was to keep the exterior look of the house as close to its original appearance as possible. After a significant amount of caulking and priming, the clapboards welcomed two fresh coats of pale yellow paint and then some glossy white trim.

The decorative windmill stood in the front yard, as if frozen in time. Snow clung to the sides of the blades and icicles dangled from the metal rungs. There was absolutely no wind but the air was bitter, bitter cold.

The swing on the front porch had received some new hardware and several replacement boards when Thomas moved back to the house. As a child, he remembered his parents going out to the porch and sitting together on the swing every night after supper. Even during the winter months they would occasionally sit out there with quilts and comforters wrapped around them and swing. Now the old swing was powdered with new snow, but Thomas had swept the porch and walkway earlier that evening and it was clear and dry.

William removed the key from the ignition and his Dad opened the front door and walked outside to greet him. Katie waited by the door, keeping warm and waiting for a glimpse of the strange dog her son had brought home.

William stepped out of the car and patted his thigh, indicating to Murphy to follow. When the longhaired dog stepped onto the gravel driveway, Katie pushed the screen door open and put her hands to her mouth. She had never seen such a beautiful creature in her entire life.

"*This* is your new dog?" she asked William as she stepped down from the porch.

"Murphy, I'd like you to meet your Grandparents. Folks, I'd like you to meet Murphy."

Thomas greeted William with a bear hug and a kiss on the cheek. Katie bent down and extended her hand to greet Murphy, who licked it only once before stretching upward and licking her face before she had any recourse.

"I always suspected that once you had a grandchild you'd forget about me," William teased.

Katie stood and hugged her son, then William wrapped his arm around her shoulder as the four of them walked up the stairs into the house.

"I assume he's housetrained," Thomas half-asked and half commented, looking at William.

"I have no idea. I assume so too."

"Well, I bet we'll find out before morning," said Thomas, chuckling.

They all walked into the kitchen and the men sat at the table while Katie removed a covered casserole dish from the oven. Murphy lay down on the floor between William and Thomas.

"If you don't want something heavy right now, you can just have dessert," smiled Katie understandingly.

Looking down at Murphy, William replied in that voice usually reserved for conversing with babies, "Oh, Murphy, I think we have room in our tummies for something heavy, don't you?"

Murphy barked in approval and everyone laughed.

Katie set the casserole on the table and removed the lid.

"It sure is good having a dog in the house again," she said, smiling down at the big white dog. "How long have you had him?"

"Well, I got him yesterday, but I'm still not sure how it actually happened," answered William. As he spooned a large helping onto his plate, he realized his answer made no sense, so he proceeded to fill them in on the events of the previous twenty-four hours.

CHAPTER EIGHT

The next morning when William woke, it took him a minute to realize where he was. When it finally hit him, he sat upright and looked down at the floor next to the bed where the dog had gone to sleep the night before. Murphy was not there.

"Murphy," he called softly, just in case someone was still sleeping

A groan came from the other side of the bed and William turned to find the fluffy dog stretching his paws and neck. His head was on the other pillow.

"What do you think you're doing on my bed?"

Murphy lifted his big head and looked at William, as if waiting for him to continue.

"If Mom sees you on the bed she'll have a fit. Now get down."

Murphy crawled on his elbows to the side of the bed and slowly stepped off.

"That's better. Now, let's go have some breakfast. I think I smell bacon."

William got dressed and walked downstairs with Murphy. Thomas and Katie were already sitting at the kitchen table drinking coffee.

"William, I can't believe you still have that old shirt," said Katie. "Good morning, Murphy," she added, smiling.

"Mom, you know this is my favorite shirt."

"It was your favorite shirt twenty years ago, Son."

William looked down at his navy blue long sleeve shirt. It was faded and very worn.

"How did you sleep, Will?" asked Thomas.

"A lot better than I have in weeks."

"I noticed that your dog likes the comfort of down pillows and quilts too," smiled Katie.

Murphy barked.

Thomas got up and opened the back door to let the dog outside.

"He seems very well-mannered," Thomas commented. "I think you've found a great companion, Will."

"He sure is a lot easier to get along with than most of the people I know," smiled William as he reached for a biscuit.

"He seems to have bonded with you already," Katie added. "Remember how Beaumont was with me? A day doesn't go by that I still don't miss that dog."

Thomas sipped his coffee and then cleared his throat. "No sense putting off our discussion, Will. Have you given any more thought to the situation with the patent?"

"Five days ago I was so sure I wanted the situation resolved, regardless of the cost. I have so much at stake with this patent. If we don't go into production, I'll need to sell the condo to begin to pay the debt. I'll lose my entire savings. The cost of this is so high."

"But what about the price?" questioned his father. "What price are you willing to pay? And I'm not talking about money. I'm talking about character. I'm talking about ethics. You know I built that company from the ground up, and I did it with honesty and integrity."

"That's what I'm talking about too," responded William. "But how do you expect me to respond to what the Patent Office did? How do you expect me to make up for that? I can't. I did everything by the book and then it all blew up in my face."

"Most things in life are beyond our control, Will. We can't change what the Patent Office has decided, and if Mr. Morgan is the legitimate patent owner, we can't change that either. If he is not interested in selling the rights, that's his prerogative. Maybe he'll change his mind at some point, but we don't know. The only thing we can do is figure out the best way to respond to what has happened."

"So, you're saying I should lose my home and my entire savings, and let the company go down the tubes?"

"I'm not saying that at all. I'm saying that you need to be accountable for your actions. If you are forced to sell the condo, so be it."

Katie looked sharply at her husband, who continued. "There is always more money to be made, Will. There will always be another product to produce or to sell. You need to look at the man in the mirror and make sure you see someone who has not lied or cheated to make a buck that day. If he has, the price he'll pay for that will continue to grow and will never go away."

"So, you want me to forget about the patent? You want me to sell the condo and pay off the debt? You're making it sound a lot easier than it really is."

"Doing the right thing isn't always easy, Son. Doing the right thing is often the hardest thing you've ever done. It's usually not convenient and it's usually not comfortable."

Murphy barked at the back door, and Katie, grateful for the interruption, got up to let him in. Wagging his tail and smiling a happy dog smile, he walked over to William and put his head on his lap.

Katie shook her head and said, "That dog acts like he's known you for years. Are you sure you want to take him back to Canton with you? We'd be happy to keep him, wouldn't we, Thomas?"

Smiling a fatherly smile, Thomas replied, "I think Murphy needs to help William look for a rental house when they get back to Ohio."

William looked down at the pure white fur that rested on his thigh. Scratching the dog behind one ear, he leaned forward and whispered, "So, what will it be? A small house in the suburbs or something farther out in the country?"

Reaching across the table, Thomas grabbed his wife's hand and smiled.

William waved goodbye as he and Murphy backed out of the driveway. His parents stood waving with one arm and with their other arms around each other. The visit had gone well and William felt like an enormous weight had been lifted from his overburdened shoulders. He had left his office in Ohio full of frustration and anxiety, but now felt a deep sense of calm and assurance. He found himself in awe of his father's wisdom and wondered why he had never fully recognized it until now. He also wondered when he would begin to feel the same righteous confidence and conviction in his own life. He hoped it was not too late for it to develop.

The return trip was uneventful and the weather was accommodating, much to William's relief. He never dreamed how pleasant it would be traveling with a canine companion. He talked to the dog like he was talking to a fellow businessman and he was amazed at the brainstorming he accomplished with Murphy.

He had made a reservation for a night's stay with a hotel that allowed dogs. He proudly escorted Murphy through the hotel lobby on his lead, to the "ooohs" and "aaahs" of other guests. The dog seemed to know that he was a very handsome creature and William swore that he walked with more of a prance when people were looking at him.

When they got to their room, the leash was taken off and William propped two pillows on the bed and grabbed the remote control. Murphy jumped up and lay next to William with his head on his leg. A smile and a sense of peace came over William that was so genuine and pure that he marveled at the feeling.

During the next day's traveling, he spent quite a bit of time thinking about what had happened in the snowstorm and how Murphy had saved his life. He wondered where the dog had come from; he wondered why no one had ever seen him before; he wondered what the odds were that he would have run into the man who owned the patent, which for a brief time had been his. Since these questions overwhelmed him, he decided it would be best to forget about them entirely and concentrate on coming up with the money he needed to cover the costs of the lost business venture.

When he got back to his condo, a neighbor saw him with Murphy and not so politely reminded him that it was against the building covenants to have pets over twelve pounds. William smiled and assured his neighbor that neither the dog nor he would be remaining in the complex.

William spent his first two days back exclusively on the phone. He contacted his buyers and informed them of the unfortunate turn of events with the patent. All twelve companies agreed to apply their credit toward existing products, which William offered at an additional fifteen percent discount.

The large building housing the new equipment was listed for sale and the machinery would be put into storage when the building sold. William's condo was put on the market and his realtor was optimistic it would be sold before the month was out. He and Murphy perused the classifieds for rental homes, and by week's end had put a deposit on a two-bedroom house twenty minutes out of town. They would be moving in the following week.

A meeting with his banker resulted in a loan to cover the other losses the company suffered as a result of the lost manufacturing rights. The bank became a lien holder of ColPro, Inc., and would rescind ownership when the loan was repaid. William knew that this arrangement would not have been possible had the bank president not known Thomas Colbert personally for the past forty years. William's appreciation for his father's reputation deepened even more.

Things at the office changed dramatically too. William took Murphy to work with him every day, and of course initially everyone was quite shocked. He told no one the story of how he came to acquire the dog, or vice versa. By the end of the month, Murphy became as natural a site in the office as any of the employees.

When the phone rang, Katie was glad she had left it on the table and as soon as she found the correct button to push, she'd be greeting her caller.

"Hi Mom, am I interrupting your dinner?"

"Yes, William, but you know you're never a bother. How are you ... and how's my grandson?"

Millie and Thomas looked at each other and smiled.

"He's just perfect, Mom. I know it's still far off, but I was calling to invite you and Dad to spend Christmas with us out here this year in our new house."

"We'd love to come for Christmas! Do you want to say hello to your Dad?"

Swallowing her food with a gulp, Millie leaned across the table and shouted, "What about your Aunt Millie?"

Laughing at the other end of the phone, William told his mother to put Millie on the phone first.

"Hey Millie! How about you coming out here with Mom and Dad for Christmas this year?"

"I'd love to. What does Murphy want from Santa?"

"Snow! He loves the snow! But if you can't bring any with you, just bring him one of those huge rawhide bones. He loves them too."

Saying good-bye, Millie handed the phone to Thomas, who got up from the table and walked into the other room to avoid being overpowered by the women's giggling. When he came back into the kitchen a few minutes later, he set the phone back in its base and sat down again at the table.

"He has never sounded happier," Thomas relayed. "I am so proud of him."

"He comes from pretty good stock, Thomas," commented Millie.

CHAPTER NINE

Thomas Colbert had been raised on the farm where he and his wife now lived. His father had been a farmer his entire life, and fully planned and expected his son to take over the spread when he was old enough. Thomas had other ideas, however, and when he turned eighteen he headed off to college on a scholarship. His father hoped that his son would at least major in agriculture or something remotely related to farming or ranching. Such was not the case.

Thomas met and married Katie while they were in college. She was an education major and planned to teach elementary school. Thomas studied business and then continued on to get his MBA. After graduation they stayed in the city where he climbed the corporate ladder to heights he never dreamed possible.

His income grew faster than anything ever had on the family farm. Even his wife had never expected their many luxuries: a custom built house, new cars, and annual vacations. They had wonderful neighbors, status in the community, and their lives were going perfectly. The only thing they wanted and just could not seem to produce was a child.

They tried for many years with no success. Their lives were full in so many ways, but they wanted a child desperately. Finally, in their eleventh year of marriage, William was born.

Katie quit her teaching job, and, although she had adored her students and believed she had truly loved them, she would soon discover the special love felt only by a mother for her own child.

William was a happy baby and grew to be a well-mannered, affectionate child. He had inherited his father's looks and personality, as well as his mother's gentleness. He graduated from high school as president of the Senior Class, captain of the football team, captain of the chess club, and was voted most likely to succeed. William Thomas Colbert was most certainly a chip off the old block. Scholarship offers poured in from colleges across the country. William decided to stay close to home, so he could continue working part-time for his Dad's company. No decision could have pleased his mother more.

William sat at his desk and was buzzed by his secretary.

"Mr. Colbert, your one o'clock is here. Mr. Grafton, from Savoy Products."

William had two appointments today with suppliers, one from Chicago and one from Dayton. Both were selling a similar product for a similar price and he would have to make a decision concerning which supplier his company would contract with for this large account. As always, Murphy lay under the large cherry desk, which extended to the floor in the front. Unless someone had been told the dog was there, they would never know otherwise.

The first supplier came in and William stood to greet him and shake his hand over the desk.

The meeting went fairly well, but the price per item was not quite as low as William had anticipated. Consequently, he assumed he would be signing a contract with the second supplier who would be arriving shortly.

The desk intercom buzzed again at 2:15 to advise William that Mr. Brickley was there. The door opened and Liz escorted the salesman into the office. As he approached the desk and introduced himself, Murphy raised his head and let out a very soft growl.

William put his hand to his stomach and smiled, saying, "Excuse me. Hunger pains."

The men sat and William listened to the supplier's presentation. Periodically, Murphy would release a soft, low growl.

When Mr. Brickley presented the contract for William to sign, William told him he would review it and get back to him within the week. The salesman was noticeably perturbed, but agreed to wait for the call. After the man left and closed the door behind him, William pushed his chair back and bent down towards Murphy.

"What was that all about, Boy? I've never seen you do that before. Are you feeling OK?"

Then, an idea came to him, and being an idea man, he picked up the phone and made a call.

Three hours later, as he and Murphy were getting ready to leave for the day, the phone on his desk rang. It was Betty, responding to his phone call of earlier that afternoon.

While he listened to Betty, he put his hand to his face, covering his mouth. His fingers spread over his jaw and the words coming from the telephone left him speechless. He thanked her and ended the call.

William stared at the dog for a long time. The man that Murphy had growled at earlier that afternoon had a previous criminal record for fraud, assault, and robbery.

"Thanks for looking out for me, Buddy."

Murphy barked as if he knew exactly what had been said.

CHAPTER TEN

It was still light when the women returned home, barely fitting through the front door. Millie was carrying a large box and Katie's arms were full with packages and bags. Thomas was sitting in his recliner reading the paper and set it down when they walked in.

"It's about time you vagabonds got back. I'm starving."

Millie walked into the den and leaned over to kiss Thomas on the cheek. With her always-present smile, she retorted, "Good to see you too, Dear Heart. We had a grand time, Thank You! Katie and I found some things we couldn't live without and a few things we have absolutely no use for, but which were such good buys that we bought them anyway!"

Thomas followed her into the kitchen and pointed to a large sack.

"What in the world do you have in that huge bag?"

"The pet store was having a sale on dog toys," answered Millie as she set the bag down on the counter. Lifting a stuffed clown toy and squeezing it to demonstrate the squeaking sound it made, she added, "I didn't know which one Murphy would like, so I bought one of each!"

Smirking at Millie and shaking his head in disbelief, he walked over to his wife and gave her a kiss on the cheek. "I've been famished for hours. What's for dinner?" he asked.

"Honey," she replied. "Have you broken a leg since we left this morning? Have you forgotten how to open the icebox door? Forgotten how to use the microwave?"

Millie laughed triumphantly, and the girls giggled like they had done when they were youngsters.

"You two are just peas in a pod. I don't have a chance when both of you are around protecting each other. I'm left alone to defend my masculinity," pouted Thomas as he opened the refrigerator door and sighed.

The women uncovered their recent purchases of glassware and old cooking bowls that had been wrapped in newspaper. "Oohs" and "aahs" could be heard throughout the kitchen.

"I'm glad I decided on this one after all, Millie," Katie said with gladness. "I'm so happy you insisted."

"You would have regretted it forever, Dear Heart," smiled Millie, and she hugged her friend around the neck.

After all the items were unwrapped and washed, Katie asked Millie to stay for dinner, and as always, Millie accepted. Katie opened the refrigerator door and Millie pushed her way past her and started pulling things from the shelves. Katie giggled and slapped her friend on the shoulder in an act of loving discipline, saying, "Why do you always have to stick your head into the ice box?"

While Katie sliced vegetables and warmed leftovers on the stove, Millie took her familiar place on the old red vinyl step stool that had been in Katie's kitchen for as long as she could remember. There she sat, an arm's reach from Katie and gabbing non-stop while the meal was prepared. From the other room, Thomas smiled as he heard the giggles coming from the kitchen.

He had gotten used to having Millie around and he had come to love her like a sister. In fact, Millie was the sole reason he and Katie had moved back to the country after all those years in Canton. Millie's husband Roger had passed away seven years ago and since they never had any children, Katie wanted nothing else but to be close by again.

On most days Millie was over before lunch and would always burst into the house with the same positive attitude and cheerful smile they had both come to love and look forward to. The first thing she would do is walk into the kitchen and open the curtains, which at first drove both Katie and Thomas up the wall. They were conditioned to keeping their curtains closed in the city, simply because their neighbors were so close and privacy was at such a minimum. After moving to the country, they found it difficult to break that old habit. Then after a while they simply got used to this new habit of Millie's.

She would then take her place on the shiny red vinyl stepstool and talk to Katie while she cooked or set up preserves or tomatoes from the garden. Millie was not much for cooking, but the ability she lacked was more than compensated for in Katie. The three would share lunch together every day, and sometimes dinner. Once a week, usually on Saturday nights, Millie would take them out to eat and of course pay for the meal. She had money but never flaunted it. She was generous and gracious and most often brought bags of food and goodies with her each time she visited. When the small store in town got in fresh produce from the nearby farms, Millie would bring over a bushel of whatever was in season: zucchini, apples, tomatoes, or green beans. The three would feast on the bounty until they were sick of it, then Katie would can it in large Mason jars and Millie would decorate the labels and date them. It was a yearly ritual that they both enjoyed.

The two women had been friends since childhood. Growing up in rural Pennsylvania had taught them two things: Rely on your friends; and when you grow up, move to the city. Their fathers were both farmers, and their mothers spent most of their second and third decades bearing and raising children. Katie was the fourth of six and Millie was the third of seven. They lived a mile from each other, or rather, their houses were a mile from each other, both on Rural Route 5, but their family's acres spread for miles on opposite sides. Consequently, the men rarely saw each other during the course of the day, but the women made it a point to get together at least three times during the week and on Sundays after church. All their children grew up together and shared each other's clothes and toys. Katherine and Millicent, however, were more like sisters than neighbors, and were virtually inseparable.

Katie was always the shy one and Millie the adventurer. Though never blatantly disobedient, Millie was notorious for pulling Katie along on her mischievous outings and escapades. One Saturday afternoon when they were twelve, Millie decided to play a prank on old man Cooper, the owner of the General Store. He was a crotchety old man who always watched them like a hawk when they visited his store. Every week they purchased a few items for their mothers, but since they were poor farmers' kids, the proprietor always assumed they would try to steal something while they shopped.

It was a sweltering mid-summer day and the girls walked into town as they had dozens of times before. Millie however, carried a winter coat over her arm and had a mischievous plan up her sleeve.

She had stuffed the coat pockets before leaving her house with wadded up scraps from her Mama's fabric box, hay, and a certain other item. She carried the folded coat over her arm so the pockets hung towards the middle and could not be seen from the outside. She had instructed Katie to make her Mama's purchases as usual but to distract old man Cooper as much as possible and engage him in continued conversation after she had purchased her canned goods.

Meanwhile in the corner of the General Store, Millie put on the heavy coat and tried to look as guilty as possible. When she manufactured a cough from the distance, Katie knew it was time to cut short her conversation with Mr. Cooper and start walking out of the store.

The plan worked perfectly and Millie walked from the rear of the store with her coat pockets bulging and her eyes staring at the floor. Old man Cooper yelled from behind the counter and raced around to the front door and snatched Millie by the collar as she tried to walk out of the store.

"What have we got here, Little Lady?" he exclaimed in disgust as he turned her around so she was facing him. "You rotten little thief. I knew your family was scum and it was only a matter of time until I caught you at what I have been suspecting for years," and he thrust his hand in her coat pocket and pulled out the contents in triumph.

It was then that both girls broke into delightful laughter and ran out of the store. There stood old man Cooper; his hand full of fabric scraps, hay, and horse manure.

The girls had kept in touch over the years and had visited each other often, but when Roger died, Thomas decided that maybe a change was in order for all of them. William had taken over most of the management aspects of the company and all was going well; Thomas had often considered returning to the country to retire anyway.

He was not sure if he could handle the drastic change when they first made the move, however. He was not used to the extreme quiet or the lack of a daily agenda. For the first three months, he filled his appointment book with normal every day activities just to feel as though he had accomplished something each day. It was not surprising to see a typical week day organized into neat time slots with notations designated to such pending appointments as:

shower and shave; go into town; go to the post office; check rain gauge; call so and so; watch show on TV at 7:00 p.m.

After a few months, however, Thomas became very accustomed to forgetting about his appointment book and even forgetting to set his alarm clock. Once he reacquainted himself to the country life, he discovered that he truly enjoyed it, and that the move had been a very good one all around.

Supper was ready and Thomas was beckoned from his recliner. The girls had really outdone themselves tonight; along with the goodies Millie had brought over earlier, Katie had made stir-fried vegetables, country fried steak, and an enormous salad. Hot corn bread had just been set on a wooden cutting board on the table.

The three sat and enjoyed the meal and the conversation, as they had done so many times before. It amazed them that they always talked endlessly and effortlessly, regardless of their frequent and often seemingly continued company. During those infrequent moments when no words were spoken, laughter was usually the filler.

Millie was always a gracious guest and seemed to sense when the time was right for her to leave. She and Katie could almost read one another's minds, and their decades of close friendship allowed them to shoot from the hip during those times when mind reading was ineffective. Tonight, no words were necessary to prompt Millie's departure. The dinner had been fantastic and the table talk had been fun, but Millie was tired and headed home before the remaining blueberry muffins made their dessert appearance.

The sky had become dark and Katie looked at the crescent moon through the window over the sink while she wiped the last of the dinner dishes. Thomas was reading the paper in his recliner; Millie had headed home an hour ago.

Millie's house was several miles away and sat on 140 acres. She and Roger had the enormous house built twenty years previously at Katie's prompting. Thomas knew he and Katie would eventually retire to the family farmhouse, and since Millie and Roger were planning on raising horses, Thomas suggested they make a move to Nebraska to eventually be near them. Thomas helped negotiate the purchase of their land and Roger, being a successful and talented architect, designed the estate. There were heated stables on the property as well as a guesthouse and three ponds. Roger had also built a workshop and several other outbuildings for storage. Millie had several workers who took care of the grounds and maintained the property. The thought of moving into something smaller never crossed her mind after her husband passed away.

Thomas set down his paper, got up from his recliner, and turned off the light in the den. Walking into the kitchen, he hugged his wife from behind and asked if she was ready to call it a night. Leaning back into his embrace, both were surprised when the telephone rang.

Katie looked at the clock before reaching for the phone. She picked it up on the second ring and said "hello."

All she heard was silence. Since the ringing had stopped, she was certain that she had pressed the right button on the phone.

"Hello?"

Total, unnerving silence. After a third and then a forth "hello," Katie pushed a button to end the call.

"What was that all about?" asked Thomas.

"I have no idea. I guess it was the wrong number," answered Katie as she set the phone back down on the counter.

Remembering the telephone's features, Thomas smiled proudly as he headed towards the base unit saying, "let's just see who dialed that wrong number, shall we?"

His smile faded immediately and he looked back at his wife.

"It was Millie."

Katie grabbed the phone and called the Police. They told her they had received a call from Millie's house twenty minutes earlier and that the response team had just arrived. Katie grabbed her coat and car keys and ran out the door. She insisted that Thomas stay home in case Millie tried to call again.

The ten-minute drive to Millie's seemed endless. When she arrived, she saw the rear door of the ambulance closing and being secured. One of the Police Officers saw Katie and walked over solemnly. There was no need for words.

CHAPTER ELEVEN

William and Murphy had become inseparable. They jogged together, shopped together and carpooled to the office every day. Murphy accompanied William on all his business calls out of the office and sat through all his meetings at ColPro. William's business associates soon came to expect seeing the longhaired white dog alongside the well-dressed businessman.

Murphy filled the void in William's life that had never been occupied by a wife or children. He was no longer lonely. Each night when he looked at the man in the mirror, he smiled at the reflection and felt as though his life was most certainly complete.

When he heard the news about Aunt Millie, he called the airline and booked two tickets: one for himself and one for Murphy. They arrived at his parent's house the following afternoon and this time there was no one waiting on the porch to greet him. The front door was unlocked and he walked in and unceremoniously announced his arrival.

Thomas came down the stairs, hugged his son, patted Murphy on the head, and thanked him for coming. He related that Katie had been given a sedative and was sleeping. The two men walked into the kitchen and Thomas poured them each a cup of coffee.

"Things are going to be very different around here," lamented Thomas.

"How about you and Mom coming out to spend some time with me and Murph? You know, a change of scenery?"

Thomas reached over to clasp his son's hand in appreciation.

"I'll suggest that to your Mom, but I don't know if a change of scenery would help. She and Millie had a bond, one of those once in a lifetime bonds."

And as he spoke, William looked down at Murphy in understanding.

Thomas continued. "As we get older, we all know the end is coming, but no one is ever really ready for that final good-bye.

It's always so difficult on the ones who are left behind. I know Millie is somewhere real special right now." Tears filled his eyes as he spoke.

This time, William was the one to reach over and grasp the other hand on the table.

Clearing his throat and wiping his eyes with a hankie, Thomas forced a smile and said, "Will, you know Millie loved you like a son."

"I know Dad, I loved her too."

"And she loved Murphy," he added, smiling as he got up from his chair and lifted the pet store bag she had forgotten on the counter the night before. Handing it to William, he said, "Millie was planning on giving these to him for Christmas."

William opened the bag and peered inside. A broad smile was met with salty tears as he stuck a hand in the bag and pulled out a toy for Murphy.

Smiling through his tears, William said, "Look, Boy! Toys from your Aunt Millie."

Murphy stood and took the toy in his mouth, wagging his tail enthusiastically.

"Son, there is one more thing."

William looked back at his father.

"We got a call from her attorney today. It appears that she left everything to you."

William's face displayed the shock of what his father had just said.

"She did what?" he said, wondering if he had heard his father correctly.

"You heard what I said. She left you the house and all the land … and it's all paid for. She left you her two vehicles and her bank accounts. All her investments."

William sat in continued shock.

"There are no conditions to the estate," Thomas continued. "You know Millie was not one to manipulate people," he said, smiling in recollection. "It's all yours to do with as you see fit."

A dozen thoughts simultaneously raced through William's mind. Six months ago a large sum of money would really have come in handy, even though he never would have wanted it to come in this fashion. Now he looked at things differently. Millie and her husband had worked hard to accumulate their assets and no one knew more than William how an entire savings could be lost in a matter of days.

"She always believed in you, Son. Your mother and I never knew about the will. We found out this morning. The attorney said to make sure you stop by to go over a few things and sign some papers before you leave town. But aside from that, you don't have to make any decisions about anything right now."

"Dad, do you and Mom need anything? What does Mom think about all this?

"She feels like the estate was given to you by your second mother. She was happy to have shared you with Millie over the years, and she believes that you and Millie were both better for having known each other."

Still, William found the news quite overwhelming.

Katie spent most of the afternoon and evening resting, as was intended. William and Murphy went on a very long walk, and Thomas sat at the kitchen table wondering if his wife would ever be the same.

No one wanted to eat much that night; even Murphy went to bed without finishing his supper.

The next morning, William was the first one downstairs and started making breakfast while a fresh pot of coffee brewed. He did not have much of an appetite even today, but hoped his parents would eat some pancakes and scrambled eggs if he set the food down in front of them.

William was still standing at the stove when his mother made her way downstairs. He held her for a long time, knowing there were no words full enough to console her broken heart.

She made a pot of Millie's favorite tea and sat at the table staring at her cup, stirring it in silence every few minutes but never drinking it.

Thomas ventured downstairs and made his way into the kitchen and paused. Wordlessly, he walked over to the curtains and opened them, as Millie had done a thousand times before. Katie looked up as the morning sun lit her wet face.

Silently, he touched her shoulder as he walked past. He said good morning to William and went outside to feed the chickens.

Occasionally he would turn around and look at the kitchen window, only to see his wife still sitting there at the table, staring through the panes. He walked into the barn, and leaning against the wall, he started to weep.

"Oh God," he groaned. "I loved her too. She was like a sister to me. Please help Katie make it through this. Please send someone to comfort her; I know I won't be enough."

CHAPTER TWELVE

It was a typical day in Everlife. There were four dogs sitting at Cambium's roots in a heated discussion. Adario, a collie; Okeana, a keeshond; Tiffan, a mixed breed; and Calais, a dachshund, had been arguing for hours and ultimately took the debate to Cambium for his opinion.

"Its got nothing to do with ego, Tiffan," declared the dachshund.

"You've got to be kidding," rebuked the mixed breed.

"I don't believe we're inferior to humans, I just think it's in our nature ... it's something we can't control," said Adario.

"So, if you believe we can't control it, you *are* saying we are inferior beings," said the mixed breed.

"No, Tiffin, that's not what I'm saying at all," said the collie. "Each of us was created with certain traits and certain instincts. In a normal situation and under normal circumstances, I would not have bitten that man. But, I don't believe I had a choice."

Tiffin spoke. "Of course you had a choice. You could have walked away if you wanted to. I've been in thousands and thousands of situations when I would have loved to have taken a nice, meaty chunk out of someone's arm or leg, but I didn't."

"But what if your human's safety was jeopardized? What if you could save their life by attacking someone? What would you do then?" asked Okeana.

"His instincts would take over at that point," answered Adario.

"But what if you were in a situation where your human's life was at stake ... *but*, let's say your human was a real creep and you weren't real fond of him anyway?" asked the keeshond.

"I think the response would be the same. At least I think it *should* be," said Calais.

"Sometimes those humans should get what's coming to them," said Okeana.

"What about the times when *we* haven't been on our best behavior? Do we deserve to be punished?" asked Tiffin.

Adario was quick to respond. "Humans have a lot more options than we do. When we're there with them, its not like we can stand up and tell them what we think. It's not like we can write them a letter expressing our feelings."

"That's exactly what I'm saying," said the keeshond. "We are inferior beings."

"Well, maybe you are Okeana, but I'm not," rebuked Calais. "Maybe you need a refresher course in self-esteem."

Cambium unfolded his arms that had been resting across his trunk and spread them wide, palms facing downward and gently lifting them up and down as if the gesture would calm the group before him.

"Friends, friends," said Cambium. "Each of you has professed your personal beliefs with much passion. I think it is time to settle this matter and move on to other topics."

"But who's right, Cambium?" asked Tiffin.

"Why, you all are correct," answered Cambium.

The four dogs looked at each other inquisitively and then looked back at the Tree.

"How can we all be right?" asked Calais.

"Each of you is basing your reality on your personal experiences. Some of you have been involved in situations that others have not. Consequently, each of you is unique and presents his or her own perspective based on experience.

"Your assignments are designed not to make you all similar in the end, but rather to utilize the gifts you each have and to improve the condition and the awareness of everyone involved.

"Okeana, since many of your experiences have involved abuse and neglect, you assume your species is inferior, and in a sense, that you deserve to be treated poorly."

The keeshond opened his mouth to speak, but thought better of it and remained silent.

Still speaking to Okeana, Cambium continued.

"Have you ever considered that your assignments never progress beyond Level III because you continue to believe that you are inferior to other species? Have you ever wondered why your Earth experiences are always a repeat of previous assignments, regardless of the form you take?"

The keeshond sheepishly replied, "Well, now that you mention it ..."

"Ahhhhh," responded Cambium. "A glimmer of realization."

The Tree then pointed to the dachshund.

"And you, Calais. You believe that all living things are equal."

The short dark dog shook his head in agreement. Cambium continued. "You are currently qualified for Level V assignments, yes?" The dog again shook his head in agreement.

"Tiffin, you are correct in saying that you have a choice. In every situation, we always have a choice as to how to respond."

The mixed breed held his head a little higher and looked at the others as if he was Teacher's Pet.

"However," added Cambium, "our choices are directly related to our life experiences and the lessons we have learned from others. If our warehouse of knowledge is limited, our choices will be limited as well."

Looking finally at the collie, Cambium smiled. "Your nature is responsible for many things, Adario. Your nature is a silent voice constantly instructing and directing you. Your nature will warn you of an impending storm and will keep safe those under your care."

Adario knew better than to believe the compliments would continue.

"However," Cambium continued, as he looked down into the faces of the four creatures before him. "Your nature is not the dominant force in your life. You are individuals; no two are alike. You each have been given certain gifts, certain abilities, and certain tendencies. You each see a situation in an entirely different fashion. You each respond to a situation in an entirely different fashion. Each of your responses is correct for you at that moment in your journey. Each response will directly influence every situation that follows. What you believe today will present itself tomorrow. What you think today will manifest itself tomorrow."

The dogs looked at each other and then looked back at Cambium. The Great Tree smiled softly and added a final thought. "Don't worry. There are no mistakes. Just opportunities to grow."

The dogs stared at the Tree, each with their heads cocked to the side.

Cambium continued. "Animals were created to be help meets for humans and to complete their wholeness as spiritual beings. Without animals there would be more sickness in the world, more hostility, more fear, less tenderness, less compassion, less wisdom, and far, far less love."

"When assignments are distributed, they are done so with both the two-walkers' *and* the four-walkers' best interests in mind. With every step we take, we have the amazing opportunity of choice; we can choose to act with kindness or we can choose to act with hatred. All things are permissible but not all things are beneficial."

"When a human chooses to act for self-benefit alone, the outcome may very well bring relative gain to that particular individual. But when actions are made without the consideration of others, an imbalance is created which eventually must be righted. When an individual exhibits cruelty or neglect or abuse or indifference towards another human or an animal, the world is affected too. When one life reaches out in anger or rebellion, we all feel its effects.

"When a four-walker is sent to a human who ultimately abuses him or her in some way, those injuries were never ordained, never predestined, and certainly never condoned. The human in question had a choice to make and the animal may have been placed in their care to provide them with an opportunity to escape their harmful tendencies or negative patterns of behavior. The choices that a particular human makes and the path a two-walker takes are decisions out of my control. Every imbalance they create in their own life will be addressed and corrected. Eventually. Every harmful or spiteful seed they sow toward any other living thing will return to them in good measure."

"Why can't I ever get past a Level III assignment?" asked Okeana. "Why do I keep repeating the same Level over and over again, just with different people?"

"Passage Wall eliminates all painful emotions and most of the negative memories with each return to Everlife, but it does not erase the recollections of the failed lessons—the times when illumination was once again postponed due to repeated negative choices. You remember portions of your journeys Okeana, but you do not recall in full."

Cambium lowered a branch and touched the top of Okeana's head with a long wooden finger and whispered to him, "Remember, remember."

Okeana's eyes opened wide in an instant as his memory was restored. He made a grimacing face of disgust and repulsion.

"Time after time I send you to become a new born puppy or a stray adult, and time after time you invariably end up with the same type of person. I never sent you to any of those humans, I simply sent you to Earth. You have never once been assigned to a particular individual."

"Why do I keep ending up with those types of people?" asked the keeshond.

"You have attracted two-walkers who share your paradigm; people whose belief systems are synchronous with yours. You were not created with your current pessimistic thoughts and your current negative beliefs. Somewhere along the line you adopted the harmful doctrines and have held fast to them. Your assignments will not change unless you change your way of thinking."

"How do I do that, Cambium? Please tell me how to do it," pleaded the beautiful gray dog.

"Okeana, I will allow your memories to remain intact until you enter the portal again. In the meantime, I would make every effort to spend your time with other dogs and cats who have successfully completed higher level assignments. There is nothing to gain by associating with others who have the same obstacles as you. Find a few mentors and watch how they deal with others; listen to the words they say; ask them questions and heed their advice."

Okeana looked at Calais.

"You're a Level V, aren't you, Calais?" asked the keeshond.

"Yes."

"Can I hang around with you for a while Calais, like Cambium said?"

"Sure, Okeana. I'd be happy to share my wisdom with you."

The remaining two dogs looked at each other and rolled their eyes.

"I believe we have adequately resolved the issue at hand. Is there anything else you need presently?" asked Cambium.

The four dogs shook their head and the Tree bid them farewell. Within a few moments his eyes and face were again covered with thick silver and gray bark.

The dogs walked away in a very amiable fashion and their chatter was now quite pleasant. While they were still within the lengths of Cambium's long roots, they became startled when his bark opened abruptly and his voice blared through the air.

"Everyone, please come to the Meeting Place."

Each of the four dogs looked at each other's necks to see their colored ID tags suddenly light up and begin flashing.

They ran back to the Tree and saw a small blue bird approaching, tweeting loudly and carrying a shiny gold envelope in her tiny beak. The bird landed on a low limb, her tiny chest heaving up and down in obvious exhaustion. Cambium raised his branched hands to his mouth like a megaphone and bellowed again.

Around every neck, ID tags that were normally invisible blinked and swung from their collars. From all over Everlife, the animals came. It took almost thirty minutes but finally everyone stood before Cambium—tens of thousands of dogs and cats. The place was a buzz.

"Everyone, a Special Request has come in," and he reached up and gently retrieved the shiny gold envelope from the beak of the small bird, who was now rested and breathing normally. Opening the envelope gingerly, he removed the letter and read the words silently, then turned his eyes back towards the crowd.

"We have a Special Request. This assignment is for a feline. It is a lengthy assignment. Level VII."

"We haven't seen one of those in a long time!" a large Irish Setter cited cheerfully.

In a distant section of the crowd, a black and white cat echoed the sentiment.

Once again, the crowd buzzed with conversation.

"Another Level VII assignment?" asked a large gray cat.

"And it's a Special Request," answered another cat.

"Yes, yes," boasted Cambium proudly. "Special Request. This is certainly an honor for the right cat. Are there any volunteers?"

Four cats walked forward for consideration. One of them was Cimmaron. He carried his fluffy tail held high and his nose straight ahead but slightly raised. Certainly confidence was nothing he was lacking.

"I see, I see," said Cambium, as he folded his lower limbs over his trunk, still holding the shiny gold letter in one hand. "It looks like I will have to make the decision myself on this one."

He continued, "Sinclair, you have performed wonderfully in your recent assignments, and I thank you for stepping forward today. Milton, you too have completed your recent assignments in splendid grandeur. However, for this particular position, I believe someone else is better suited. Please return to your seats with our thanks."

The crowd applauded.

"Cimmaron and Minstral. You both have exemplified the criteria for Level VII qualified felines and I know you both have vast experience with lengthy assignments. But only one of you has had past experience with a Special Request assignment."

Cimmaron sneered at Minstral, a large tortoise shell with brilliant gold eyes who sat gleaming with pride.

"However," continued Cambium, "since Minstral has had prior experience with a Special Request assignment, I feel it would be most beneficial if Cimmaron was granted the opportunity to participate in this renowned and distinguished event."

Cimmaron stuck his pink nose higher in the air and smiled politely at Minstral, as if to congratulate him for taking second place.

As Minstral turned to head back to his seat, Cambium reached down and lightly patted the large orange cat's head and smiled. "Cimmaron. You will be leaving tomorrow. Congratulations on this Special Assignment. Peace be with you."

The crowd erupted in loud applause.

Soon, the animals dispersed and returned to their daily activities. Most walked away, chatting with friends. Okeana, however, remained at the Meeting Place, trying his best to act casually.

"Cambium," whispered the keeshond. "Cambium."

The Tree awakened to find Okeana back at his roots. Cambium surmised that the dog had additional questions concerning his past assignments. Nothing could have been a more errant assumption.

"Remember a little while ago when you restored my memory, Cambium?" inquired the dog.

"Yes, of course," assured the Tree.

The dog looked to his right and then to his left. Cambium looked to the left and right as well. Slowly and cautiously, Okeana tiptoed closer to the Great Tree, peering again to the sides and then behind him to make sure no one else was there.

"I assure you Okeana, we are quite alone," said Cambium softly. "What troubles you so, Child?"

"It's the memories, Cambium. I remember everything. And I mean *everything*," said the stout gray dog hesitantly. After looking once more to his left and right to confirm that no one was within earshot, Okeana continued. "I even remember the '*hellos*'," he said quite ashamedly.

"The 'hellos'?" queried Cambium.

"Yes, Cambium, the 'hellos.' You know … the greetings?"

"The greetings?" inquired the Tree, still quite unsure as to where the dog was going with this conversation.

Lifting a paw to his mouth and gesturing to Cambium to bend forward a bit, the keeshond whispered, barely audibly enough for the Tree to hear.

An expression of understanding shot across Cambium's face and he straightened once again, almost chuckling.

"Ahhh," he said in a muffled tone. "The '*hellos.*' Now I understand."

A look of relief came to Okeana's face and he stepped backward a few feet and sat, awaiting Cambium's explanation.

"Well Okeana, there are many differences between the species, and as you know, dogs happen to have a very whetted sense of smell. Other creatures have different gifts; for example, the eagle and the hawk have excellent vision. They are essential to us in Everlife for they return to us with detailed accounts of what they have seen during their visits to Earth. They are not usually given assignments, although this has been known to happen perhaps once or twice a century. However, canines such as yourself, who routinely participate in assignments, return to us with information not only concerning your assignment human, but with information and data about other assigned dogs and cats.

Shaking his head and rolling his brown eyes, the keeshond questioned. "What in the world are you talking about, Cambium?"

The Tree smiled and nodded in understanding.

"Dear Okeana. Upon your return to Everlife after each assignment, your painful memories are erased by Passage Wall. However, all the data and information you accumulated during your time away is transmitted when your hand is scanned on an Arrival Post. Everything you saw, everything you experienced, is all recorded. Future assignments to humans are partly determined and arranged using the information provided by each returning animal.

"I'm still not following you, Cambium."

"When you ... *greet* ... a fellow dog on Earth, you identify them by their scent. Every meeting with every animal you have contact with during every one of your assignments is recorded as a scent record in your brain. When your hand is scanned upon your return to Everlife, the information is downloaded and we are able to document and monitor the locations of all the animals with whom you've had contact. This is one of the tools we use to signal their participation in the Meetings of the Full Moon."

"But Cambium. Why do we have to sniff them ... *there*?"

"There are universal identifiers, Okeana. Every home has a house number by the front door and every business has its name near the entrance. Photographs of people are taken from the front, not from the back, because the face is the part that is unique. Yet many automobiles and many dogs look alike. So humans place license plates on the rear of their vehicles to identify them. In the same fashion, dogs were designed with an invisible scented registration tag, also located at the rear of the body."

The dog did not seem appeased.

Cambium continued.

"Do not allow your memories to cause you shame Okeana; you were simply accumulating data for our DMV system."

"Your DMV?"

"Yes, our Dog Movement Verification system."

CHAPTER THIRTEEN

Millicent Wilson had always done things her own way, and her last wishes were no different. She had arranged everything long in advance, and per her request, she was cremated and there was no memorial service. Everything she owned was given to William to do with it what he pleased.

It took Katie almost a month before she was emotionally ready to walk into Millie's home. There in the foyer, she was met with the familiar fragrance of the house, as well as mixed feelings of comfort and extreme sadness.

She remembered her grandmother's house and the distinct aroma it had, not that it was an offensive odor by any means. Everyone's house had its own distinctive scent and our memories were often tied to those familiar scents from the past. One Christmas many years ago, Katie was given a homemade afghan by her grandmother. When she unwrapped the box and opened it, she was amazed by the unmistakable and familiar scent that had been woven with the yarn. Memories poured into her mind like her grandmother's hot cocoa, and she wondered how long the smell would linger.

Millie's house always smelled of lilac. She had lilac bushes outside her kitchen windows and in the spring the entire house was filled with the scent. When fresh lilac was unavailable, candles, potpourri, oils, and fancy sprays were used to disperse the smell of lilac to the far corners of the house. Even in Millie's absence, the fragrance lingered.

Katie inhaled deeply when she noticed the smell of lilac in the foyer. She smiled for the first time in weeks, to the relief of her husband. Yet after the smile faded, the tears returned.

As promised, William flew back to the farm several weeks following Millie's passing, and of course brought Murphy with him.

He and his parents were just finishing up with lunch when the doorbell rang. Murphy lifted his head in attention and followed William as he got up from the table to answer the door.

"Hi, is Mrs. Colbert in?" asked a woman standing behind a large crate.

"Yes, she is. May I say who's asking?"

"My name is Sandy Ellis … I have a fruit stand at the Farmer's Market."

William went to get his mother and returned with her to the front door. Thomas followed, remaining behind them in the foyer. When Katie and William stepped onto the porch, the woman continued.

"I know this is not a good time Mrs. Colbert, but I have a bushel of fresh peaches for you. Millie Wilson ordered them for you several months ago. They're already paid for. Like I said, I know this is not a good time, but I didn't know what to do."

Katie held back the tears with all her might but when one slid past her eyelid and fell to her cheek, she knew her words would be equally difficult to control.

William thanked the woman for coming and carried the heavy bushel of fruit into the kitchen. Thomas wrapped an arm around his wife to comfort her.

"How about we open the crate and have a fresh peach?" he asked. "You know Millie would have that box torn apart by now," he said. "There'd be peach pits all over the counter and a pie ready for the oven."

Katie smiled and nodded in agreement, still stifling the tears.

They sat back down at the table while William opened a kitchen drawer and after some searching, pulled out a long flat head screwdriver. Bending down, he shimmied the tool under one of the wooden slats and lifted it. He repeated the procedure on the other two slats and then reached inside and grabbed a peach.

He smiled and tossed the peach to his dad. Trying to make conversation, he commented on how beautiful the fruit was and reached down to pick one up for his Mother. The smile left his face and his words stopped in mid-sentence when he noticed something under the top layer of fruit.

He gently moved a peach, then another, staring in disbelief.

There was a tiny orange kitten lying between the layers of fruit. It was the smallest kitten William had ever seen, probably only a few weeks old. It had a white bib and another area of white above its tiny pink nose. Dark orange stripes of fur wrapped around the body and the legs like ribbon, and a splash of white topped the tip of the tail. It was the most adorable kitten William had ever seen.

But it was dead.

William fell backwards onto the floor and put his hands over his mouth.

"William, what is it?" asked Thomas.

William's anguished silence impelled his parents to walk over to the wooden crate.

"Oh, dear Lord," gasped Katie, shaking her head in disbelief.

Murphy slowly walked towards the crate. Assuming he would ravage the dead kitten, William began to shoo him away, but the dog kept coming.

By now, William's tears were falling from his cheeks to the floor. Thomas and Katie leaned against one another; there were no words to express their horror.

Murphy continued to cower towards the crate. William felt helpless.

The dog slowly peered into the wooden bushel. The orange and white kitten lay motionless, his head sloping downwards over the leaves of a large, ripe peach.

Murphy's snout went down into the crate and William bent forward to pull the dog's head from the box, again attempting to dissuade him.

"No, Murphy, no!" snapped William, as he reached in between the peaches and lifted the lifeless creature into his hands.

Katie swooned and Thomas was fortunate to catch her and steer her to a chair before she fainted entirely.

As William held the tiny kitten, Murphy sniffed it repeatedly. Then, with his wet black nose, he started to nudge the motionless orange body. William's head fell to his chest in total resignation. Murphy whined tenderly and with his warm pink tongue, he began to lick the still kitten.

They were amazed at the tender expression of compassion displayed by the white beast whose mere size loomed over the kitten. Murphy's gentle grooming seemed almost sacred, and it continued with no further reproach by William.

It took a minute or two for him to realize it, but William noticed movement in his hand. At first he assumed it was coming from the dog's licking motion, but he soon realized he was wrong. The kitten opened his eyes and began to move.

William stood and walked over to the table, his face now saturated with salt laden tears.

"Look!"

Katie saw the kitten and her face lit up like it had not in months. A motherly "oooh" escaped from her lips, and she reached forward, taking the small creature from her son's hands.

Looking at his parents, William smiled and softly said, "Now you know how I felt when you asked me how I got Murphy."

CHAPTER FOURTEEN

William pulled into his driveway and told Murphy that it sure felt good to be back home. Murphy barked in agreement.

They walked into the house, leaving the luggage by the stairs to be taken up later. They headed towards the kitchen and William opened the icebox. Nothing in there looked appealing. He opened the freezer. Nothing looked very appealing in there either. He picked up the water bowl from the floor and washed it thoroughly before refilling it with filtered water. Murphy had a drink and then looked up at William, as if to inquire about dinner.

"I don't feel like going out again, Murph. How 'bout we just have peanut butter and jelly sandwiches tonight and then we'll go shopping tomorrow and fill the fridge?"

Murphy barked in agreement.

The telephone rang and William answered on the second ring. Very few people had his home phone number, so he knew it would not be a business call.

"Hello?" he said into the receiver.

"Hey Son, just wanted to make sure you got in alright."

"Yeah, Dad, we did. I was going to call you in a little while. How's the kitten?"

"He's doing great, Will. We took him to the vet after we dropped you off at the airport this morning. We had to buy a tiny feeding bottle and some special kitten formula, but the veterinarian said the little guy will be just fine."

"Did you, uh, tell the vet about the, uh, story?"

"No Son, we decided to keep that to ourselves. Some folks would never believe a story like that and I can't say I'd blame them."

"I know what you mean, Dad."

"Guess what your Mom decided to name the little thing."

"Don't tell me she's named him Murphy Jr."

Chuckling, Thomas answered, "No. She's named him Peaches."

"Peaches? Well, I guess that's a real appropriate name for him, don't you think?"

Still chuckling, Thomas replied, "I think it suits him just fine. Well, I won't keep you. Give my grandson a hug for me and we'll talk to you soon. We love you, Son."

"We love you too, Dad. Bye."

Looking down at Murphy, William shook his head, saying, "It's another of life's great mysteries."

Peaches did well eating from the bottle, but after a few weeks, he was anxious to try some solid food. He had doubled in size, but still squealed instead of meowed, and still had his baby fur.

He followed Katie everywhere. When she cooked breakfast, the kitten sat on the red vinyl stool and watched. When Katie opened the refrigerator door, he was in between her feet looking inside to see what had been placed on the shelves since the last time he had looked in there. When Katie left one room and walked into another, the little cat followed her. When Katie brushed her teeth, Peaches sat and watched. He even liked to talk on the telephone, and when Katie called her son to wish him a Happy 48th Birthday, Peaches sat on the counter anxious to join in the conversation.

"Good morning, Son! Happy Birthday!"

"Hey Mom, thanks. How are you and Dad doing?"

"We're fine, William. Your furry brother would like to wish you a Happy Birthday too."

Right on cue, the kitten hollered into the telephone with his baby-cat squeaky bellow. William laughed and Katie put the phone back to her ear.

"He's quite the conversationalist, isn't he?" asked Katie.

"You may not be so thrilled with his vocal abilities when he gets a little older, Mom," chuckled William.

"If my little Dear Heart wants to express himself, that's fine with me," sing-songed Katie, more to the cat than to her son.

Still snickering, William replied, "I think I'm feeling some sibling rivalry for the first time in my life."

"I better let you go, Son. Don't you have an appointment with your therapist this morning?"

"Ha ha, Mom."

"Happy Birthday, Dear. We'll call you tonight so your father can wish you a Happy Birthday too. We love you."

Katie ended the call and carried Peaches out of the kitchen and upstairs. She was more attached to this cat than she had even been with Beaumont. They had become as inseparable as William and Murphy.

Christmastime came and Thomas, Katie, and Peaches flew out to Ohio. William had left Murphy in the house while he went to the airport, and when he returned home and pulled into the driveway, the dog barked loudly from behind the den window. Thomas laughed from the passenger seat and Katie looked at Peaches through the door of the sky kennel and asked if he was ready to see his brother's house. Right on cue, the cat bellowed a long meow in reply.

Everyone had been silently apprehensive about this trip. Peaches had never flown and had rarely left the big farmhouse. No one knew if the animals would remember their first encounter and they were wondering if any fur would fly or if any hissing or spitting would take place. William assumed that Murphy would be social, and it seemed to be the consensus that Peaches would be the one to instigate if something did come about.

As William and Thomas carried luggage into the house, Katie carried the cat carrier into the foyer while Peaches hollered the entire time.

Murphy stood by, staring down at the carrier, his tail wagging a mile a minute. Katie unlatched the kennel door and out walked Peaches, now six months old, just as composed and confident as ever. Murphy barked, obviously calling attention to himself, and the orange cat walked over and sniffed his large black nose in greeting. Peaches voiced one loud meow and one low growl, then walked past Murphy and proceeded to investigate every inch of the house. Everyone laughed and realized that their worries had been wonderfully unfounded.

Katie toured the house and expressed her approval and delight to William. He had made the abode restful, inviting, and very comfortable. It warmed her heart to see so many of Millie's things scattered throughout the house too.

William had put up a real Christmas tree, much to his parents' pleasure and surprise. Peaches was particularly intrigued by it and climbed up the trunk and onto the branches on more than one occasion. As always, Thomas had his camera ready and captured one of those priceless moments on film.

The weather was obliging and the Colberts awoke to a fresh snowfall on Christmas morning. Thomas got up early and started a fire before the rest of the family stirred. The warmth of the roaring fire contrasted dramatically with the snow and ice clinging to the glass windowpanes.

William knew how excited Murphy would be when he saw the snow, so he insisted that his parents stand by the kitchen windows before he opened the back door to let the dog outside. Katie held Peaches in her arms as William unlocked the door. Murphy ran outside and laughter erupted when, as predicted, Murphy stuck his black nose deep into the snow and started running around the backyard. Periodically, he would lift his snout and turn toward the house to see if he was still being watched. Then he would stick his nose down into the snow again and continue with the game.

"He was certainly created to enjoy the snow," commented Thomas as he sipped a cup of hot coffee. Peaches hollered in reply while he too watched Murphy through the window.

"Yes, Dear Heart. And you were created to be my precious Peaches and to stay inside where it's warm and toasty," said Katie smiling. The cat turned to her and meowed in reply.

Murphy stayed outside playing while William poured himself a cup of coffee and served his mother a cup of tea in one of Millie's lilac-themed mugs. Outside, the big white dog barked at the falling snowflakes and jumped into the air to catch them.

"When we do the things we were created to do, every moment is spectacular," said Thomas as he watched Murphy rolling in the snow.

"Sometimes I swear that dog is a person," confessed William. "A person disguised in a thick fur coat."

He sipped his coffee again and turned back towards his parents, who were staring at him.

"Don't worry. Your son has not lost his mind," he said reassuringly, while silently supplicating a response of understanding from his parents.

Thomas reached across the table and in familiar fashion placed his hand over his son's and squeezed.

"William, the older I get, the more about life I find incredible, and sadly, the less about life I truly understand. I once believed that my life was mine to do with as I pleased; to choose a path I selected and to make whatever changes I saw fit. Now I'm not sure if I ever had any options at all. I look back on the challenging times in my life and they don't seem like a big deal anymore. I look back at the events that seemed so important and now they don't seem to have been very important at all." Thomas returned his gaze outside and continued.

"I'm an old man and I had really hoped to have figured out all of life's big questions by now. The truth is," and he turned to look at his wife, "the only thing I know for certain is that I have loved fully and that I have been fully loved. To know for certain those two simple realities I believe is to have perhaps discovered the secret of the ages."

After a long pause, William spoke.

"Dad, do you think animals have souls?"

Thomas looked at his son and thought deeply before answering. "If a soul breathes with the fire of loyalty … if a soul whispers with the embers of compassion … if a soul abides with the dedication of devotion … if a soul is defined by reckless abandon and the ability to choose to love unconditionally … then most certainly, animals have souls."

Thomas sipped his coffee again and then motioned William to turn around and look outside. There sat Murphy in the middle of the yard, perfectly still, staring directly at the two of them.

It had been a long cold winter and a thin layer of ice had covered the windmill in the front yard for weeks without any indication of melting. The winter had dumped its share of snow on Nebraska, but the severe storms were few and short-lived. The temperatures remained below freezing for most of the season though, and a three-inch layer of stubborn snow still blanketed the yard around the farmhouse. But when the crocuses stretched their bold purple and yellow petals through that crusty snow, both Katie and Thomas were relieved to see the hinting of spring.

Finally the snow melted. For several weeks now, everything green slowly awoke from its icy slumber and colored the landscape again. It was a Thursday and Thomas went into town, as he had done every Thursday since they moved into the farmhouse. His first stop was usually the library and his second stop was usually the feed store. After returning a few books and checking out a few more, and after loading the chicken feed and wild bird seed, he decided to extend his comfort zone and venture into the large home furnishings store that had recently opened on the other side of town. After all, he decided, it was spring and that meant it was the season for change and growth. Today Thomas would broaden his horizons. It was the time to be bold.

When he walked through the doors of the store he was taken back by the enormity of the building. After several moments of looking around, he was amazed at the incredible selection of items.

He must have appeared totally overwhelmed and while his mouth was still agape, a kind saleswoman approached him.

"Sir, what may I help you find today?" the smiling woman asked.

Shaking his head, still in disbelief of the store, he finally stammered an answer.

"Right. OK. Yes, yes, yes. I came in for curtains. New curtains for my wife's kitchen. I mean, our kitchen. New curtains for our kitchen."

"Let's walk over to that department, Sir, and I'll show you what we have."

Thomas walked past a section of bed pillows. He counted four long rows of them; he was shocked. There were various thicknesses of pillows, various lengths of pillows, various fillings of pillows, not to mention various prices for these bed pillows.

Then he walked past a section of bed linens: sheets, pillowcases, blankets, quilts, shams, bedspreads, comforters, and dust ruffles. He counted fourteen rows in that department alone.

By the time he finally arrived in the kitchen curtain section, Thomas was actually exhausted.

"What kind of window dressing is currently in your kitchen, Sir?"

"Window dressing?" asked Thomas.

"On your windows, Sir. Does your wife have blinds, drapes, curtains, or shades?"

"She has the kind of curtains that you open by pulling a string," and without thinking about it, he began the motions with his hands of pulling down on the string.

"So, your wife has some traditional drapes in the kitchen, then. Are you looking for a different color or would you like a different style of window dressing?"

"I had no idea this would be so complicated," sighed Thomas.

Smiling with understanding, the woman continued.

"Are the drapes in the kitchen sheer, semi-sheer, or are they lined?"

"What's the difference?" asked Thomas.

"Let's make this a bit simpler. When your drapes are drawn closed, do they let in a lot of light, a little bit of light, or no light at all?"

"No light at all. That's why I want to replace them."

"Well, we're making a lot of progress now! Do you want a window treatment that covers the entire window again or are you looking for perhaps something that covers only the very top or the bottom half of the window?"

"How about something that leaves the top half open all the time?"

The sales clerk walked over three aisles, escorting Thomas to the sheer and lightweight curtains.

"These curtains are available in a variety of colors and fabrics," she said, pointing to the swatches hanging above the shelves. "Some of them are available with tabs on the top like this, or for use with a more traditional curtain rod."

"I think I like the more traditional style," suggested Thomas.

"If you want to install a new curtain rod, we have dozens to select from a couple aisles over. If you want to go the easy route, you can just use a tension rod, which uses a spring to keep the curtain rod firmly in place."

"Easy sounds really good," smiled Thomas.

Ten minutes later, Thomas walked out of the store with all the supplies he needed to surprise his wife in the morning. He hid the shopping bags behind the truck seat and planned to get up early the following day and hang the new curtains while she was still in bed.

When he returned to the house that afternoon, Katie was sitting at the kitchen table looking through a photo album. Thomas could tell she had been crying, and Peaches was lying on the table with half of his body on the album, rolling around and meowing. Thomas walked over and gave her a kiss.

"You doing OK?" he asked.

Katie smiled and said, "Yes. They were happy tears."

Peaches looked at Thomas and hollered, producing a chuckle from both of them.

"Sometimes I really think he believes he's the boss," said Thomas.

"That's because he is," replied Katie, rubbing the cat's neck. "And I don't think you'd want it any other way, would you Dear Heart?" she said to Peaches.

Evening came and went uneventfully, and in the morning, Thomas got dressed and went downstairs early to remove the old drapes and hang the new curtains as he had planned. When he walked into the kitchen, he noticed a large stream of morning light coming into the otherwise dark room.

The back door was open.

He closed it and went upstairs to their bedroom. Peaches was not in bed with Katie.

He woke her and asked if she had been up yet this morning. She had not. He asked if she had seen the cat this morning. She sat up and looked around on the bed.

"He must have gone downstairs with you," said Katie nonchalantly.

"I haven't seen him this morning Katie, and I just went downstairs and the kitchen door was open."

"What do you mean 'open'?" asked Katie, obviously becoming very concerned now.

"The door was open. Wide open."

Neither she nor Thomas remembered leaving the kitchen door unlocked, let alone wide open. Katie walked outside and started calling for the cat, softly at first, as if she was afraid of what she would find or who would answer. Then she started running in the tall grass and shouting for Peaches.

There was no response.

She turned to face Thomas, who stood by the doorway. "You left the back door open last night!" she yelled accusingly as she began to cry.

"No I didn't. I closed it when I brought in the eggs last night."

Katie paced back and forth in the grass, obviously in thought. She looked up in defense of his silent accusations.

"I know I didn't leave it open. I didn't go outside last night after you came in. I just ..." and her sentence ended unfinished. Thomas could tell she remembered.

Her pacing stopped and she looked at her husband. "I opened the door to throw those apple cores into the yard, but I never stepped outside. The phone rang and I remember turning around and pushing the door closed with my elbow because my hands were slimy."

"It's all my fault," she said weeping. "I guess the door was never closed and the wind blew it open during the night."

Thomas walked through the yard and up to the hen house calling for the cat. They both continued to call his name. But there was no response.

Peaches had never left the house, let alone crossed the property line of the farm, some twelve acres to the north. The textures he felt as he walked were new to him: some smooth and soft, and others rough and brittle. As he walked instinctively for a reason he did not understand, he thought of nothing and considered nothing. He simply walked.

When he approached a barbed wire fence, he sniffed it and rubbed his cheek against it. Big mistake. He would definitely remember not to do that again.

He slowly and carefully stepped over the lower wire, lifting each limb cautiously and turning to make sure his tail did not catch on the middle wire as he walked into the neighbor's field.

He had no idea how far he would be traveling or even where he was going. He just walked.

When Peaches came to a paved road, he stood at the edge and watched the vehicles whoosh by.

Unfortunately, he had emerged onto the shoulder of the road at a particularly dangerous stretch of highway. To his left, the road was clearly visible for at least a quarter mile. The road to his right, however, was not visible at all because he was sitting at the top of a huge hill.

He sensed the danger of the cars and trucks but was so preoccupied with looking for the vehicles that he neglected to listen as much as watch. There were no vehicles approaching from the left and Peaches started crossing the road. The pavement was hot under his paws and he reached the painted double yellow lines in the middle of the highway. He stepped over them with a feeling of moderate conquest and headed towards the other side of the road. Suddenly he noticed trembling in the pavement under his hands and feet.

The grinding of gears echoed loudly and the moan of a diesel engine rang violently in Peaches' tiny ears. He turned and saw the shiny grill and massive headlights of a tractor-trailer looming down upon him.

Whether his little orange legs propelled him from the road or whether the turbulence created by the massive eighteen-wheeler jolted him to the shoulder was unclear. Either way, he had escaped. Just barely.

He watched the truck as it continued speeding away, making a mental note to be more attentive to outdoor sounds in the future. Peaches had certainly misplaced his street sense, or perhaps had lost it all together.

He turned and walked away from the treacherous highway and into the adjacent woods. There he noticed the sounds of insects and birds, the latter which he found delightful as well as fascinating.

Eventually the fascination wore off and his mind became preoccupied with the journey and nothing else. He stopped for a drink when he found water but he did not eat. Periodically his pupils would dilate and his body would crouch down low to the ground when he saw a chipmunk or a bird close by. His claws would emerge from his delicate white fur and his jowls would chirp in an ancient hunting song. But he never reacted further and merely watched. Somewhere in the deep recesses of his memory, his mind played scenes of other hunts and other feasts, but these memories were too distant for Peaches to presently recall with clarity.

CHAPTER FIFTEEN

The alarm clock went off on the nightstand and William rolled over and moaned.

"Time to get up, Boy," he mumbled to Murphy, as he swung his legs off the bed and slid his feet into his slippers.

Murphy stretched and moaned before climbing off the bed. He followed William downstairs and was let out the back door. William put coffee into a filter and filled the brewing machine with water. He turned and went back upstairs to shower and shave; it was all part of their morning routine.

In ten minutes, a towel clad William went back downstairs to let Murphy back in, but when he opened the door, Murphy was not there. This had never happened.

William stuck his head outside and looked around. The dog was nowhere in sight.

"Muuuurpheeeee. Come on, Boy. Muuuurpheeeeee."

There was no response. He shook his head and walked through the house to the front door and looked outside. There was no sign of the dog there either.

Although Murphy was very sociable, he was not a wanderer. He had never strayed from the yard and had never gone beyond William's sight. William began to worry.

He got dressed in stages. He put on his underwear and then went to the window to look outside. Then he put on his pants and shirt, and went to the window to look outside. He then put on his socks and shoes, and went back to the window to look outside. Finally, he put on his tie and belt and went downstairs.

He walked out into the back yard again and hollered. No response. He walked around the house while continuing to call. No response.

He walked back into the house and poured himself a cup of coffee. Sitting at the kitchen table to review his schedule and appointments for the day, he looked out the window and wondered aloud, "Where did you go?"

Liz, his secretary, was used to his phone calls asking her to reschedule meetings and appointments, but the concern in his voice was upsetting to her and she asked what was wrong. William simply told her that Murphy was missing.

When the cup of coffee was finished he poured another and loosened his tie. Holding the large mug with both hands, he began to pace.

When Murphy crossed the property line far behind the house, he had no idea where he was going or who he would be encountering. His internal compass pointed him due west and he walked in silent obedience.

His slightly raised nose breathed in the new smells with excitement and the wind in his fur was delightful. His emotions were torn between his desire and obligation to remain near William, and this unexplainable new calling to hastily leave his friend and his home. Murphy wished he understood his actions. Soon, however, the anguish would dissipate and Murphy would be left with a sense of calm assurance.

While William worried and paced throughout the kitchen and den, Murphy cantered with a light step and an even lighter spirit. He felt so alive, so rejuvenated, so free. He had no worries, no cares, and absolutely no concerns. In fact, his mind no longer considered even one thought. He just briskly walked towards an unknown destination.

Canton was less rural than the Nebraska farmlands, but compared to a large metropolitan city, this part of Ohio still had its fair share of pastures and undeveloped real estate and woodlands. Murphy soon came upon a relatively new development and although he somehow knew he should avoid people, it was difficult for him to blend into his surroundings. After all, a longhaired white dog is easy to spot against a background of green.

He walked out of a wooded area and onto a lawn of thick grass. Two children playing in the adjacent yard saw him immediately and squealed with delight. The younger of the children, a toddler of three perhaps, ran towards Murphy with her arms outstretched in preparation of wrapping them around the fluffy white visitor when she reached him.

The dog stopped and watched the little girl as she approached. Closer and closer she came. He knew he should not stop to visit, but he did not know why. He looked ahead to the left and saw a high fence surrounding the yard next door. He looked to the right and saw a woman step out of her back door, wiping her wet hands on her pants as the door closed behind her, and walk hastily across the patio towards the thick green lawn.

Directly in front of Murphy was a straight shot to the street, but he would have to dart past the other children rather abruptly to avoid the pending encounter with the toddler.

"Sarah!" shouted the mother to her little girl. "Come over here. Don't go near the doggie."

As often is the case with small children, the toddler suddenly lost all hearing capability and continued running wildly toward the dog.

A gate opened in the high fence next door and two more children emerged, these a few years older. Not wanting to miss the excitement, they too ran towards the white fluffy surprise visitor.

The added complication made Murphy's escape more necessary, as well as more delicate. With a quick cut to his left and then his right, the trespassing canine avoided the fearless little girl who closed her arms around him as he darted past. Sarah fell to the soft ground with a handful of long white fur and eyes full of instant tears of disappointment.

Murphy ran towards the street, and after checking for cars in both directions, he crossed it and headed towards the woods that lay ahead.

William's pacing led him from the kitchen to every other room in the downstairs. He opened the front door repeatedly and stepped outside. Then he retraced his steps and opened the back door and stepped outside. There was no sign of Murphy anywhere.

He paced and sipped his coffee; he was on his second pot. He went back into the family room where his eyes were immediately drawn to Murphy's wooden toy box that was kept on the fireplace hearth. Then he looked a bit higher and walked toward the wooden mantle.

There, a dozen framed photographs sat on proud display. There was one of his mother and Millie, taken when they were twelve years old. Next to that one was another image of the two friends, this one taken some fifty years later. There were two shots of his parents, one formal photograph taken the year his Dad retired from the company, and one that William took one summer at the farm of his folks leaning up against a split-rail fence.

All the other photos were images of either Murphy alone or Murphy with him. One was taken candidly while he gave a sales presentation and Murphy lay at his feet. William's favorite shot was the one he took of Murphy last winter during a blizzard. The dog was standing proudly in the snow with a look of serious contemplation on his face, and his long white mane was being blown by the strong winds. William believed that there was never a nobler dog to be found.

His dad had taken two of the other pictures and had given them to William for his last birthday. The black and white shot was taken from behind during one of William's visits to the farmhouse. In it William and the dog were walking down the dirt road near the farm. It was dusk and the two were obviously in deep discussion when the camera was clicked. The scene captured a man looking down towards his dog, while the dog was looking up at his man. William reached a finger forward and touched the glass over the photo.

The ringing of the telephone pulled William from that blissful moment on the dirt road and set him back into his present reality. He was not pleased with the change of scenery.

"Hello, Son. I just called your office and Liz told me I could reach you at home. Are you feeling OK?

"I'm fine Dad. Is everything OK with you two?"

"Well, that's why I'm calling, Will. We're fine but something has come up and your Mother is pretty upset about it. I thought maybe you'd have some words of wisdom for me."

"That'd be a first, Dad. I'm the middle-aged bachelor, remember? You obviously know more about women than I do."

Forcing a smile and then pausing for a moment, Thomas continued.

"Peaches took off during the night. He managed to slip out the back door and we can't find him. I don't want to think the worst, but your Mom is pretty beside herself."

"Dad, I'm not going to be any help at all. You're not going to believe this, but when I let Murphy out this morning, he never came back. I'm pretty beside myself too, that's why I stayed home. I just couldn't bear the thought of him coming back while I was gone and having no way of getting in the house. He's never been outside alone except for when he's taking care of dog business."

"Oh, Will, I am so sorry. Do me a favor, huh? Let's keep this phone call between us for right now. If I find out something at this end, I'll call you. And you do the same, OK?"

"It's a deal, Dad. And let's hope they come home real soon."

Thomas concurred and the two men said good-bye.

William continued to call for Murphy, just as his parents continued to call for Peaches five states away. But neither animal came home that day.

On and on walked Murphy. He paid little attention to the noises he heard as he hiked. By dusk, his stomach began making noises of its own and the dog was inclined to listen to those noises more so than the others around him. Stopping to survey the dining possibilities, he soon discovered that his options were negligible. Offering a silent suggestion to his empty stomach to be patient, he stooped to sip from a small brook before continuing on his way.

By the time he had put a dozen more miles behind him, the sky had become dark. He found a relatively comfortable spot under a pine tree, curled up into a ball, and closed his eyes.

A sound sleep came easily and quickly, but a loud commotion nearby woke him suddenly and he rose to his feet assuming a defensive stance. Five yards in front of him, two raccoons were obviously in disagreement concerning a canvas bag that lay on the ground in between them. Murphy opened his nostrils wide and inhaled deeply; there was definitely food in that canvas sack.

He took a few steps toward the raccoons, neither of them realizing his presence, let alone his intent. By the time the masked thieves noticed Murphy, the dog was only a few feet away.

It was the smaller of the two raccoons who first saw him. The creature stood on his hind feet, stretching upward to appear taller.

Murphy crept toward the bag. The second raccoon finally spotted the invader and looked to his comrade for suggestions. Mimicking his smaller friend, the second raccoon stood on his hind feet too, also reaching his hands upward to display his height and presumed threat.

If dogs could snicker or chuckle, surely a smile and giggle slid from Murphy's mouth at that moment. He raised up onto his hind legs to demonstrate his size, and realizing their inadequacy, the two raccoons returned to all fours and sprinted away in defeat.

Murphy looked down at the canvas bag. "Newton Natural Foods." Standing in front of the bag, he put a paw on the bottom handle and gently stuck his snout under the top handle, opening it. After a long sniff and a brief moment of reconsideration, he pulled his nose out and walked around to the bottom of the bag. Lowering his head, he bit securely on the bottom seam and slowly lifted the bag.

Fortunately for Murphy, whoever had gone shopping today at the health food store had both diverse and excellent taste. Falling out first was a loaf of bread and a few muffins, each individually wrapped in waxed paper. The muffin assortment was followed by several small bags of dried fruit and nuts. Behind these, toppled out a package of organic cream filled cookies – the kind William liked to dunk in milk. Of course William always shared these vanilla cookies with his dog.

As most people would do after a long hike with no food, Murphy decided to have some cookies first. It took him several minutes to get the package open and admittedly, most of the cookies were broken by the time he reached them. Regardless, they tasted phenomenally delicious and surely satisfied both his immediate need for food as well as his sweet tooth.

He eyed the muffins next. There were four of them and he sniffed each to identify their flavor. Banana, corn, carrot and blueberry. He would definitely eat the blueberry muffin first. He had never had a corn muffin before, but thought he would try that one second.

He chewed leisurely and appreciatively. By the time he was through with the first three muffins, he was thirsty and needed to find water again.

When nighttime blackened the sky over Peaches, he curled up on a leafy bed beneath a tree and slept. He had no idea how much farther his journey would take him or how many more days he would travel. Sometimes, ignorance was most certainly bliss.

By the morning of the fourth day, Peaches fur was becoming entangled with burrs and quite dungy. Somehow he knew that by nightfall, he would be arriving at his destination. So he proceeded forward with excitement and determination.

CHAPTER SIXTEEN

William sat in his recliner watching the evening news mindlessly. Three days had passed since Murphy disappeared. He had placed an ad in the local newspaper for a lost dog and included a substantial reward. He had contacted the local animal hospitals and shelters with Murphy's description, but no one had seen him.

Thomas and Katie had done the same. No one had seen Peaches either.

Thomas got up from his recliner and walked into the kitchen. Katie sat at the table expressionless, staring out the window into the darkness. Setting his hands on her shoulders and gently massaging them, he suggested they go sit on the front porch and watch for Peaches to come back. She knew how hopeless the situation was at this point, but in appreciation of her husband's tenderness and compassion, she agreed.

They had spent endless hours sitting together on the porch swing since they moved to the farm. Their years together did not diminish their love for each other, nor did it abate the mutual devotion they shared. In times of gladness they sat together and rejoiced as they swung. In times of pain, they sat together and swung, sometimes talking things out and sometimes being silent. Thomas came to understand that more often than not, the times of silent togetherness proved to be the most comforting.

So they rocked in wordlessness.

Katie was the one who finally broke the stillness.

"That sure is a big moon tonight."

Thomas nodded in agreement.

CHAPTER SEVENTEEN

There was a large clearing in the forest covered with soft grass and a few scattered rocks. The trees bordered the brightly-lit meadow like soldiers posted around their sleeping battalion. The moon rose upwards, higher and higher into the clear night sky. And the animals came.

They did not know why. They did not even know how. They simply came; directed and guided by an inner voice. Some had traveled for several days; others had only come a short distance. Still, they came because they could do nothing else.

Their numbers grew to perhaps three thousand and the clearing filled to overflowing. They did not speak, they did not touch, and they did not communicate in any way. They felt no fear, no anxiety, and no desire to respond or to interact with the other animals. They simply came, laid down, and slept.

When the number of guests fated to attend had arrived, the Meeting of the Full Moon began.

The animals were awakened by a silent whisper. One by one, they sat up and lifted their heads towards the sky. Then they closed their eyes.

The heavens gently released a mist of tiny light speckles that fell softly toward the Earth. As the white drizzle fell on the animals, it seemed to suffuse into each of them and then instantly disappear. This cascade of delicate radiance lasted for several minutes. When it was through, the animals once again curled up on the ground and fell asleep.

In clearings all across the country, Meetings of the Full Moon concluded in the same manner, with the animals curled up and sleeping. In the morning, they would all head back to their homes.

CHAPTER EIGHTEEN

William sat at his desk at the office, his chair turned towards the window, staring out but seeing nothing. His intercom buzzed and he swiveled his chair around to push the button on his phone.

"Yes, Liz."

"Mr. Colbert, someone just delivered a ... package, Sir. May I bring it in?"

"Yes, Liz, bring it in."

The office door opened and the woman walked in with a puppy in her arms. It was a beautiful golden retriever, complete with collar, leash, and a red ribbon.

William stood and walked around to the front of the desk.

"Who dropped him off?" he asked.

"I don't know, Sir. He didn't leave his name. I assumed you knew about it."

"No, Liz, I didn't order a dog. I already have a dog," he said as he turned and walked towards the window.

"Mr. Colbert, maybe you can take him home to keep you company ... until Murphy comes back."

William turned and walked over to the puppy, who was still in Liz's arms. He reached out slowly and touched the dog on the head tenderly.

"Why don't you take him home to your boys," suggested William, and he turned and walked over to the large window again.

It had been nine days since he last saw Murphy. There had been no responses to the newspaper ad; there had been no sightings by the animal shelters. There had been no report of an accident by the highway department or the local Police.

His parents' house had become as quiet and desperate as his had.

He tried to pour himself into his work, but it seemed meaningless. His employees and business associates tried to cheer him up, but he discarded their efforts.

Driving home without his dog was depressing. Walking into the house without him was heart-wrenching. Waking up without him was nothing short of devastating. With each passing day, the loss became more difficult; he could only imagine what his parents were going through.

He sat in his recliner with the television remote in his hand for most of the night. He was almost asleep in his chair when the kitchen phone rang. It was his mother.

"Will! I know it's late but I had to call you! Peaches came home! Your father and I were in bed and I heard a meowing out back. It's him, Will! He looks fine too! Our Peaches has come home!"

William was relieved for his mother, but their good news seemed to make his situation more bleak. He tried to be happy for them; he genuinely was, but in reality he was more sorry for himself.

"If Peaches was able to survive this whole time, I'm sure Murphy is just fine too."

"We'll see, Mom. We'll see. I'm happy for you. Give him a hug from his brother, OK?"

The phone call ended and William turned off the TV and went upstairs to bed. He doubted he would sleep, but he thought he would at least lie down. When the alarm sounded at 6:15 a.m., he was shocked that he had actually dozed off.

He went downstairs to make coffee. A strange feeling came over him and he opened the back door. No one was there. He called for Murphy. No one came.

He went back upstairs and showered as usual. With a towel wrapped around his waist, he started descending the stairs.

That is when he heard the bark.

He took the remaining stairs three at a time and nearly fell at the bottom as he grasped the handrail and turned the corner sharply.

"Murphy, Murphy!" he yelled as he raced into the kitchen and threw open the back door. But no one was there.

His hope plummeted and his heart sank to a depth he could not have imagined possible. He stared outside for an endless minute, and then closed the door and locked it.

Then he heard the bark again.

He ran to the front door and flung it open. There stood Murphy.

When the phone rang in his parents' house, they could not find the receiver. After the tenth or eleventh ring, when William was just about to hang up, his Mother answered.

"Mom! Murphy's back! He looks fine ... no limping, no blood anywhere. He's a little dirty but aside from that, he's perfect!"

"This is a day for celebrating, Son. I'm sure you and Murphy will do something special after work today ... maybe split a pizza?"

William laughed and said, "After he has a nice bath!"

"William, I love you and am so happy for you, for all of us. But, I need to tell you something and I've been putting it off for a long time."

William's smile vanished and he held the phone tightly to his ear.

"Mom?" he replied.

"Son, we hate this telephone. Is it OK if we put our old one back on the wall?"

William laughed so long and hard he thought he would explode.

"Mom. I will personally reinstall your old phone next time I see you. And from now on, you're either going shopping with me for a Christmas present or you're getting gift certificates."

"It's a deal," said Katie, much relieved.

The workers arrived the following morning at William's house. Their flat bed truck was piled high with cedar. By the time William and Murphy returned home from the office that evening, there would be a six-foot fence surrounding the back yard.

CHAPTER NINETEEN

Thomas was the first to notice the subtle changes in Peaches. The cat talked more now, a lot more. He also stayed closer to Katie and started sleeping on her pillow at night, instead of at the foot of the bed. There were times when Thomas woke to find the huge orange cat actually sleeping on his wife's head. Fortunately, he was able to capture one of those moments on film.

Peaches also started pitter-pattering with his hands, which he had never done before he ran away. Both Thomas and Katie noticed that he also seemed to purr a lot more.

When Katie would leave the house, Peaches would lay on a bench by the living room window, with his face in between the curtains. There he would remain, waiting for her to come home. Nothing made Katie feel more welcome than seeing that fluffy orange and white face in the window when she pulled up to the house.

He also developed a habit of sticking his little pink nose inside every bag or box that made its way into the house. One day Thomas came home with a bag from the pet store and deliberately set it down on the kitchen table. Peaches immediately jumped up onto the table and worked the bag open with his paws. When he looked inside, he saw a rawhide bone and a toy baseball, both of which he assumed were Murphy's. Also in the bag were some small Wiffle balls with bells in the middle, and a bag of toy mice that smelled like catnip. The mice were an instant hit and Peaches threw one in the air and then batted it down, time and again. Thomas watched him jump around like a circus cat, at times laughing so hard that the noise brought Katie in from the other room. They both sat and watched the cat play with his new toy for a good twenty minutes.

Every morning Peaches would follow Katie downstairs to the kitchen. She would make a pot of coffee for Thomas and a pot of tea for herself. Peaches would jump onto the counter near the window and stand on his hind legs, resting his white furry paws on the new curtain rod. He would then push down with all his might until the curtains fell to the floor. Thomas would tighten the tension on the rods and Peaches would somehow compensate and push harder. Every morning, down came the curtains. No one needed to verbalize the similarity between this and Millie's daily routine. Consequently, the cat was never scolded.

It was amazing for them to discover—or rediscover, actually—how much joy and love a creature could bring into a home. They had each been raised with pets but they both realized that Peaches was an extraordinary cat; one of those pets you are likely to encounter only once in a lifetime ... if ever.

The summer heat was less sweltering than it had been the previous year. William and Murphy had gone camping three times out by the Lake and even the mosquitoes seemed to be fewer and farther between this year.

On the morning of his 50th Birthday his Mother called, as she had done every year for the past three decades. When he hung up the phone, he allowed the reality of his birthday to settle into his awareness. The years certainly passed by more quickly than they did in his youth; or was it just that the days experienced by older people were cherished more than those of the young? Regardless, William found himself in a heavy ponder for several minutes after the phone call ended.

ColPro, Inc. was growing steadily and sales were up 34% over the previous year. Although it would take several more years for William to re-coop his losses from the Eugene Morgan fiasco, he had no regrets and no desire to re-write the past. He had learned that those chapters most difficult to write, were the ones most likely to produce the greatest rewards.

Murphy was now four years old, as best as anyone could guess. The veterinarian's initial examination of the dog estimated him to be about two at that time. It took the past two years for the apprehension to ease for William every time the phone rang; the first three months had been the worst. In the back of his mind, William always expected Murphy's owner would finally call and claim him. After all, a neutered purebred dog must belong to someone, somewhere. Right? After two years though, William decided that if anyone did come forth to claim him, there had to be some sort of statute of limitations concerning such a situation. At least he hoped there was.

As summer wound down, the nights became more comfortable for sleeping, but the days were still plenty long for work and play.

As transpired every morning, William stretched and muttered across the bed, "Time to get up, Boy." The two males had such similar waking routines it was almost comical. Both stretched their arms and legs while simultaneously groaning loudly. They then would lift their head and then set it back down. Then ever so slowly, their bodies would creep along inch by inch and approach the side of the bed.

This day they had both slept in because it was Saturday. Saturdays were meant for drinking coffee, walking in the park, and grocery shopping. William and Murphy loved Saturdays.

Their first stop was the feed store. The shop owner was always glad to see Murphy and always treated him to a special dog cookie.

William had recently developed an interest in birds, mostly due to a book of Millie's he had picked up from her house the last time he was there. To his surprise, she had over a dozen books dedicated to identifying and attracting birds to your yard. She even had a few books devoted to building birdhouses; apparently Roger had planned to pursue their construction some day. But often times, some days never come.

William carried the birdseed out to the car and Murphy followed close behind. The dog always turned heads wherever they went. William glowed like a proud Papa when a passerby commented on the dog's beauty or good behavior.

The afternoon temperatures were rising rapidly and William decided that a cool treat was in order. Pulling up to the drive-through window at the ice cream stand, he asked for two vanilla cones. The cashier looked at him, then looked at the dog sitting in the front seat, and then looked back at William, who obligingly smiled and said, "He likes vanilla ice cream too."

As they drove off, William looked over at Murphy and said, "I guess she'd never seen a dog order ice cream before." William's left hand held his ice cream and the steering wheel. His right hand held the other cone, and since this was not the dog's first ice cream, he was quite adept at licking it gently, giving William time to turn the cone periodically. William rotated the cone and the dog lapped away, just as a child would. People driving by pointed and stared, which gave William more delight than even the cold dairy treat.

By the time they were done with their shopping, it was time to think about supper. William decided to stop at a Chinese restaurant and place an order to go. He made sure to order enough to last the entire weekend, and as always, he asked for extra fortune cookies because Murphy liked them even more than dog biscuits.

The smell of the food filling the interior of the vehicle was nothing short of divine. Murphy kept sniffing the large bag and looking over at William with pitiful begging glances. The dog was reminded that they had to wait until they returned home before tearing into the small white boxes of delight. By the time they reached the house, they were darn near starving.

The heavy brown paper sack sat on the kitchen table unopened while William took some of Murphy's food from the icebox and put it in a clean bowl on the floor. Then the cartons of Chinese food were opened and William made himself an enormous plate. Of course he would also give his dog a bite of beef and vegetables, a bite of shrimp lo mein, a mouthful of fried rice, a won ton from the soup, and a few fortune cookies.

The food was fantastic, and William had just grabbed another egg roll when the doorbell rang. He had always been a soft-spoken, genteel man and although he was exceptional in dealing with people, he preferred his solitude and rarely had company. So the interruption was both curious and surprising, as well as somewhat annoying.

Murphy stood at attention and followed William to the front door. Through the beveled glass it was obvious that the person ringing the doorbell was a man. With an egg roll in one hand, William turned the knob with the other. When the door opened, William immediately realized that the man standing on his porch was not a neighbor asking for a cup of sugar or to borrow a ladder. The man at the door was Rusty Morgan.

William had no idea how to respond. He wondered if his facial expression could possibly be revealing the four or five thoughts synchronously running through his mind. Apparently, the only discernable look on his face must have been one of total confusion, because Rusty smiled and said, "I guess you don't remember me. I met you about two years ago ... in a diner outside of Davenport." William continued to stare, his eyes expressionless and his right hand still holding the egg roll.

Rusty extended his hand and said in question form, "Rusty Morgan? I sat next to you one afternoon in a diner where the waitress spilled your lunch in your lap."

William realized that his honest look of shock proved more effective than any deliberate ploy of playing dumb he could possibly had enacted. His countenance eased somewhat and his face resumed a more natural expression.

"Oh, Rusty. From the diner. Uh ... won't you come in," said William as he stepped back into the foyer and gestured with his egg roll for his unexpected guest to enter.

Murphy sat behind William as still as the dragon statue had sat outside of the Chinese restaurant. Rusty walked into the house and bent down a few feet in front of the dog, extending his hand to be sniffed. "Hi Murphy," said Rusty, "it's a pleasure to meet you."

Murphy sniffed Rusty's hand and then barked and wagged his tail. William wondered what in the world was going on, but tried to act nonchalantly as he led his guest to the kitchen and motioned for him to have a seat.

"Have you had supper? We're having Chinese. We have plenty," said William.

Smiling, Rusty looked at William and said, "You said 'we.'"

"Excuse me?" William said, still somewhat in shock.

"You said 'we' have plenty. That word has a pretty nice ring to it, doesn't it?"

Letting down his guard a bit, William looked at his dog and then back at Rusty. "Yes. Yes it does," he replied.

"I ... I actually would love some Chinese food. You know how difficult it is to get a good meal when you're on the road."

William went to the cupboard for an extra plate and bowl for his guest, and grabbed another set of silverware. Taking the other little white boxes from the bag, he smiled and said, "Dig in." Then, after a moment of thought, he added, "and I promise not to dump it in your lap."

Rusty spooned the food into his plate and ladled the soup into his bowl. Finally, realizing that William was staring at him and not eating, Rusty spoke.

"I guess you're wondering what I'm doing here."

William stared at his guest, trying desperately to think of the most appropriate response. He realized his hesitation fit perfectly in his attempt at innocent naiveté. Finally, he answered.

"The question had crossed my mind."

"Do you know who I am?"

Taking as much time as he could while still trying to play dumb, William answered, "You're Rusty from the diner. Your dog was expecting puppies."

"My parents named me Eugene," said Rusty as he spooned a mouthful of fried rice into his mouth. I never cared much for the name, so I have always used my middle name."

William picked at his food hoping that his innocent host routine would continue working. Rusty continued.

"Mr. Colbert, I own the patent that your company tried to buy a couple years ago," he said, looking directly at William, awaiting a response.

Although he was doing his best to act surprised and shocked, inside William was relieved that the game could end here and now. He then realized there was still one unanswered question.

"How do you know my dog's name?" he asked.

Starting to feel more relaxed, Rusty's smile grew bigger.

"I saw you and Murphy on the News a few days after I met you. Since I knew you didn't have a dog when you pulled into town, I did find it rather curious that you had one when you left. When they mentioned your name, I knew I had heard it before but I couldn't remember where. Then the next day I happened to get a real nasty phone call from your attorney. Then it dawned on me where I heard your name."

William fumbled with his fork after that last comment about the attorney.

Rusty chuckled and continued, "It's OK. He called me back a few days later to inform me that he was no longer representing you. I did ask him a few questions about you though, and I hung up realizing there was no way you knew who I was when I sat down next to you in the diner."

William felt relief again. He looked his guest right in the eye and said, "Mr. Morgan, I had no idea who you were that day in the diner." That much at least had been true.

"I then hired a private investigator to follow you," declared Rusty.

Almost choking after that comment, William struggled to respond. "You did *what*?"

"I paid to have you followed. On and off for over a year. I'm a pretty good judge of character, William, and although you were really stressed when I met you, and although you seemed a little snobby, I didn't sense any deceit in you, or any maliciousness."

Oh my, thought William. He had certainly pulled the wool over Rusty's eyes, it seemed.

"I thought it was more than just coincidence," added Rusty, "that we had run into each other the way we did. But since I'm only human, I wanted to make sure of a few things and to have you checked out."

Trying to sound offended, William said, "I can't believe you hired someone to investigate me." As the words fell from his lips, they rang loudly with guilt and irony.

"Sometimes you can't rely on your own judgment," said Rusty.

"I know exactly what you mean."

"Anyway, I accumulated a two inch file on you," continued Rusty, while lifting a fork full of egg Fu young. After eating that mouthful, he added, "sorry, but I needed to know."

"Needed to know what?"

"I needed to know if Murphy was for real."

"Murphy?"

"Yeah. I saw you drive off with him on the News, but I figured you'd dump him somewhere as soon as you got the chance."

William toyed with his food. Rusty continued.

"After a couple of weeks I decided to have you investigated. When I got the first set of photographs I realized you kept the dog."

"The *first* set?" asked William.

Rusty's face took on a look of slight embarrassment and begged silently for understanding. William did not oblige, since he actually did feel violated by the disclosures.

"I had you followed for about eighteen months, actually. Not every day mind you; it was expensive enough just having you monitored once or twice a week."

William felt modest fury but each time his anger reared, it was squelched by the reminder that he had done the same despicable thing to Rusty. So his guilt kept him silent.

"I wasn't sure how you'd take it once I told you all this," admitted Rusty. "You're taking it much better than I would," and he picked up another egg roll and took a bite.

"Anyway," he continued, "it became clear to me that you kept the dog. I was quite surprised, to tell you the truth. Then, when the second and third sets of photos came in, I realized you had grown to love Murphy. It was at that point that I started thinking that maybe we could work something out."

"Work what out?" asked William.

"The patent."

A dozen emotions washed over William in a matter of seconds and he had to replay the words he had just heard. He waited before responding.

"You changed your mind about selling the patent?"

"Maybe."

"Maybe? You came all this way and showed up at my front door to say ... maybe?"

"No. I came all this way and showed up at your front door to say I wanted to talk."

"Why in the world do you want to talk now?"

"Haven't you ever changed your mind about something, William? Haven't you noticed that as you get older, you find yourself changing your mind about most things? Don't you feel differently today than you did a year ago? Two years ago?"

William spoke softly and thoughtfully. "I am no longer interested in your patent."

"So, you've changed your mind about that too, huh?"

"Apparently so," said William, still shocked at what he had just said.

Katie had a pot of tea brewing and had just fed Peaches. Thomas was outside in the yard; he had agreed to attend a farm auction with her later that morning.

The tea was ready and Katie poured herself a large cup. She had brought a few of Millie's things back to the house recently, and one of them was this coffee mug, which had been one of her friend's favorites.

She and Katie had taken a trip to New Hampshire one year to see the foliage, and of course their days were full of shopping and antiquing. In one particular shop, everything was handmade on the premises by the proprietor. She had a potter's wheel in the rear of the shop, along with a kiln. She made dinnerware, candle holders, bowls, salt and pepper shakers, and everything in between. She also offered custom design and personalized items, which had appealed to Millie tremendously.

The proprietor drew silhouettes of each woman and would later incorporate them into the item selected by either etching or painting. She also asked them each many questions and scribbled notes on a pad while they answered. The cost was astronomical as far as Katie was concerned, and she tried to dissuade Millie from confirming the order, but Millie was insistent.

Three weeks after returning home from their trip, Millie received a package in the mail from the artist. It was a large coffee mug that held fourteen ounces and was a dusty sand color. The top of the mug was slightly lipped and the body was thinner at the top and wider at the bottom. The handle was twisted and somewhat ornamental, with a small squashed dollop of clay added near the top to accommodate your thumb. Directly across from the handle there was an etching of the two women facing each other. On the other areas of the mug there were tiny paintings of the items the women had described during their conversation with the artist: strawberries, blueberries, oak leaves, chickens, a mailbox, hearts, a baby, a picnic basket, and a bird house. This morning, as Katie looked at the mug in front of her, she was so glad that Millie had insisted on buying it.

Peaches walked into the kitchen meowing loudly, which he tended to do frequently and seemingly for no apparent reason. The old telephone rang on the kitchen wall and she walked over to answer it. It was William.

"Hello, Sweetheart. How are you and my grandson?"

"Just peachy, Mom, how's my little brother?"

"I won't tell him you said that. We are all fine, thank you for asking. Do you want to talk to your father?"

"Yes, Mom, I do. Is he busy?"

"Retired men are never busy William, just constantly under foot. Hold on and I'll fetch him for you."

Thomas was beckoned from the yard and smiled at his wife as he reached for the phone.

"Hello, Son. I smelled the cinders last night, what's going on?"

"You're not going to believe who paid me a visit last night, Dad. Not in a million years."

"OK. I give up."

"Rusty Morgan. The guy with our patent."

"You've got to be kidding."

"Not in a million years. He wanted to talk about the patent."

"What did you tell him?"

"I told him I wasn't interested."

The lengthy silence disturbed William.

"Dad, are you still there?"

"Yeah, Will, I'm here. I'm just in shock is all."

"What do you think I should have done? Didn't we let go of that plan two years ago?"

"Yes, yes we did, Will, but that was then. At the time, the man was not interested in selling. Now he is."

"Well, we didn't actually get that far, Dad. He never said he would sell it … he just said maybe."

"Considering the circumstances of this particular situation, a maybe sure seems like a yes to me."

"Are you saying you want me to pursue it?"

"That's your call, Will. I'm just surprised you let it slip through your fingers."

"Now you're making me second guess myself, Dad."

"That's not my intention Son, you know that. Why don't you think it over for a few days? Whatever you decide is fine with me."

Feeling confused, William ended the phone call with his father. Both men sat rubbing the back of their head repeatedly.

A week passed, and then another. William's thoughts were centered around Rusty's visit and the patent. There were so many options to consider; so many scenarios; so many possible outcomes.

Firstly, he had no idea if Rusty really would sell the patent. Unfortunately, William had slammed the door on that conversation very hastily. If the patent was now for sale, did Rusty want to sell it outright? Did he want to be partners? Were there conditions, and if so, what were they?

The machinery that had been built for production was in storage. The building where the equipment was initially set up had been sold for a loss.

William lost money on the entire venture—a lot of money. He had lost his home as well. However, he felt that the lessons learned and the changes that had resulted from the very trying situation had left him a stronger, more understanding person. He felt he gained something he had always seen in his father, which, until now, William had been unable to isolate or identify. That elusive trait his Dad so aptly carried and with which he sublimely radiated, was character.

Character: a trait that cannot be taught, but which must only ultimately be personally developed. Good looks were genetically received (or manufactured), but character ran deeper; character was part of the soul. It was something you either had or did not. It was something that could not be purchased or coerced, for if one tried to acquire it in those ways, the attempt would certainly be negated by the means.

William was not sure how or when he began feeling like a man of character, but was sure he had acquired a minimal degree somewhere along the way; certainly not as much as his father possessed, but most assuredly, at least a little.

He had done much thinking and growing over the past couple of years. Ironically, most of his deep and introspective thoughts centered around his dog. Sometimes he watched Murphy while he played or slept, as a parent watches their baby or child. William pondered many things during these times of quiet observance. Most often, he considered the "what ifs." What if the patent had not been rescinded? What if his car had not broken down? What if he had not met Rusty Morgan in the diner? What if Murphy had not forced him off the road? What if he had frozen to death? What if he had not keep Murphy? What if Millie had not passed away? What if he had married Samantha? The "what ifs" seemed more numerous than one man could comprehend or consider.

Sometimes when he watched Murphy, he would silently ask himself another set of questions. These were the "why" questions and they were as plentiful as the "what ifs." Why did the patent fall through? Why did he just so happen to run into Rusty Morgan in the diner? Why was he saved from falling off that bridge? Why did Murphy stay with him in the snow? Why? Why? Why? Sometimes William felt like a wondering three-year-old boy instead of a full-grown man.

Through all the contemplation, however, William seemed to have come to a peaceful place of blind acceptance. Although the pages from his past occasionally reared their ugly heads of doubt and questioning, he was finally able to bind those pages together into a chapter called, "over and done with." After he did this, the pages that followed were much easier to write, and most often were threaded with seeds or deeds of something called *character*.

Sometimes when Murphy was sleeping, his feet would move like he was running up a flight of miniature stairs and his face would twitch like he was talking to someone. William wished he could peek inside those dreams and discover what adventures and conversations his dog was having.

There were other times when William wondered what animals were thinking, his dog in particular. He wondered if Murphy actually considered him his friend; he wondered if the wagging tail and the seeming smile on the dog's face were truly indications of joy or contentment, or just reflexive actions caused by ancient wolf genetics.

William began observing animals more and more, as well as their interactions with their owners. He noticed that on the whole, pet owners smiled a lot more than non-pet owners. He noticed that people who owned pets tended to be more outwardly physical and affectionate. He realized that people who did not like animals in general could simply not be trusted.

The alarm on William's nightstand chimed at 6:15 a.m. as usual, and he reached over and thumped the "off" button. He groaned with morning grunts and worked his way towards rolling out of bed, throwing the covers back on top of Murphy.

"Time to get up, Boy," he said as he put his slippers on and walked towards the bedroom door.

"Come on, Murph. Time to get up."

William was just about to set his foot on the top step when he realized Murphy was not next to him. His heart sank as he turned around and froze in the doorway. The quilt was covering everything but the white dog's head, and there he lay under the covers, motionless.

A lump formed in William's throat and his heart seemed to fall into his stomach. He walked towards the bed and extended a hand forward to stroke the soft white fur.

"Oh, Murphy," he softly uttered as his hand touched the dog's head.

Suddenly a deep sleeping groan came from beneath the blankets as the dog stretched his arms and legs and extended his head back. With an inexpressible sigh of relief and pure delight, William fell onto the bed in exhaustive reprieve.

"Boy ... you just gave me the worst scare of my entire life," he said as he rubbed the dog's ears and kissed him. "You were just sleeping. I thought you were ... well ... I don't even want to talk about it. It's time to get up, OK?"

This time as William walked to the stairs, his best friend was at his side.

CHAPTER TWENTY

As usual, Murphy was let out the back door while William started the coffee. The gate in the high cedar fence was padlocked from the inside, and since William never had the need to open it, the dog was quite secure in the back yard. So, with sanguine assurance, William left Murphy outside once again while he went upstairs to shower and get dressed.

Forty minutes later they were en route to the office. As always, many other drivers and passengers heading to work or school pointed and waved at Murphy, who sat alertly in the passenger seat in true shotgun fashion.

William's day began with an informal staff meeting and was followed by a lengthy overseas phone call. He was flipping through the pages of a large file when his office phone rang.

"William Colbert speaking."

"Hi, Son. It's me."

"Hey Dad, you don't call me at the office very often anymore, is everything alright?"

"I'm not sure, Will. Your mother woke me up during the night saying she wasn't feeling well, so I drove her to the hospital."

"What are the Doctors saying?"

"They aren't saying anything. All the tests they ran so far came back normal. They should know more later this afternoon."

"How was she feeling when you left the hospital?"

"You know your Mother; she never complains about anything. She seemed real weak though, Will. I'm not sure what to think. The only reason I came home was because she insisted I come feed Peaches."

"I'll be there as soon as I can, Dad. The next flight out is in about three hours; do you want me to meet you at the hospital?"

"She's in room 301. I'll be back over there as soon as I feed Peaches."

"Call me if you hear anything. Tell her Murphy and I will see her later this afternoon."

"I'll do that, Son," said Thomas as Peaches looked up at him and meowed loudly. "I need to feed the cat, Will. We'll see you later."

Thomas fed Peaches, who picked at his food without eating more than a mouthful. The cat walked around the house hollering for Katie, whose absence was obviously as distressing to the cat as it was to him. When a knock at the front door interrupted their lamenting, they both seemed relieved by the distraction.

A freckled woman stood on the porch with her red headed five-year-old son, the boy fully clad in Cub Scout attire, complete with ribbons and pins.

"Good afternoon, Mr. Colbert," said the confident boy. "I'm taking orders for some wonderful popcorn and chocolate products to help support my Den." Opening a small catalog, he added, "May I show you a few of our best sellers? Perhaps you would like to order extra for friends and family this year?"

Thomas was always a gentleman and always exceedingly polite, especially with children. He looked at the woman and then back at the little boy.

"Johnny Grassmeyer, you are a natural salesman, dear boy. I imagine you are one of the top selling Scouts in the area."

"Yes, Sir, I am. But that's only because our products are such high quality. They sell themselves."

"I imagine you are planning a career in marketing or sales when you grow up, Johnny?" asked Thomas, while smiling at the little boy's mother.

"Oh no, Sir. I plan on becoming a veterinarian."

Just then Peaches appeared between Thomas's legs and meowed loudly.

"What a beautiful cat," exclaimed Mrs. Grassmeyer. Her son concurred.

William and Murphy were on an airplane heading west by dusk. As always there would be a rental car waiting for them at the airport.

When William walked off the plane and saw his father waiting for him at the gate, he knew the worst had happened.

The two men sat at the kitchen table drinking coffee and talking in between their tears.

"You know darn well that she's filling Millie in on everything that's been going on around here," said William.

"Oh, knowing Millie, she probably found a way to continuing getting the newspaper," smiled Thomas.

Peaches walked over to Murphy who was sleeping on the kitchen floor. It would have been typical for any cat to swat the dog on the nose as he walked by, and Peaches was certainly prone to mischief himself and made no secret of it. However, on this occasion, the cat simply sauntered over to Murphy and lay down next to him. Thomas was the one to notice it first. He gestured to William who turned around to see the two creatures curled up together into one huge ball.

"Peaches is going to miss her terribly," said Thomas.

Reaching his hand across the table in familiar fashion, William clasped his father's hand.

"He still has you, Dad."

"It won't be the same. Those two ... well, let's just say it was something special."

Thomas paused for a few moments, as if debating whether or not to say what he was thinking. "This may not come out the way I mean it," said Thomas, "but I am thankful that Peaches outlived your mother."

"I was thinking the exact same thing, Dad."

At his father's insistence, William and Murphy flew back home within a week. William had new machinery being delivered and he needed to be there to inspect it upon arrival. Friends and neighbors secretly promised William they would drop by every couple of days to look in on his father. William planned to visit again in a few weeks.

Initially, Thomas did not feel Katie's absence because he continued expecting to see her at every turn. When he came downstairs in the morning, he expected to see her in the kitchen. When it was time for lunch, he expected her to walk into the den and tell him that his meal was ready. When nighttime came, he walked into the kitchen repeatedly looking for her. When the phone rang, he thought he would hear her voice. Eventually, the denial was sadly replaced with reality and he struggled a great deal.

Having to do his own cooking and laundry was not difficult, but being alone proved to be the most difficult thing he ever had to face.

He always enjoyed the quiet house when Katie and Millie were out gallivanting, but part of that appeal was the assurance that after a few hours the house would be filled once again with buoyant chatter and laughter. Now the quiet was never ending.

When Millie passed, Katie and Thomas noticed the drastic noise difference in the house. To compensate, Thomas began spending more time in the kitchen with his wife, where the two women had spent so much of their time together. He started reading the paper at the kitchen table and bought a small television for the kitchen counter so he could watch his shows there in the evenings while Katie washed the dinner dishes. Now Katie was gone and even the television set was unable to dispel the silence.

Peaches noticed Katie's absence as much as Thomas did. The cat sat at the refrigerator door and hollered endlessly. He was not hungry, he was just accustomed to his daily ritual of sticking his head in there when Katie opened it a dozen or more times a day.

He sat on the red vinyl step stool and hollered. He sat by the front window and hollered, always looking outside for Katie to come home. His morning routine of taking down the kitchen curtains persisted, even though it no longer brought a smile to Thomas's face.

When the telephone rang these days, it would most likely be William. Today was no exception.

"Hi Dad, how are you?"

"I'm making the best of it, Will. How are you and my Grandson?"

"We're thinking of coming out this weekend if that's OK with you and Peaches."

"Are you sure you're able to get away from the factory?"

"Absolutely. I was thinking of taking the late flight out on Friday after work. Then, we'll have the whole weekend together. What do you think?"

"I think it sounds swell, Will. I'll wait up for you and maybe even try my hand at baking a pie for you."

"Oh, Dad. Please don't do that. I don't want to see the house up in flames when I pull in the driveway. Just pick one up at the store, OK?"

"You doubt my baking abilities?" asked Thomas.

"I trust your purchasing abilities much more, Dad," chuckled William.

"I'll take a peak in the deep freeze and see if I can find one of Mom's pies in there."

"That sounds perfect. See you in a few days. Call me if you need anything."

"Will do. I'll wait up for you. I love you, Son."

"Love you too, Dad."

When William's rental car pulled into the driveway, the farmhouse was dark. Granted it was after eleven o'clock, but his father said he would be waiting up for him. Needless to say, William's mind weighed heavily with concern. Even Murphy seemed apprehensive when he stepped out of the car.

They walked up the porch stairs and pulled open the screen door. William turned the doorknob and found it unlocked, which in itself was quite typical and was nothing out of the ordinary out here in the country.

He walked in hesitantly and flipped on the hall light switch, refraining from calling for his Dad in case he had fallen asleep in the recliner, which he did frequently these days.

When Peaches ran to the foyer hollering, William's stomach sank and he started hollering too.

"Dad! Dad!"

William checked the recliner in the den and found it empty.
"Dad! Dad!"

William flipped another light switch and ran up the stairs to check the bedroom, and found it empty.

Peaches continued to holler from the hall and William followed him into the kitchen. Another light switch came on; no one was there.

Peaches jumped onto the counter and placed his pink padded hands on the window and hollered, scratching the pane fervently.

William pulled the back door open, flipping the switch for the outside spotlights as he ran outside.

"Dad! Dad!"

William ran to the barn calling for his father. A raccoon scampered through the tall grass, his black mask ensuring his anonymity.

Walking into the hen house and reaching his hand inside to feel for yet another light switch, William began to lose all remaining hope.

The lights flickered on and tiers of chickens began clucking softly on their perches, wondering why their rest had been disturbed. There he saw his father leaning against a few sacks of toppled feed, which were once neatly stacked. Even though his back was facing the barn door, William could tell by the unnatural slump that his beloved father was gone.

William made breakfast for Murphy and Peaches before placing the ground coffee and filtered water into the coffee machine. Neither of the animals ate with their usual fervor this morning.

A large mug of coffee was carried to the kitchen table. Peaches did not even push the curtains down this morning. William looked at Murphy, who was staring at him from a few feet away. Peaches was laying on the table, inches from the coffee cup.

"You two are all I have left of my family."

Murphy tilted his head. Peaches meowed and reached a furry hand forward to touch William's arm. William stared out the window.

There were very few loose ends to tie up concerning his parents' estate. William was informed that his parents had made two slight modifications to their original will of fifteen years ago. The first alteration was that Peaches was to spend the rest of his life with William and Murphy. The second revision was that if either animal outlived William, the estate would pay for their upkeep for the rest of their natural lives. William smiled when the changes were read to him.

He found homes for all the chickens and although he doubted the need, he had deadbolts installed on the doors. He returned back home to Ohio the following Friday with Peaches in tow. The cat would have the weekend to adapt to his new home, and William planned to stay home with him until Monday morning when he and Murphy would leave for the office.

His first day back at work was hectic and he was totally ineffective. He was too distracted to concentrate and too preoccupied to care. He had Liz reschedule all his upcoming appointments and meetings, and by eleven o'clock he and Murphy left the office and were on their way home.

When they pulled into the driveway, Peaches was at the front window. Even through the glare of the glass, William could see the cat's tiny mouth open and could lip-read his "meow." Peaches had adjusted beautifully to his new surroundings, especially considering he had been in William's house only once previously. And just like in the farmhouse, he sat on the bench by the window when he was left home.

The front door opened and he ran to greet William, who bent down to lift the large fluffy cat to his shoulders. Murphy followed them into the kitchen and was let out the back door. Peaches purred heavily and rubbed William's neck; William had never owned a cat and was already beginning to understand why so many others did.

"Peaches, what would you say to going camping with Murphy and me?"

A loud "meow" in William's ear was interpreted as an "I'd love to. Let's go."

William had taken Murphy camping several times over the past two years but had obviously never taken Peaches. He had no idea what to pack for an outing with a feline but assumed that anything in addition to a litter box and food would be strictly optional. The campground was a forty-five minute drive, and even if it took an hour to load the truck and stop at the store on their way out of town, they would still get there long before dusk and would have plenty of time to set up camp. The forecast called for possible showers, but if the weather proved accommodating, he and Murphy would even get a swim in before supper.

Murphy was accustomed to traveling by car or truck; in fact it had become second nature to him. Peaches, on the other hand, had ridden only minimally by car. William carried him in the travel kennel from the house to the truck and would keep him in the kennel until the tent was completely assembled at the campsite. When they stopped at the grocery store, Murphy was placed on guard duty. William returned to the truck with two sacks of food and thanked the dog for watching over his little brother, rewarding him with a peanut butter flavored dog treat from the bag.

They then headed out of town, away from the phone, away from the television, and toward a place in the woods where William hoped he would begin to find his center again. Murphy curled up on the back seat next to the small kennel and Peaches eventually quieted down. When they turned into the entrance of the Park, William knew he had chosen well by getting away for a day or two.

He parked the truck near a large group of pine trees and looked over toward the lake. To his delight, he saw only one small boat out on the water, quite a distance from shore. There were no other campers in this area of the Park, which pleased him even more.

Murphy jumped off the back seat and looked around. Lifting his nose into the air, he inhaled deeply and looked at William, wagging his tail. He definitely recognized this place.

William set the kennel on the ground and his first order of business would be to set up the tent. Murphy walked around the campsite, sniffing every pebble and every rock thoroughly. Apparently each stone had a story to tell.

The sky remained clear and the rains did not come. The two-room tent was erected and the rain flap was fastened to the screened peak, just in case. William set the cat carrier down inside the tent and opened the door. Peaches walked out nonchalantly, as if he had walked out into the tent a dozen times previously. His tail lifted gracefully upward and he walked in and out of Murphy's legs, rubbing against the soft white fur and meowing.

"Unbelievable," said William.

He looked at the cat and recalled how tiny and weak Peaches had been when they first saw him. There was no way anyone would recognize the cat if they saw him now. His fur was long and silky and he was huge, even for a male. His arms and legs were long, so he stood very tall too. The orange stripes around his legs were still dark and symmetrical. When he sat up straight, the orange rings around his right arm matched perfectly with those of his left. His white bib and the other white areas on his stomach and legs were a beautiful contrast to his orange fur. His eyes were light green and when he looked at you, you were certain he was deeply thinking. Of what, even Katie had never known. Tipping the scales at sixteen pounds and with his soft beautiful fur, Peaches was most certainly a very attractive cat.

William always felt that Peaches conceded his good looks, as did Murphy. Both animals seemed to walk with a strut that said, "Hey, look at me. Aren't I good looking?"

William smiled as he set the litter box and small bowl of water in the corner and changed into his swimming trunks. He had every confidence that Peaches would be fine while he and Murphy went for a dip in the lake. The dog preferred the snow but also enjoyed cool water. Since his coat was bi-layered, he never really got wet all the way down to his skin.

William swam ardently, his body attempting to release his penned up pain and emotion. With the water splashing on his face and dripping from his hair, he was unable to feel the hot tears pouring from his eyes. Murphy sensed the man's need for solitude and privacy and after only a brief swim, Murphy went back to shore and patiently sat. William emerged from the lake feeling emotionally and physically exhausted. Murphy met him at the water's edge and together they walked back to the campsite.

Peaches was calmly sitting in the tent behind the zippered screen door and meowed loudly to welcome his family back.

William told him to be patient and that they would all eat supper in a little while.

The iron fire pit was soon filled with charcoal and sprinkled with lighter fluid. When the match was dropped and the huge fire erupted, both Murphy and Peaches stepped back several paces and watched with extreme trepidation. When the flames abated, the animals calmed once again and laid down waiting for supper.

William took two large coolers from the bed of the truck and spread a checkered vinyl tablecloth over the nearby picnic table. Opening the first cooler, he removed the plastic bowls filled with the animals' food. He placed Murphy's food on the ground and then unzipped the screen door to feed Peaches. He then sat on the bench and waited for the coals to glow.

Staring into the fire was bittersweet. William recalled the times spent sitting around the wood stove growing up, as well as the last Christmas he spent with his parents. Just as the flames spread upwards from their Earthen bed of the camp fire, reaching higher and eventually disappearing into the air, William's thoughts and memories replayed over and over in the flicker of the fire, only to ultimately fly away leaving nothing but lonely reminiscence.

The coals grew deep orange and red in their luster. William opened the second cooler and removed containers of potato salad, coleslaw, and hot dogs. As he emptied the clear plastic package and stacked the frankfurters on a plate, he smiled as he recalled the similar items he saw in a certain gas station shortly before his life changed by meeting Murphy. How ironic that a common item like a hot dog could trigger such a vivid memory. Regardless, it did.

He opened the lid of the potato salad and nibbled with a plastic fork, still looking deeply into the flames. He would put the hot dogs on the grill in just a few more minutes.

A gentle breeze wafted the savory smell from the picnic table over to Murphy, who lifted his nose to investigate further. Oh yes, definitely people food.

William's back was to the table and to the dog. Murphy had already eaten his food and although he normally was well mannered and virtuous, the aroma from that plate of hot dogs proved to be irrepressible. Ever so slowly he crept up the wooden bench and leaned forward toward the plate. With one eye on William's back and one eye on the hot dogs, he opened his mouth in a gentle rift and took his prize.

Summer surrendered her heat and lush greenery to autumn, who painted his canvas with hues of gold and red. As the leaves dropped from their former moorings of security, the skies began to blow with the foreboding of another nasty winter.

William discovered just how deeply he missed his parents. He spent Thanksgiving quietly with no turkey, no dressing, and no pumpkin pie. He resolved that he would not allow Christmas to pass with the same melancholy. It took a great deal of emotional effort but he decorated for Christmas and even put up another real tree. He wished he could step back in time, just a year, and spend one more holiday with them. If that were possible, he would savor their time together and pay very close attention to the details he took for granted for so many years. He would breathe in deeply the aromas of the Thanksgiving meal and the cinnamon scented pinecones his Mother bought for Christmas every year. He would watch the steam rise from the gravy as he ladled it onto his plate. He would purposely study with detail his Mother's face and pay close attention to his Father's tender words and kind gestures. Just once more William wanted to sit by the fire, sipping hot coffee with his parents, reminiscing about earlier times. Just once more William wanted to answer the phone and hear his Mother's voice wishing him a Happy Birthday. But even dreamers eventually realize that wishes are melting snowflakes, resting on your hands for only a moment, ultimately slipping through your fingers.

No one called on William's 51st Birthday that summer, or for the next four years. His employees bought him gifts and nice cakes, but his smiles were shallow and fabricated, manufactured merely for the moment.

CHAPTER TWENTY-ONE

The alarm went off as it had so many mornings for so many years. William was beginning to understand the sentiments other people had expressed when they reached their mid fifties or sixties—sentiments that surfaced in the early morning just before dawn. The alarm clock would sound and the desire for continued sleep would be overruled by obligations to get up and go to work. As a younger man, William never understood those feelings; now at fifty-five, they seemed to be strengthening with every passing morning. Murphy seemed to empathize and share the sentiment. For the past few days, he too was slow to crawl out of bed.

He reluctantly followed William downstairs. This winter had been dry and relatively mild, which was a welcomed change from the past three winters. However, last night's storm from the west deposited fourteen inches of powdery snow and William knew Murphy would be thrilled. As the back door opened, a gush of cold air blew into the kitchen uninvited. William pulled the lapels of his fleece robe together over his chest and tightened the belt around his waist. Murphy hesitated before stepping over the threshold, turning his face upward to look at William before walking outside into the foot of new snow.

The door closed behind him and William headed toward the counter to make a much-needed pot of coffee. Once the gurgling sounds began, he headed back up the stairs to shower.

The hot water should have helped to wake him and prepare him for the day ahead, but instead, the warmth made him sleepier. When the showering was completed, the thought of slipping back into his flannel pajamas was more appealing than he could imagine.

With a towel around his waist and his bathrobe back on, he slid his damp feet into slippers and went back downstairs to let Murphy inside.

The aroma of the coffee opened his sinuses and cleared his mind. The thought of staying home was not as strong as it had been ten minutes ago, William would wait twelve hours before flannel once again warmed him.

He cracked open the back door to see if Murphy was waiting on the stoop; he was not. William then opened the door a little wider and gave a quick whistle. Still no response. Once again pulling his robe closed across his chest, he opened the door halfway and looked outside. Murphy was not there.

He flung the door open and stepped outside.

"Murphy?" he called, somewhat hesitantly.

The snow was still falling and it was so desperately cold.

"Murphy!" he called again, this time much louder.

There in the yard to the right, barely visible, Murphy lifted his head and William saw his dark brown eyes against the white background.

"Come on, Boy. It's cold."

The dog's head fell back into the snow.

"Murphy?" William said softly.

He released the hand holding his robe and ran into the yard, sliding and losing one slipper, then abandoning the other before reaching the dog. He dropped to his knees and bent over his companion, stroking his head and encouraging him to stand. Murphy looked at him but made no effort to move.

"No, Murphy, no," William pleaded.

He tried to lift the dog but Murphy groaned. He tried once more but the dog resisted. Murphy lifted his head and looked at his friend. William leaned forward to kiss his face and rub his ears. Murphy raised a paw and rested it on William's arm.

They looked at each other, both silently wishing they could express the love and fear they each felt. Murphy lifted his paw higher and touched William's cheek, seemingly to wipe away the tears. As his paw fell back towards the ground, Murphy closed his eyes and lowered his head into the cold snow.

CHAPTER TEWENTY-TWO

Flanders had been sitting at Passage Wall with the impatience of a pup waiting for a new toy. At any moment his best friend Lanagan would be returning to Everlife. Flanders could not recall the last time he was this excited. Even though Everlife was full of joy and there was never any pain here, there were still days that even surpassed the normal bliss of Everlife. Today was one of those days for Flanders.

Waiting seemed to take an eternity, which ironically was something with which Flanders was quite familiar. When the moment finally arrived, he had to restrain himself from not lunging forward and grabbing hold of Lanagan's neck and pulling him hastily through the wall.

A shiny black nose poked through the liquid metallic portal, followed by a brilliant white snout and face. Closed eyes and upright ears came next, followed by a thick silky mane. Broad shoulders and the front limbs appeared simultaneously, then came the torso and hindquarters. As the fluffy tail exited the wall, the large white dog opened his eyes and looked at Flanders and smiled. The enormous black dog nuzzled his friend with such force that he almost knocked him over. White fur mingled with black fur and Lanagan's head brushed under Flanders' neck, like two horses playing on a cool fall morning. When the greeting was done, they walked together and Flanders asked the question they had been wondering about for years.

"How was the Level VII assignment?"

"Oh, Flanders. I can't begin to tell you about it. The thing that worries me is that I'll forget all about it; you know how that goes? We come back and before we know it, the memory fades and all the feelings go away. Right now, I feel like I could talk to you for hours about William and my assignment. And I still have all the emotions too; I wonder when they'll start leaving me."

"Remember my Level VI assignment?" asked Flanders. "You left shortly after I returned from that one. Well, I never lost the memories *or* the feelings."

Stopping in his tracks, Lanagan looked at his friend with a puzzled expression.

"You still have the feelings?" asked Lanagan.

"Yeah, I do."

"Have you talked to Cambium about it?"

"No, but I talked to Calais and Mendon about it. They said the only time you remember the emotions is when you complete a Level VI or Level VII assignment. Of course neither of them has ever gone past Level V, but that's what they've heard."

"Do you know anyone who's completed a Level VII assignment?" asked Lanagan.

"I've heard about them, but you're the only one I know personally who finished one."

"I need to go see Cambium to check in. I don't think I'll mention anything about the memories just yet. I'll wait a while and see what happens with them."

Peaches walked around the house hollering for almost a month. He followed William everywhere and actually began sleeping with him during the night. In the evening when William watched television or read in his recliner, Peaches curled up in his lap. There were times the cat seemed to look right through William's eyes and into his pain—and his soul.

At the office, William spent a great deal of time staring out the window. He wished he had someone to talk to, someone who would understand.

A thought occurred to him and he pulled a file from his desk drawer and flipped through several pages before finding the one he wanted. With a finger marking one particular line on the page, he picked up the telephone and dialed.

"Hello?" said the voice on the other end.

"Rusty. It's William. William Colbert."

There was a lengthy pause before Rusty responded.

"William. What a surprise. You don't sound so good. Is everything OK?"

Leaning his head forward to fall into his hand, William could not find any words.

"William? What's wrong? Is it Murphy?"

"He's gone, Rusty. He's been gone for over a month. I thought I'd be over it by now. I don't know anyone else who would remotely understand."

"I do understand, William," and he paused before continuing. "Would you like some company for a few days?"

"I wouldn't be a very good host."

"I understand, believe me I've been there. Are you still living in the same place?"

"Yes, for now."

"Are you planning a move, William?"

"I might be, but I'm here for now."

"When would be a good time for me to fly out?"

"No time is better than any other, Rusty."

"You hang in there, Buddy. I'll give you a call after I book a flight, OK?"

William hung up the phone, dropping his head to his desk.

It had been three years since Rusty had interrupted William's Chinese dinner and surprised him with a knock at the front door. How ironic that the man William wanted to deceive and ruin five years ago was the same man he turned to during his time of grief. And how unbelievable that Rusty would drop everything and come to the aid of a virtual stranger. The two men shared a common bond somehow and although both had met many other people during their lives with whom they shared numerous interests, Rusty and William recognized their unique connection.

William was relieved when Rusty arrived empty-handed, sans a puppy. Rusty did, however, bring photos; not surveillance shots of William, but hundreds of photographs of his dogs, past and present. Interspersed was an occasional photo of a human, a few of his late wife, and the rest were of his children.

His son Paul was regional manager of a national grocery store chain and lived in Omaha with his wife and three kids. Suzy, his older daughter, quit her job after her first child was born and never rejoined the work force. Her husband was a salesman for a laundry soap company and they lived very comfortably on one income. Donna, his youngest child, was quite the entrepreneur and owned several apartment complexes in three states, as well as her own line of women's athletic apparel. She and her husband had no children but had two golden retrievers.

Rusty did his best to keep the conversation going. His distraction techniques, however well intentioned, were not very successful.

"My heart is broken, Rusty." I never had a wife or children like you, and I don't grieve for what I never had. My life has been full and I never longed for a family the way some people do. I was quite content living alone before I got Murphy, and after he showed up I never considered myself as someone who lived alone anymore. He was more than a companion; he was almost like the brother I never had."

"What are your plans now, William? I know it will be a while before you even consider getting another dog, I'm not talking about that. You mentioned on the phone that you were contemplating a move. Where are you planning on going?"

"I'm seriously considering moving back to my family's farm house. I also own another piece of property out there too and I need to decide what I'm going to do with it. If I had someone I trusted to take over the company, I'd leave tomorrow. You know how it is though; no one cares about the family business like family does, and although I have some awesome people working for me, I never found anyone I wanted to leave in charge of my Dad's company."

"You'll find the right person, William, I know you will. Just be patient. In the meantime, I was wondering if you wanted to discuss a little business venture. Involving that patent."

CHAPTER TWENTY-THREE

Lanagan and Flanders laid on a large rock near the western border of WinterQuad. The snow was falling lightly and the sky was overcast and dreary. The scene suited Lanagan perfectly.

"Are you going to talk to Cambium today?" inquired Flanders.

"I'm thinking about it. What do you think I should do?"

"Well, I don't see any other option. You've been back for a year and you've retained your memories *and* your emotions. You still want to go back to William, don't you?"

"Yes, more than anything."

"I've been asking around and no one has ever heard of Cambium ever allowing a repeat assignment to the same human."

"There *has* to be a way, Flanders. There has to be a way for me to see William again."

"I think you should go talk to Cambium. If there's a loop hole he's the only one who'll know about it."

Lanagan had pondered the situation daily for the past year. He was preoccupied with the idea and although his friend had never expressed it, Flanders was beginning to worry about him.

The day that Lanagan finally decided to talk to Cambium, he felt as much trepidation as he did resolve. Walking toward the Tree, he whispered quietly the words he had rehearsed over and over for months. Finally, the time had come and he would speak those same words to Cambium.

Lanagan stood twenty feet in front of the Tree's massive trunk and awakened him.

"Cambium ... I need to talk to you."

Immediately, the creaking and splitting began and the large eyes appeared, followed by the nose and mouth. If the face ever revealed itself in another fashion, no one had ever seen it do so.

The white dog sat down and waited for the Tree to speak.

"Lanagan, what a pleasant surprise. I do not suspect, however, that this is a social visit?"

The dog's heart pounded as vigorously as his thoughts raced. All his planning and all his rehearsing was thrown by the infamous wayside and he blurted out his words, leaving his practiced speech and all his diplomacy behind.

"Cambium, I want to go back."

"Go back where?"

"I want to see William again."

"Ah, yes. The William Colbert assignment. Level VII. You performed well, Lanagan."

"I wouldn't call it performing. I'd call it learning to trust and learning acceptance and learning to love."

"I would call it all those too, but I assume the purpose of your visit today does not involve semantics."

"I want to go back."

"You cannot."

"Cambium, I know the rules and I know they exist for a reason. But, I also know that everything changed for me after I returned from my last assignment."

"You cannot go back."

"But why?"

"I think you know why."

"My … my heart is broken, Cambium. I miss William more than I've ever missed anyone. Why can't I go back?"

"You told me you knew the rules and you told me you realize they exist for a reason. Correct?"

Lanagan shook his head in agreement.

Cambium continued. "There are no exceptions, Lanagan."

"There *has* to be a way. There *must* be a way."

The Tree closed his heavy barked eyelids and pursed his lips. His trunk seemed to swell and then ebb as if in exhalation. When the lids opened again, Lanagan was still sitting defiantly at his roots.

Bending forward and lifting a branched hand to his mouth, the Tree whispered to the dog.

"Long ago, there *was* a way to go back. A way did exist to return to the other world."

Lanagan jumped with joy.

"I KNEW IT! I just knew there had to be a way!" he exclaimed.

"Now, now, dear Lanagan. Your rejoicing is premature. I said there *once* was a way to go back. The way has long been adjourned."

"But Cambium. Why can't you just initiate the old way once again?"

"I wish it was that simple."

"But, it *is* possible?"

"Perhaps."

Looking hopeful and reservedly excited, Lanagan took a step closer to the Tree.

"What was the old way?"

"The OFAD."

"The what?"

"The OFAD, Lanagan, the OFAD ... to Observe From A Distance ... the ancient art of seeing through the eyes of another. Long ago, there was an ... arrangement of sorts. Do you remember when I allowed for the shifting of species from dog to cat and cat to dog?"

Lanagan shook his head.

"A very long time ago, there was another permissible species shift, this one involving crows."

"Crows? You let dogs take assignments as crows?"

"No, not assignments, but OFAD voyages. Eons ago, animals who completed Level VII assignments had the option of seeing their two-walker again ... but there were rigid restrictions and limitations involved."

"What kind of restrictions?"

"The OFAD could only take place after the four-walker had been back in Everlife for at least six months, and as I indicated, the only animals permitted to go were those who had completed a Level VII assignment. The decision to participate in an OFAD took a considerable amount of contemplation because of the risks."

"What kind of risks?"

"Quite often, a bereaved human acquires another pet after their other has passed through. This was why OFADs were discontinued thousands of years ago; the returning four-walker most often deeply regretted going back."

Lanagan swallowed hard.

"I resorted to erasing the memories of all the animals who had ever taken an OFAD voyage and discontinued future OFADs indefinitely. However, under the right circumstance Lanagan, I would consider the option again."

The dog pleaded, "If I promise to not tell a soul and if I promise to never mention any remorse about my going, would you let me do it, Cambium? Please?"

The Tree reached out his long arm toward the neck of the beautiful white dog. As the wooden fingers touched the neck, the invisible collar changed to a golden translucency and Lanagan's ID tag appeared.

"This is very curious," said Cambium. "Are you aware that your ID tag has changed color?"

The wooden hand lifted the collar from the dog's neck and held it so he could see.

"I thought Level VII was royal blue," said Lanagan.

"Level VII *is* royal blue. Your tag is now purple."

The collar was returned to the dog's neck where it once again disappeared.

"Why did it turn purple?" asked the dog.

"I don't know. I'm sure the deeds of your last assignment are still effecting the lives of the people who knew you dear Lanagan, but why it turned purple, I cannot say."

Whispering, the dog asked, "What about the uh … you know … the voyage?"

Answering with another whisper, Cambium replied, "There is only one way to reinitiate the OFAD. I must consult with a certain crow. I will have your answer tomorrow."

The green eyes once again hid themselves under the rough ridges of bark and the face in the tree disappeared.

CHAPTER TWENTY-FOUR

Back when OFADs were commonplace, there was one crow in charge of all the comings and goings, in charge of handling all the reports, and in charge of providing updates to Cambium on all crow activity. The crow was an ancient bird, only a day or two younger than Cambium, whose origins laid most certainly on the far left of the time line, by anyone's standards.

His name was Olde Crow, and although his name was neither particularly profound nor extraordinary, Olde Crow's reputation and accomplishments were.

Everyone knew the story well and they had all sat under the tutelage of Olde Crow for centuries. But time and distance often have a way of replacing truth and wisdom with indifference and folly. Very few inhabitants of Everlife now mentioned the famed bird, but soon they all would recall the amazing story.

It was difficult for them to imagine a time before days and even harder to imagine that first moment. No one other than Olde Crow was capable of retelling the story in detail, because he himself had been there.

It was midnight on the fourth day of creation. The first stars twinkled from the distant skies and the new moon reached its unseen hands to the Earth, pulling the waters to make them move. Rivers began to flow and the sea swelled for the very first time. Waves suddenly rushed to the shore, crashing on rocky coasts and skimming over the soft, newly formed sand.

The Creator stood along the bank of a broad river, watching the cold, raging water. A hand stretched out toward the dark current and called forth a creature with a thought. The roaring river instantly calmed and a drizzle of sparkling dew and light rose from the still water. From the midst of this array arose a shiny glow of black light. The Creator released another thought, and wings shot out from the sides of the oval black light.

The form, still incomplete and lifeless, floated across the vast river toward the bank. Slowly it moved closer to the Creator, ever developing and changing. The body became contoured and took shape; a head and face emerged. Twig-like legs sprouted from the lower portion of the body and short talons appeared at their distal ends. Wings pushed through the dark skin and stretched outward, followed by feathers which burgeoned and lengthened, each becoming long and flat. Smaller feathers pushed through and covered the creature in short, stout down. The feet hung inertly and the two expressionless dull eyes stared blindly into the night sky.

From the riverbank, the breath of life was blown toward the creature. The beak opened and the life force entered the bird. His chest expanded mightily and his small black eyes became bright and shiny.

The glow surrounding the bird evaporated into the darkness and the newly formed creature stretched his wings and flew the rest of the way to the riverbank.

The Creator smiled and said to the bird, "You have been called forth from the calm river of water, so you shall be called 'crow.'"

Midnight gave way to dawn and the sunrise lifted itself into the sky bringing deep reds and orange to the landscape. The creature stared in amazement and awe. Soon other crows were brought forth from the calm river. After all the crows that were destined to be created that day had emerged from the peaceful river, the water suddenly raged once again and splashed against the rocks along the bank.

Other species of ornithalia were created later on that fifth day. First Crow played an important role in sending off each species of bird to the exact place on the globe where they would inhabit. Each of the different species had been given certain intrinsic abilities and instincts unique to their environment and survival needs. First Crow made sure they all understood migration and weather patterns and then sent them on their way. (He was not sure how he had come to know the information he was sharing, but he never considered asking.)

First Crow continued providing instruction to the new birds for the next two days. When all of them had flown off to their new homes, First Crow said good-bye to the Creator and began flying away too. His flight was abruptly halted and he turned to look behind him. The Creator smiled and said "no." First Crow would most definitely be taking a journey but it would not be where the other crows had gone. Crow opened his beak to speak but the words never left his mouth. He blinked his eyes and the next moment he was floating effortlessly through Passage Wall.

Emerging on the other side, he gently wafted to the ground and stood there looking around this huge expanse. In the far, far distance stood an enormous Tree.

Crow pushed off with his feet, flapped his wings, and took to the air once again. He flew over to the wooden monstrosity and landed on one of the lower branches. Startled from sleep, Cambium awoke.

The bird looked all around, trying to determine the source of the loud, cracking noises.

"Ahhh, hello. You must be Olde Crow," came a bellow from within the Tree.

The bird lost his footing and fell thirty feet down to the ground.

"Who said that?" asked the bird, looking around.

"It was I, Olde Crow."

The bird stood on the soft green grass several yards in front of Cambium, looked up and saw the face in the Tree.

"Who are you?"

"I am Cambium."

"Why did you call me 'Olde Crow'?"

"Are you not the oldest of all creatures?"

"I suppose so."

"And are you not a crow?"

"Well, yes."

"So then, you are Olde Crow."

"Very well. And what is this place?"

"This is Everlife," answered Cambium. Then, after pausing for a moment or two, he continued. "There have been many firsts this week and surely your arrival here today is one of them. You are the first creature to have entered this place through Passage Wall without having completed a life on Earth. Do you understand what I am saying?"

"I'm beginning to," answered Olde Crow.

"Do you know why you are here?"

"That, I do not."

"Oh," said Cambium, rather surprised and obviously disappointed. "I was hoping you would."

With a look of condescending frustration the bird retorted, "You don't know why I'm here either?"

"Unfortunately, I do not. I was simply told to be expecting you."

"Well, here I am."

"Apparently so."

"What am I to do now? Where am I to go?"

"That, I do know. You are to report to the area called Black River. It is several days journey from here."

"Black River?"

"Yes," smiled Cambium. "I was told that place is … for the birds."

"How do I get there from here?"

"I was told that once you reach an elevation far above my branches, the path will be revealed to you. Fly well, Olde Crow. Go in peace. We will meet again."

The bird flexed his legs once more and pushed off from the ground, extending his dull black wings. He flapped them just one time and was airborne. Higher and higher he climbed. He looked around and around, surveying the seemingly endless lands that comprised Everlife. He looked one way and then another. As far as he could see there was land, land, and more land. Off in the distance to the west he saw what appeared to be a rose colored fog.

Olde Crow then noticed something he had hitherto overlooked. Floating high above him in all directions, were hundreds of thousands, perhaps millions, of gleaming translucent spheres of sparkling light. It was as if miniature stars had fallen from the heavens and were being held captive by sheer, pearl colored orbs.

Cambium was the solitary being in this portion of Everlife for quite some time. However, in other portions of Everlife, other creatures began appearing relatively quickly; enormous creatures at first and then smaller wild animals. Their lives on Earth had ended and they now found themselves in Everlife. It took many ages, but eventually dogs and cats started to appear in Cambium's section of Everlife. Assignments were distributed and continued for ages and ages. Inevitably, a dog approached Cambium after completing an assignment, with the desire to see her human again. As the centuries passed, more and more dogs and cats expressed a desire to return to Earth to see their two-walker.

One day Olde Crow was summoned by the Great Tree and presented with a proposition. Originally, crows were mild-mannered, timid creatures, always traveling alone during the darkest hours of the night. These birds were seldom seen and even less often heard, for their voices were low and meek. Cambium suggested that since the crow was such a secretive individual, that it would perform the perfect reconnaissance mission. The crow could silently observe from a distance and then return with a report of his findings.

Olde Crow selected a small group of crows for this trial arrangement, and Cambium began sending them on short-term OFAD missions with the selected animals. A crow would stand on top of the dog or cat and together they would walk through Passage Wall. On the other side of the portal, only the crow body would emerge. The dog or cat would see through the eyes of the crow and would be aware of and in partial control of their host body. But after several trial journeys, it was determined that most frequently there was very little observing done during the OFAD due to the limitations of darkness and the hiding tendency of the crows.

Olde Crow suggested a few modifications to the crows' habits and personality and asked for a volunteer to test the new characteristics. One crow stepped forward and received the modifications. An additional color was added to the black feathers: a layer of purple was placed over the pitch undercoat to represent the transition from darkness to daylight. Secondly, a new voice was given to the crow; a voice that called loudly to the people he was watching. No longer would the bird be silent and timid; this new voice would beckon and haunt, summon and taunt.

The result of the revisions exceeded all expectations. No longer did the crow return from an OFAD journey with an inadequate or incomplete sighting.

Before long, all the crows wanted the alterations. More and more OFAD missions took place. The birds were proud to "call and watch," or "caw" as it came to be known.

However, as the years passed and the number of OFADs increased, so did the incidences of regret and remorse felt by the animals after returning. They came back to Everlife disappointed and downhearted at what they saw or heard on their mission. Cambium and Olde Crow deliberated over the situation for weeks and ultimately decided to discontinue all future OFADs. All memory of the OFAD was erased from every dog and cat, and Cambium and Olde Crow did not discuss the matter even amongst themselves ever again.

Now, centuries later, the matter was to be revisited.

CHAPTER TWENTY-FIVE

Olde Crow received the message from Cambium and sent a reply back to the Great Tree. Olde Crow stated that he was willing to discuss the matter, but that there were conditions. Firstly, he demanded that Lanagan present his petition to him personally. The second condition was more complicated; Lanagan would have to travel to Black River to meet with the Crow.

Because of his special place in creation, Olde Crow was held in high esteem, and like Cambium, often mediated debates and was the one approached when questions or problems arose in the other regions of Everlife. The birds did not routinely receive assignments like some of the other animals, but they did enter and exit Everlife in the same manner. The crows currently had very little contact with the dog and cat population. Now, Lanagan learned that he would have to consult personally with Olde Crow if he had any hope of seeing William Colbert again. He would soon discover that the feat of traveling to that meeting place would be vastly more difficult than he had ever considered.

Olde Crow lived in the far reaches of Everlife, and although every animal had free reign of the expanse, it was virtually unheard of for a domestic four-walker to venture to the safari area or for a polar bear to venture to SummerQuad. Everyone had an area specifically designed to meet their individual species preferences and even more so, additional regions and recreations were available for different breeds.

Olde Crow lived in an area of Everlife where no canine or feline had ever traveled. Sure, they had all heard of Black River and of the black caves—as well as the violent weather changes—but if that was not deterrent enough, there were the stories of attacks.

Cambium was in charge of Lanagan's picturesque part of Everlife and everyone knew that the Tree ran a pretty tight ship, so to speak. When the playful games and antics of other species became intolerable, Cambium would post a time of LOSA. Such was not the case in Black River.

Lanagan wondered if the stories were true; he hoped they at least had been embellished. He assumed that all parts of Everlife were safe and secure, however, he also knew that some species liked to play a bit more roughly than others do, and such was the case in Black River.

Lanagan would have to cross hundreds of thousands of diverse acres including jungle, mountains, and perhaps the desert. No one was sure if the ocean area was on this side or the other side of Black River. He asked Cambium if it would be possible for him to transform into a bird for the journey but was not really surprised by the answer he received.

It would be Lanagan's decision when to embark on his quest to Black River. None of the other animals had any idea that there had once been such a thing as an OFAD, but they soon learned that Lanagan was planning a journey to Black River. They also discovered that the purpose of the journey was to meet with Olde Crow. Flanders knew that his best friend was keeping something from him but he knew better than to press the issue. Eventually everything would be out in the open for all to know and understand.

Cambium had been bombarded with inquires as to the nature of Lanagan's trip, but like the dog, he said only that he could not discuss the matter at this time. Even if Lanagan made it to Black River, and even if he met with Olde Crow, and even if he completed the return journey, Cambium could not be certain whether any arrangements would be made or if any agreements would be reached. Until Lanagan arrived safely back in Everlife and was able to talk to him, even Cambium would not know the outcome of the undertaking. Consequently, the Great Tree was feeling anxious about the entire situation and was silently hoping that all would go well for Lanagan and that he would return with good news from Olde Crow.

When the day finally arrived for Lanagan to begin his journey, he was as nervous as he was concerned. To say he was having second thoughts would be an understatement. Part of him wanted to leave well enough alone and forget about the possibility of seeing William Colbert again—to forget about OFAD missions and forget about the crows. But another part of him—a part nearer to his heart and further from his reasoning—wanted to set out as soon as possible and face whatever crossed his path and to deal with whatever he had to, to accomplish his objective, which was to see his friend William again.

As he walked from WinterQuad with Flanders, he asked his friend if he was doing the right thing.

"Do you think I'm crazy?" asked Lanagan.

"Of course you're crazy, Lanagan, but that's not a recent discovery," smirked Flanders.

"Do you think I'll make it back?"

"Yes, I believe you'll make it back. Oh, did you mean alive?"

"Very funny, Flanders, very funny. I'm about to step out of our area of safety and protection and cross into the unknown, and you're making jokes."

"Oh, come on, Buddy. You know I'm just trying to ease the tension a little. Of course you're going to make it back."

"Alive?" asked Lanagan.

"I don't think it'd be possible to get really hurt, do you? Those other parts of Everlife really can't be that different than how things are here. Can they?"

"That's just it, Flanders, no one really knows."

"Oh, Cambium knows, he just refuses to tell you."

"I agree."

"Do you think it would be possible to …? You know." Asked Flanders.

"That's what I'm wondering too. I asked Cambium about it and he refused to answer. He just said it was a risk I'd have to take."

The dogs walked and talked while making their way to the Meeting Place. When Lanagan grew silent, Flanders resisted the temptation to fill the silence with empty words, knowing his friend needed the quiet pauses perhaps more than he needed conversation.

Lanagan wondered how his life would change because of this journey. He wondered if his voyage would affect everyone else or ultimately only himself. He wondered what he would say when he finally saw Olde Crow. He wondered what the ancient bird would say to him.

He wondered what the animals would be like in the far regions of Everlife. He wondered if they could talk. He wondered if they were civilized. He wondered if they were allowed to bite or scratch visitors or to sting them or tear them apart. Was it possible to be injured in the other regions of Everlife? Was it possible to be killed there? Maybe that was the most important question of all.

Lanagan was so relieved that Flanders was here to see him off. He was glad that his friend had remained in Everlife during the weeks proceeding today too. Unbeknownst to either of them, Cambium was responsible for keeping Flanders at hand by not sending him off on another assignment.

When the two dogs emerged from the outlining area of saplings and tall grass and entered the huge clearing of the Meeting Place, they both froze in their tracks. Every other dog and cat in Everlife had turned out to bid him bon voyage. When a few of the animals stationed sentry at the outskirts of the expanse saw Lanagan, they cheered and applauded. Within a few moments, everyone realized he was there and they too began to celebrate.

A wide path opened amidst the multitude of animals, and Flanders and Lanagan humbly walked towards Cambium.

The Tree greeted Lanagan with a branch across his trunk and a bow of respect. Miss Mallory scurried to the back of the Tree and led a small contingent around to the front, which brought out a special sled-like contraption that Cambium had built especially for the dog. It included a beautiful purple harness to strap around his body for pulling, and it had four wheels for use over dry terrain and four metal runners that were attached to the hubs. When the sled approached snowy or icy conditions, the metal runners could be unlocked from their upward position and rotated downward and locked into place. In their locked and extended position, the flat runners would glide over the snow like a traditional dog sled.

Adario made canvas saddle bags for Lanagan to carry on his back. Other friends had filled the bags with food and notes of encouragement. The sled was laden mostly with food and water, as no one knew what Lanagan would face once their portion of Everlife had been traversed and he ventured into unknown territory. Also included in the saddlebags were a small tent and a pillow.

Lanagan sat in front of the Great Tree, looking at the sled and supplies and looking around in amazement at all the animals who came to see him off. He was so overwhelmed and humbled that he could not speak.

Cambium lifted an arm to quiet the crowd.

"Everyone—dogs, cats ... and any other creature who may be present—today truly is a momentous day. Today, one of your beloved friends will begin a journey into the unknown. Although he will be carrying your gifts and good wishes, he is venturing out alone and no one, including myself, knows what he will find on the other side of the foggy divide. May his bravery and determination, along with your prayers, bring him safely home to us. Lanagan, go in peace. We hope to see you again when your journey is completed."

The crowd erupted in applause and cheers. Lanagan smiled hesitantly at Cambium and thanked everyone for their gifts. Two canine bystanders lifted the harness and secured it around the white dog. He slowly walked away from the Tree, pulling the contraption behind him in the direction of the foggy barrier.

He walked past the outskirts of the Meeting Place with a crowd behind him. Flanders walked alongside him silently. After a few miles they noticed the dense fog in the distance. Everyone knew its significance: the boundary of their area of Everlife was approaching.

A few animals had wandered in this direction before but none had ever been this close to the murky divider. After all, there was absolutely no reason for them to ever consider leaving this perfect place.

Lanagan turned towards Flanders, who had stopped a pace or two behind him.

"Well, Buddy, I guess this is good-bye," said Lanagan.

"No, this is bon voyage. I'll see you in a couple of weeks, right?"

Trying to sound optimistic despite his extreme trepidation, Lanagan forced a smile.

"Sure. See you in a couple of weeks."

He looked behind him and saw the thousands of other four-walkers who were standing a safe distance away, perhaps thinking that the fog might suddenly shift position and swallow them.

The silence was eerie and Lanagan hoped it was not foreboding. He turned to face forward again and stared into the fog. Then, stealing one more brief glance back at Flanders, he lifted his right paw and stepped forward.

The silence continued as each step took him farther from safety and deeper into uncertainty. Soon his face breathed the coolness of the murky fog and he disappeared into the barrier. This time he walked alone.

CHAPTER TWENTY-SIX

When Lanagan emerged on the other side, he was relieved not to have been torn to pieces immediately. He opened his eyes and slowly stepped forward. He noticed several contrasts right away, the most obvious being the darkness. This section of Everlife was so different; he could not see the sky and it was so dark. Not like nighttime, but like the darkness caused by being in a building with few windows. Trees grew so closely to one another that it was difficult to see where one stopped and another began. Leaves and vines were everywhere; in all directions there was greenery so extensive that it blanketed the entire landscape. He was sure it was daytime here; he was just underneath so much vegetation that there was very little light.

Another unexpected difference was the noise level; it was strikingly loud here. The most abundant sound seemed to be avian; birds of all sizes and colors were tweeting and singing like he had never previously heard. They swooped down at him and flew around him, as if they were a scouting party investigating rumors of infiltration.

The air was very dense too. It was not simply a matter of humidity; the air felt heavy and visibility was exceedingly limited.

Large boulders were scattered throughout the grounds, and they were surprisingly free of moss and the clinging undergrowth. Lanagan backed out of his harness and left the wheeled sled where he stood. He walked to a large boulder and climbed to the top, where he took a few minutes to survey this strange place.

Without the perspective of having the barrier behind him, all sense of direction was lost. The view in front of him looked exactly like the view to either side or behind him. If he were not careful, he would climb off the rock and walk back in the direction from where he came. For a split second, before stepping from the rock and moving forward, he strongly considered that option.

His paw stepped onto the ground and a branch snapped in two, freezing his breathing and stopping his forward motion. After a few moments' hesitation and a few additional moments of reconsideration, he took another step forward into the dense foliage.

There was no possible way to navigate through the jungle towing the sled, so he left it behind and tried to find a distinguishing landmark nearby so he could find it again on his return trip. Ah, his return trip. The possibility of even completing half of his journey seemed very unlikely to him at the moment.

He did keep his saddlebags on his back.

Birds continued to fly low and dart across his path as the hours passed. In between ducking under low limbs and pushing his way through the tangles of vines, he repeatedly crouched to avoid the annoying low flying birds. His forward progress was slow and tiresome. How many miles had he walked so far? Three? Four? A dozen? He had no idea. As soon as he came to a clearing, he would open the backpack, have a snack, and rest his sore paws.

Another hour of this grueling excursion passed and he came upon a group of rubbery plants with thick shiny leaves. As he pressed past them, he found himself at the edge of what appeared to be an ancient ruin, maybe a temple. The remaining walls were made of stone, each section carefully carved with word pictures that relayed stories of earlier times.

Lanagan walked towards the ruin, stepping through a shallow stream that passed through the temple relics. The cool water was soothing to his sore feet, and after each step, small trickles of blood were left behind with his footprints.

The largest section of upright wall stood to his left, and although it was the tallest remnant standing, it was the least decorated. Toward the top of the wall, near where perhaps the ceiling had rested, was a border of leaves and what looked like weapons of some sort, perhaps spears. Beneath the elaborate border was a large section of flat, unadorned stone. However, in the bottom third of the enormous slab was an elaborate crest surrounded by a vine-like plant with berries or fruit.

There were many sections of wall lying on the ground, most facing downward. Lanagan moved to the next section of standing wall, this one being the first of four adjacent slabs. Each section contained three large, square artist renderings of a story. He looked from the first slab to the second, then to the third and finally to the fourth, trying to make some sense of it all. He could not. After significant consideration and much frustration, he realized the story was meant to be read vertically. After basking in a brief moment of accomplishment, he proceeded to tell the story aloud.

"OK. The bright sun shines over the river. The bright sun shines over many rivers. The rivers become one larger river and flow. I guess the bright sun went away. OK. Small seedlings grow along the banks of one larger river. The seedlings grow taller and taller. Someone comes and cuts down the tall plants. Small seedlings begin growing again along the banks of the large river. Oh. The guy who cut down the tall plants seems to be running from something along the banks of the large river. Hmmm. Now the seedlings are tall again. But, I wonder what happened to …"

As that last word was uttered, Lanagan's ears rang with the most terrifying sound he had ever heard. The roar split the air around his head, and with the sudden rush and power of a freight train, he was thrown to the ground. In a whir of roaring and a blur of slashing and biting, his attacker sliced and gnawed him mercilessly.

Finally the brutal assault ended and Lanagan lay bloodied on the jungle floor. Standing above him, eyes looming down and mouth still growling with fury, stood the victorious tiger.

The animal lowered his head to within inches of the dog's face. After one final growl and an even more threatening stare, the tiger walked away, looking back one time with an additional snarl and the showing of his enormous teeth.

Lanagan strained to get up from the ground and onto his feet. He ached everywhere. Blood dripped from his jowls, his sides, and his hind leg. He slowly crept to the tiny stream and collapsed into the cool water.

Sleep covered him like a soothing balm. He dreamt he was on William's bed and that it was a Saturday morning when they could both sleep in. He heard William tell him it was time to get up, that he was going downstairs to make coffee.

He opened his eyes and instead of seeing the image of his friend getting out of bed and walking towards the bedroom door, he saw the massive stone wall and felt the stinging of his wounds and the pain that seemed to cover every inch of his body.

Slowly rising to his feet, he eased one paw in front of the other and walked out of the stream. Where he had lain, the sand had become crimson with blood.

Aside from being in excruciating pain, Lanagan was also ravenously hungry. Where was his backpack?

He looked all around. He limped up and down the streambed. Surely the pack was too heavy to have been swept away by the slow, trickling current. Where was his saddlebag then?

He fell back onto the moist ground. He was severely injured and had now lost his provisions. In his misery and seeming defeat, he wished he had never agreed to this impossible journey.

Sleep overtook him once again. This time, when he awoke, although still in extreme pain, his resolve had returned and he rose to his feet grimacing but with renewed determination.

He turned to look back in the direction of the misty barrier, and with a deep inhalation and a wincing or two of pain, he walked forward towards the Black River.

As had occurred the previous day, large birds of many varieties swooned down and in front of him. Was it his imagination or were their dives a little less aggressive than they were yesterday?

His stomach panged with hunger and he looked to and fro while he walked. Up ahead to his right he saw some sort of fruit bush. The berries were dark in color and by the look of the trampled ground beneath the plant, other animals frequented this place to eat. So Lanagan was reasonably confident the fruit was not poisonous.

He stretched his neck and hesitantly opened his mouth just enough to pull one of the succulent purple balls from the plant. He purposely rested the tiny fruit on his tongue for several seconds as a precautionary measure before allowing it to fall onto his back teeth. Since Lanagan continued breathing, he concluded that there was apparently no poison on the skin of the fruit. He finally allowed the berry to fall in-between two sets of ready teeth. He closed his eyes and his jaw simultaneously.

Seconds later, his eyes shot wide open and he declared to no one but the birds, "Blueberries! They're blueberries!" and he feasted until his face was purple and his belly was full.

Feeling refreshed and somewhat accomplished, he confidently stepped farther into the jungle, hoping beyond all reason that he was going in the right direction.

The traveling continued to be arduous and time consuming. After several hours of stepping over and through vines and overgrowth, something caught his eye up ahead and he quickened his pace in anticipation.

"It's a path," he whispered, "a real path." He had no idea where it would lead, but since it appeared to be relatively straight and well traveled, he assumed he had nothing to lose by following it.

For several more hours he walked. He saw no sign of any other tigers but he kept his ears on the alert and his eyes canvassing the jungle constantly. His feet were bloody and painful and his body still ached with every movement. But he found more wild blueberry bushes along the path, which kept his stomach satisfied and his outlook positive.

When dusk approached, he knew he needed to rest. An area off the path to the left caught his attention and he cautiously walked towards it. Steam rose from the solitary pool and when he sniffed the water he knew immediately that the pool was a mineral spring. Dismissing from his mind any thought of hidden quick sand or a trap, he walked into the pool of hot water and allowed the healing spring to engulf him.

Far beneath the water went the battered and bloodied dog. He held his breath for as long as he could, and when his white head finally breached the surface, his body relaxed in relief and appreciation. He rested his head on the bank and kept his swollen and slashed body beneath the water. And he slept.

Dreams filled his head once again. He walked with William along a dirt road; he played in the snow; he licked a vanilla ice cream cone; he chased Peaches around the Colbert's farmhouse. Every dream centered on his family—his human family.

A persistent multicolored bird with an enormous voice woke Lanagan many hours later and he was promptly reminded of his current predicament. He stretched his arms and legs, then his neck and tail. When he climbed out of the water, he shook until his coat was nearly dry. Patches of fur that had surrounded his wounds fell to the ground. His gashes were starting to heal and most had stopped bleeding. The pads on his hands and feet were still painful, but at least some of the blood that had stained his fur had been washed away by the mineral spring.

Returning to the path was easy, once he remembered he had seen the hot spring to his left. By lunchtime he realized that he had apparently, and with success, crossed the jungle lands. Spread wide before him lay the next section of Everlife—the northern mountains.

CHAPTER TWENTY-SEVEN

The panorama was breathtaking but overwhelming. How could he climb over those mountains? They were not only enormous but were also snow covered and their faces seemed sheer on all exposed sides. Again he turned to look behind him. He had come so far but he still had so very far to go. With a deep breath, he walked from the jungle toward the dense forest of tall, thick trees.

The quiet of this area was a drastic change from the jungle. Lanagan found the silence more unnerving than the persistent racket that had haunted him for the past two days. Here, no birds flew overhead but the wind grew stronger and louder with each step he took and it screamed in its own muffled, sinister way as it blew past his ears.

Temperatures plummeted too. Had he not been in his given form, he would certainly not survive this leg of the journey. There would be little to no food in this region and Lanagan walked blindly forward, hoping only that he would somehow make it through.

The only positive thing about the northern region was that it was easy to stay on course. The mountains loomed in front of him and he knew he needed to simply end up on the other side. He had no idea whatsoever how that would come to pass, but he knew he needed to keep moving forward. Retreat and defeat were simply not an option.

Lanagan walked slowly and deliberately, often turning his head and closing his eyes because the gusts of wind were so severe. By mid-afternoon he found himself in a steep valley between two mountains. He was hungry, tired, and feeling dismayed.

He sat for a few minutes to relax, thinking the rest would benefit both his body and his mind. However, after the first minute passed and as he remained stationary, his mind wandered into defeating thought and took up camp there.

If he did not continue moving forward he would succumb to the oppression. So he lifted his hindquarters from the ground and once again walked forward.

When the fierce wind was not blowing, the deafening quiet was baleful. The current silence was interrupted by the sudden sound of a tree cracking nearby. Turning his head toward the crash, a great gush of air filled Lanagan's lungs in an automatic and instantaneous preparation to flee. His front paws lunged forward as his recently straightened backside flexed with tensile determination to propel his body from the pending doom.

Before he had time to think, his limbs sent him twenty feet from the grizzly bear who was in hot pursuit. All thoughts of oppression and defeat were replaced abruptly by only one thought—run!

He bolted past trees right and left. He jumped over boulders and fallen logs. He darted this way and that, and once even backtracked for a quarter mile in an attempt to delude the fierce predator at his heels. He ran until he simply had exhausted his physical resources. He hid behind a tree and slowly peered around it to see if the bear was still behind him. It was not, but as Lanagan surveyed his surroundings, he realized he had absolutely no idea where he was and in what direction he had run.

He turned around and around, squinting to see something familiar or at least a shadow so he could tell which way he needed to go. Everything around him was bathed in the shade of the massive stony cliff that loomed above him. Once again, he solemnly nursed thoughts of surrender and defeat.

As his mind continued its sabotage, he noticed an area of increased darkness ahead near the base of a mountain. He took a step towards it, looking both ways and letting his feet touch down slowly and delicately with each step. There was no sign of the bear.

He got closer to the darkness and discovered it was a cave. More considerations flooded his thoughts. If he decided to enter the cave, would it be a place of refuge or would it lead to his ultimate demise? There was no way to be certain, but he walked into the cavern anyway.

His steps continued with much caution and trepidation. To his great relief, his eyes adjusted to the darkness and although detail was obscured, he was able to make his way forward with relative ease. However, as corners were turned and he moved deeper into the cave, his limited vision vanished and he found himself in total darkness.

He stepped sideways, inch by inch, closing the gap between himself and the cold stone wall. He had no choice but to continue forward.

The ground beneath his tender feet became damp and soon he heard a muddled sound in the distance. With each step, the faint noise grew louder and echoed against the cave walls.

He rounded a corner and the air became less musty. Gradually the level of darkness decreased and once again his eyes adjusted and he was able to see where his steps were taking him.

Drip, drip, drip. The sound continued more distinctly. Soon, his feet trod in a tiny stream of cool water. Bending down to take a drink, he hesitantly gazed at the walls on either side of him, making sure there were no ancient stories carved on these rocks.

After the rousing drink he continued walking forward. Around the next bend, light shined down over the wet walls in rays from an apparent opening above his head. He paused to consider the possibilities of his current location in the cave. For all he knew this stone tunnel could go on forever or could wind up leading to a dead end. Turning around and retracing his steps was certainly plausible, if not highly logical. However, if his desire was to see William Colbert again, there was no choice but to keep moving forward.

Traveling in that direction proved to be the best choice, because within the hour, the big white dog and his wet feet exited the cave and found themselves on the other side of the mountain. What now stretched before him was the third section of his journey to Black River. The ocean.

CHAPTER TWENTY-EIGHT

Lanagan had never seen the ocean before and found it beyond amazing. He stood there staring for at least an hour, so completely awed that he could do nothing else.

When the wonder subsided and his awareness returned, he pondered aloud, "How in the world am I going to cross the water?"

He had swum hundreds of times, but even an accomplished swimmer would not survive crossing an ocean. He could not see past the horizon; for all he knew the waters went on for thousands of miles. Crossing them was certainly out of the question, so Lanagan stepped onto the sandy beach and simply started walking.

The first stretch of beach was beautiful and the salt water was therapeutic to his sore pads. But after a few miles, the sun grew hot and he resorted to plunging into the waves to cool off. There were several areas on his body where his fur had either been ripped out during his fight with the tiger or scraped off while he scampered through the forest to escape the bear. There were other areas where the fur had fallen out simply to assist in the healing process near the puncture wounds. When the salt seeped into these exposed areas, Lanagan screeched in pain and dashed back to the shore. His consolation was that he was cooler and refreshed and knew the salt would aid in the healing of his cuts and abrasions. He shook vigorously to release the water from his fur, but as the sun beat down on him, his thick double-layered white coat became sticky and matted. He decided that his next move must be to find fresh water.

He turned from the water's edge, inland, in the hopes of finding enough water for both drinking and bathing. The hot sand burned his hands and feet as he walked. The tiny silica crystals of the beach became more compressed the farther inland he walked. Soon he felt small pebbles under his pads and reeds sprung from the sandy soil forming nearly impassible green barriers. Their edges were sharp and serrated on both sides and cut his skin easily where the fur was absent. Making his way through these green spears was more difficult than trekking through the jungle.

After at least a dozen new crisp cuts to his face and sides, he escaped the platoon of killer reeds and found himself on the edge of a marsh. Ducks quacked and dove for food in the slimy green water. As he walked closer, he sniffed the air for both salt and predators, and then lowered his head for a quick taste of the murky liquid. His initial supposition was confirmed: it was fresh water. He lowered his tongue and drank slowly for several minutes before once again raising his head. When he did, he found himself face to face with the largest crocodile he had ever seen.

Panic, fear, and indecision filled his mind in equal portions. The white dog stood motionless, his eyes locked in contact with the piercing stare of the reptilian creature directly in front of him. The enormous green leathery beast opened his mouth and lunged forward. The jaws clamped down on the dog's neck and shoulders and he yelped in agony once again.

The croc thrashed and shook the dog, both above and beneath the water. Lanagan kicked with all his might but his defenses were useless against this ravenous monster. The crocodile swung his prey back and forth, back and forth, and then with one final fling, the crocodile threw the dog back onto the land. Lanagan lay motionless.

The reptile crept up in its slither-like manner, his face inches above the still dog. Lanagan opened his eyes and realized he was breathing his last breath. His pride proved to be stronger than his fear, and he mustered one final growl and bared his teeth at the creature in defiance.

"Have you had enough?" asked the crocodile.

The dog's eyes widened.

"Excuse me?" queried the dog, lifting his head off the damp and bloodied ground.

"Come on, let's get you up," said the green monster as it grabbed Lanagan by the scruff of his neck and lifted him off the ground.

"Gee, thanks," said Lanagan sarcastically. "So, is this the polite conversation that comes before the death blow?"

"No hard feelings, chap. Just doing my job."

"Your job?"

"I was told that I might be seeing you and if I did, I was to give you a little bit of a scare."

"A little bit of a scare? You almost killed me."

"Nah, if I was aiming to kill you, we wouldn't be having this nice conversation."

"Who told you to scare me off?"

"That would be the Constable."

"The Constable?"

"Constable Prescott. He's the administrator over these parts."

"And where exactly are 'these parts'?"

"You're still in the ocean sector. We were all told that as long as you didn't high tail it back into the northern mountain region, we were to give you a little bit of a fight, but then to let you pass."

"Let me pass?"

"Rumor has it you're going to see Olde Crow."

"Yes, yes I am. How far away from here is Black River?"

"Ah, my friend, you still have to cross the ocean, but I can help you with that part of the journey."

"You can? How? Do you have a boat?"

"No, but we've got whales."

"Whales?"

"Yeah, whales. They're like real big fish. Haven't you ever heard of a whale before?"

"Of course I've heard of whales. I've just never seen one."

"Well, today's your lucky day then. Hop on my back and I'll take you back to the beach. Those reeds can be mighty harsh."

"Yeah, I know," lamented Lanagan as he stepped on to the back of the crocodile. "Why is there pain and bleeding in this part of Everlife?"

"There's not, not normally anyway. Olde Crow asked Cambium to give you an Earthly body when you walked through the foggy barrier. He wanted to see how determined you were to see him and to go on your OFAD."

"You know about that?"

"Ah, Lanagan, everyone knows about it. Everyone throughout all the regions of Everlife. We're all behind you."

"I can't say I've been thrilled with the way you show your support."

"Just doing our job, just doing our job."

"How come you know about OFADs and everyone else's memory of them was erased?"

"The only ones who used to go were dogs and cats, and they're the ones with no recollection. The rest of us still remember everything."

In no time at all, the two animals were on the shore. When Lanagan looked out towards the water, it looked quite different than it had an hour before. Twenty feet from the water's edge, dolphins danced above the water, vocalizing in their familiar language and seemingly smiling as they sang. Scores of whales floated in the deeper water, waiting as close to the shore as possible. Directly in front of them and up to the shoreline were dozens and dozens of sea turtles, all looking at Lanagan.

"Here's where we say farewell, chap," said the crocodile. "Maybe I'll see you on your way back. And … uh … sorry about the injuries. They're not life threatening."

"Uh … thanks," said Lanagan as he walked towards the water.

One of the turtles stepped forward, her movement slow and lumbering.

"I am Matriarch," said the creature. "My family and I will carry you out to the whales. The whales will take you to the other side of the sea. There, a welcoming party will escort you to Black River."

Lanagan approached Matriarch, marveling at her immensity. She was at least ten feet long, maybe more. Her hands were sleek and dark, easily measuring five feet across and simply enormous. From the tip of the right flipper to the tip of the left measured at least fifteen feet. Lanagan neared her slowly, and apprehensively jumped on top of her enormous shell, but promptly slid right down the other side. A round of giggles escaped from the other turtles.

"Perhaps you might just lay across my shell?" suggested the accommodating turtle as she offered her leg as a step stool.

This time, Lanagan stepped onto the hind leg of the animal and she obligingly lifted her hand and placed it behind her shoulder to assist him as he climbed. Emitting a groan as she heaved him upward with her limbs, Lanagan sprawled across her shell and then slowly turned himself around so he was facing forward.

"Can you hold on to my shell? Here." said Matriarch pointing to the area of lipped shell behind her ample head.

"Yeah, I think so."

"Hold on," said the turtle as she turned around and walked towards the water.

Once she was buoyant, the creature was an example of grace and agility. Lanagan smiled and turned to the crocodile, lifting his right hand to wave. Letting go of the shell just momentarily nearly cost him a tumble in the water, so he lifted his head in an alternative gesture of "good-bye."

With the sea air rushing past his face and the knowledge that he had actually lived through the ordeals of the jungle, the mountains, and the ocean, Lanagan's heart was lighter than it had been in months.

Matriarch reached the pod of whales and swam alongside an exceptionally large humpback. The whale lowered itself down into the water to approximate the level of the shell on which Lanagan was riding. The turtle turned her head and told the dog, "Go ahead and jump. You can use your claws if you have to; his skin is thick and you won't hurt him."

Slowly rising to all fours, Lanagan evaluated the jump and pushed off with his hind legs. The turtle was pushed back and down a bit into the water, but provided the perfect launching pad for her passenger. Thankfully, Lanagan landed on the whale with minimal sliding and came to a stop just about in the center of the mammal's broad back.

A low, raspy voice came from the mouth of the great mammal, sounding like a foghorn.

"Put your front paws in my blowhole and flex your wrists to use your hands like a hook."

Lanagan crept up to the hole, which was bigger than his head. He did as he was told and latched his paws inside.

"Ready?" asked the whale.

"Ready," answered the dog.

"Let's go!" bellowed the whale and they were off.

Lanagan whooped and hollered in delight. He was unaware that whales could swim so quickly and smoothly. Just when his arms were too tired to hold on any longer, land finally appeared in the distance.

Just as before, dolphins escorted the whales and another team of sea turtles waited in the shallows to take the passenger to shore. This time the jump from the whale to the turtle was more calculated and precise. As if he had been riding these massive and wonderful creatures all his life, he grabbed onto the shell lip and rode comfortably and effortlessly to the brown sands of the second shore.

After thanking the sea animals profusely, he turned to face the welcome party. He was not sure what he expected, but what stood before him was certainly nothing he would have ever predicted.

The small furry creatures stood at attention, backs straight, knees locked, and arms at their sides. Although they held no weapons, their formation strongly resembled a company of soldiers and many even wore colored sashes across their tiny chests.

There were dozens of them, perhaps hundreds. They stood silently and calmly as if awaiting instruction. They stood with their necks extended and their wee little noses stuck straight up towards the sky. Lanagan wondered if they were waiting for him to speak.

"Hello," said the dog, "my name is L—" but before he could utter the word, every one of the soldier moles opened their tiny mouths and shouted, "Lanagan!" and then they all returned to silence.

Taken aback with shock and surprise, the white dog looked behind him to see if any of the turtles, dolphins, or whales had remained. They had not. He faced the platoon of moles once again.

"Yes, I am Lanagan. I have come to see Olde Crow. Is this the place they call Black River?"

One of the moles stepped forward from the ranks of small brown creatures. His head bore a yellow beret and a blue sash hung from his right shoulder across his chest. Lowering his head to approximate eye contact with Lanagan, the mole spoke.

"My name is Kout. Welcome to the land of Black River."

Lanagan opened his mouth to say "thank you," but before he could speak, the entourage of moles began to sing.

Welcome to the land of Black River
Home of the infamous Crow
May light walk with you as you travel
And your heart lift as you go.

Follow us to the land of Black River
Someone waits ahead for you
We admire your perseverance
And your journey's almost through.

Row by row, starting in the back, the moles turned on their heels and began marching toward the lush greenery of Black River. As they turned, they continued their welcome.

You are welcome here in Black River
We hope you will enjoy your stay
Until you leave we're here to serve you
We hope to see you again some day.

By now, every row of tiny blind rodents had turned and was walking from the beach. Their song continued, but since Lanagan was standing behind them, he could no longer make out what they were saying.

When he reached the area where the beach ended and the thick vegetation began, he was relieved to see a clearly defined path on which the moles were traveling. Each of his lengthy strides was equal to about fifty mole paces, so he walked very slowly and took tiny steps as he followed in the rear.

After perhaps two hours of this monotonous procession, the moles stopped in their tracks without warning. Lanagan nearly tripped over his own feet trying to stop his forward momentum and avoid squashing the moles in the last several rows. The mole in the yellow beret walked from the point position back toward the rear where Lanagan was stationed.

"This is as far as we are to take you."

"How do I get to Olde Crow from here?"

"One hundred yards ahead, this path will separate into three. You must pick one and continue on that path until you find Olde Crow."

"But which one should I take?"

"That is for you to decide."

"That's just great. I thought the last leg of the journey was going to be easy."

"If you prefer, I can have you escorted back to Everlife and guarantee that no harm will come to you as you retrace your steps."

"No, no," said Lanagan, realizing that his frustration had crept into his heart and pushed his feelings of appreciation and assurance to the side. "Thanks for everything, I mean it."

The yellow-capped mole shouted, "Dismissed" to his company and they scattered in all different directions from the once organized procession. The rustling they made in the low ground cover ceased in a matter of fifteen or twenty seconds, and there was no longer any sign of them. Once again, Lanagan was alone.

With his feet firmly set, he extended his arms forward along the pebbled path and lowered his chest to the ground in a much-needed stretch. With a groan and a shake to wake him up fully, he then sprinted until he came to the path's divergence.

He looked from one path to the other, then to the next. All seemed equally traveled, and all seemed equally similar. He took a few dozen steps down path number one and then returned to his starting point. He did the same for path number two and path number three. He could see no difference.

He tried to rationalize, theorize, hypothesize, and philosophize which path to take. He stood there for at least thirty minutes, maybe more, trying to figure out which trail to choose. In the end, he decided there was only one logical option.

He closed his eyes and started running in a tight circle, as if to chase his tail. Around and around and around he went, until he realized the sheer silliness of this circling and he burst out laughing. When he could run no longer, he fell to the ground and lay still until his dizziness subsided. In a few moments when he opened his eyes, he would walk down the path that he was facing.

Opening his right eye first, he peeked to see where he was laying. He did not see any of the three paths in front of him. He slowly opened his left eye and there, farther to the left, was path number three. He got up and said proudly to himself, "OK. That matter has been settled," and he took his first of many steps down the well-trodden path.

For the most part, his hike was pleasant and effortless. Dozens of animals hopped, crawled, flew, or otherwise crossed the path where he walked. Dozens of others looked and pointed from the outskirts. To each, he nodded respectfully, smiled, or said "hello."

One particularly inquisitive squirrel jumped directly in front of him and sat in the middle of the path.

"You're Lanagan, aren't you?"

"Yes. What's your name?"

"My given name is 'Ceelo', but everyone around here calls me Acorn."

"Well, that seems fitting. It's nice to meet you, Acorn."

"Everyone says you're going to see Olde Crow."

"That's right, I am. You wouldn't happen to know how much farther down this path he is, would you?"

"I'm not sure you can get to his cave from this path."

Lanagan's heart sank to the pads of his feet and he looked at Acorn with utmost despair.

"Acorn, are you sure I can't get there from here?"

"No."

"Do you know anyone else around here who you could ask for me?"

"Maybe."

"Maybe?"

"Well, O.K. I'll go ask. Are you going to wait here?"

"I'll wait in this exact spot. How long will it take you?"

"I don't know. How long will you wait?"

"Acorn!" said Lanagan in a rather frustrated tone.

"Give me five minutes," said the young squirrel, and he dashed off into the trees.

Lanagan sat and looked around. He was intensely hungry by this point; he must have been walking for at least three hours and his last meal of blueberries had been two days ago. The sun was beginning to set and he had hoped to be wherever it was he was going by nightfall. With each passing minute, that hope grew more dim.

A rustling in the leaves and the sound of someone approaching sent Lanagan abruptly to his feet. Thoughts of the tiger, the bear, and the crocodile attacks raced across his mind. This time, however, the one whom shot out again from nowhere and landed in the middle of the path was Acorn. Then, with a somewhat less dramatic entry, came a second squirrel who sat adjacent to Acorn on the gravel trail.

"Mr. Lanagan," said the second arrival, an obviously older and more refined squirrel. "I see you've met my son. Please forgive his rather flippant attitude and lack of manners. How may I be of assistance?"

"Well, Ma'am, I'm trying to find Olde Crow. Do you know how I can find him?"

"Certainly, Sir, I'd be happy to assist you."

It was not necessary for Lanagan to listen attentively, because all he needed to do was continue on the current path for two more miles. The path would end on this side of the actual river. Once he reached the river, someone would be there to escort him to Olde Crow.

The big white dog thanked the gray squirrel and continued walking down the trail, wondering if once again, the journey's end may actually be forthcoming or if he would be running into more obstacles.

Forgetting his hunger pangs for the time being, he trotted with a confidence in his step and perhaps a slightly premature feeling of accomplishment. During these final few minutes of his quest, he allowed his mind to wander to the possible outcomes of his meeting with Olde Crow.

There were two obvious possibilities: The crow would either allow Lanagan to go on an OFAD or he would not. Considering that the crow had consented to a meeting with him in the first place gave Lanagan enough reason to believe that an OFAD would most likely be granted. What remained now were the stipulations, regulations, and formalities of the OFAD itself. Of those, there were endless possibilities, and Lanagan grew mentally weary considering only the first five or six that entered his mind.

So with his head occupied with several options and his hands and feet occupied with walking, he was taken by surprise when the path ended and a wide river splayed before him. His first impression was that the river was not black. His second thought was, "Where's my escort?"

Looking to his left and right, and even straining to see the other bank, he saw no sign of anyone. Once again, frustration filled his veins.

Adding insult to injury was the fact that his hunger pains returned. There was nothing edible anywhere around him. He could walk along the riverbank searching for food (or maybe even his escort), but he wondered if he might miss the convoy altogether if he ventured away from the path. After much deliberation he decided to stay where he was.

Dusk turned to night and darkness surrounded him in dense silence. The only sound he heard was the very slow moving of the river. Curling up in a tight bundle, he closed his eyes and fought to stave off his hunger.

Whether it was emotional exhaustion or intense physical fatigue that plummeted the dog into deep sleep was uncertain. Regardless, when sleep came, it took him fully and completely, leaving no possibility of immediate release.

When his arms and legs finally extended and his back stretched to open the ball shape he had curled into, Lanagan was amazed that it was almost dawn. He had needed that deep sleep more than he would ever have imagined, even more than food.

He walked to the river and dipped his mouth into it for a cool drink. When his thirst was sufficiently quenched, he lifted his head to a sight of both broad and dramatic proportions.

Flying toward him from across the river was the largest flock of crows he had ever seen. In the distance, they approached by the thousands, in rows evenly spaced. They flew in at a height just above the tree line; but as they approached the far river bank, the front row dove downward toward the river and then flew across it, only four feet above the surface of the water. Lanagan ducked and watched row after row fly low across the river and then over his head. When the final row had come and gone, he stood up straight again and continued watching the skies.

Off on the horizon, a tiny speck appeared in the distant sky. As it approached, Lanagan noticed the wingspan and its black and purple shiny feathers, so he knew it was not Olde Crow. As it reached the far bank, it did not dive as the others had done, but merely landed on the river's edge. It stood in silence, as did Lanagan, who was waiting for some sort of profound event.

Another dark speck appeared in the distance. Likewise, when it approached the far bank, it gracefully landed and stood silently. Assuming another crow would make its entrance in the same fashion, Lanagan watched the far sky and waited.

Nothing came. After several minutes, he huffed lightly to himself with impatience and mumbled aloud that he was going in search of breakfast. He turned around and took a step forward, almost stepping on the bird who was standing directly in front of him.

It was Olde Crow.

CHAPTER TWENTY-NINE

Lanagan was not sure how much of his recent outburst had been witnessed by the great bird, but he assumed it had been everything. If a big white dog could possibly blush in embarrassment, that moment would certainly be now.

"Good Morning, Lanagan. I am sincerely glad to see you."

"Olde Crow. Yes, Good Morning, Sir. It's great to see you again too."

"I trust you are sufficiently hungry and that a nice big breakfast is in order?"

"My stomach and I would be eternally grateful."

"Eternity is a very long time, Lanagan."

"Yes, Sir, it is. What I meant was ..."

Reaching a black wing tip out to touch the dog on the shoulder, the crow smiled and said, "Don't take everything so seriously, Lanagan. It was just a joke."

Relieved, the dog tried to relax, tried to regain his composure. The journey to Olde Crow had been long and difficult and he was physically and emotionally exhausted. He tried desperately to appear nonchalant and calm. He wondered if he was succeeding.

Olde Crow walked toward the water's edge and reached down with the same wing tip and touched the cold water. The small spot in the river suddenly hardened and darkened. Then the blackness spread outward and to the left and right and across to the far side of the water. Within seconds, the water had become a coal black sheet of solid rock.

"Shall we?" asked Olde Crow as he motioned with his long wing for the dog to cross the river.

"So ... I guess this is why they call this place Black River," mentioned Lanagan.

"I believe I could have come up with something a bit more creative, but no one ever asked for my input," lamented Olde Crow.

The bird was just as Lanagan had remembered, even though it had been centuries since their last meeting. Olde Crow was a little bigger than most crows, or maybe it just seemed that way because he carried himself so erect. He was also quite a bit blacker, because he never did opt for the crow modifications. He remained soft spoken too, unassuming and very genteel.

There was one thing different about him this time, however. Some sort of medallion hung from a silver chain around his neck. Not wanting to be obvious about it, Lanagan casually glanced at the pendant and made a mental note that if the opportunity presented itself sometime later on, he would inquire about the new piece of jewelry.

When he and Olde Crow reached the other side, the two crows standing on the bank nodded to their leader and flew away.

The ancient bird led Lanagan up a hill to a substantial cave. There, near the entrance, was row after row of wooden benches, placed in a semi-circle, with a wooden podium centered in the front. Without needing to be asked, Olde Crow volunteered the explanation.

"The old bird is still called upon to teach now and then."

Lanagan knew the crow was being very modest. He remained respectfully silent and followed the bird past all the benches and far back into the cave. There a large, low table sat, with bowls of fruit, nuts, breads, and casseroles.

With another gesture of his wing, Olde Crow motioned to Lanagan to eat. With a sigh of gratitude and much appreciation, the dog stepped toward the table and surveyed the buffet. The thick casseroles were cut into bite-size chunks, which he easily lifted onto his plate. To them, he added large spoonfuls of fruit, berries, nuts and muffins. He then lifted the pewter plate off the table with his teeth, set it on the floor, and began eating eagerly.

Olde Crow jumped onto the table and picked berries with his beak, and also nibbled on a Danish. "My cook only uses whole grains and honey in the sweets, so help yourself to some guiltless pleasures."

Lanagan could only moan in response because his mouth was so full. Olde Crow smiled.

Breakfast lasted a good half-hour and when they both were satisfactorily stuffed, Olde Crow hopped onto a large perch. A contented Lanagan sat on a soft rug and looked up at his host.

"Lanagan, I know you have traveled far to see me. I know you have suffered while on this journey. The trials were necessary to measure your heart and the depth of your love for your friend".

"As you know, OFADs were discontinued many centuries ago for a multitude of reasons. If you and I decide to reinstate the OFAD, we must do so for the right reason and we must consider the impact it will have in another thousand years. My spirit tells me that you have a pure heart and that your motives are sincere. I have also heard many speak of your identification tag. Is it still purple?"

"Yes."

"May I see it?"

Lanagan stepped forward and lifted his head to stretch his thick, downy neck. The crow jumped down from his perch and using his long feathers like fingers, he reached up and separated the white fur to expose the tag.

"In all my days," said Olde Crow as he held the tag, "I have never seen one of these in this color," and he released the tag and fluttered back to his perch.

"What does it mean Olde Crow?"

"Lanagan, there are many mysteries in this universe and many things still to be learned. With all our acquired knowledge and with all our seeking, we are still but babes when it comes to understanding the unknown."

"But Olde Crow, you were the first creature. You had mysteries revealed to you by the Great Creator Spirit. Surely your knowledge exceeds that of any other."

"Knowledge, perhaps. But the river of knowledge is shallow and narrow. You are dealing with the river of life itself, which is endless in length and deep beyond comprehension."

"So no one can tell me what's going on?" asked Lanagan perplexed.

"It appears that your story is not over, Lanagan. You must be patient and let it unfold."

"Unfold? Unfold? How am I supposed to do that? I'm stuck here in Everlife and my best friend is in Ohio."

"Do you feel connected to him, Lanagan?"

"In a way I cannot explain or describe, Olde Crow."

"You and William are kindred spirits, Son. Nothing can ever separate you from that truth."

"Well, it sure looks like a couple galaxies are separating us right now. That's why I want to go back."

"You know that is forbidden."

"I mean on an OFAD."

"I see. What do you think the OFAD will accomplish?"

"It will allow me to see him again."

Growing impatient and somewhat annoyed, the dog summoned his remaining willpower to keep the tone of his voice amiable. "It will make me feel better."

"Ah. You want to feel better. Cambium tells me your memories are still intact. Is this true?"

"Yes."

"And the accompanying emotions?"

"Yes."

"Has this ever happened to you following any other assignment?" asked Olde Crow.

"No, it never has."

"And how does it feel, Lanagan?"

"It *hurts*. It's like seeing a photograph of someone you love, but not being able to touch them. It's like eating your favorite food but not being able to taste it. Every night I can't wait to go to sleep because at least in my dreams, we're together."

"Passage Wall did not erase your ability to dream either?"

"No. I dream about my last assignment all the time."

Olde Crow turned and began pacing on the perch. When he reached the end of the knurly branch, he turned and walked to the other end, clutching and releasing the perch with each tiny step.

"Do you remember anything about the old OFADs?" asked the bird.

"No, Cambium erased everyone's memory in our part of Everlife, but he told me about them."

"Did he tell you about the crow modifications?"

"Yes."

"Before permitting the return of the OFAD, I must once again deeply consider the repercussions and the long term effects. I need more time to make my decision. You may stay here in my cave while

I am away. When I return, I will have an answer for you, one way or the other."

"How long will you be gone?"

"I have no idea."

Lanagan nodded in agreement. Olde Crow sprung from his perch and Lanagan watched him as he flew away, continuing to watch even after the distant black speck in the sky disappeared completely. Even then, he just sat and stared for a good long while.

No one came by the cave that first afternoon, so Lanagan had plenty of solitude—which meant plenty of time to think. Initially he was extremely optimistic about Olde Crow's upcoming decision, but as the day wore on, he realized that the longer the bird was gone, the less likely it was for a positive outcome.

Regardless of his progressing melancholia, at around dusk the need for sustenance reminded him that he had not eaten since the breakfast buffet. He made his way back into the cave and ate; perhaps a bit less enthusiastically this time, but still heartily.

The night sky brought with it renewed hope, as well as cooler temperatures. Lanagan sat at the cave entrance gazing out at the stars, wondering if William was somewhere looking up at the same dark sky. When he fell asleep that night, he had no dreams.

Morning came in an instant, as if night had not even come and gone. He woke up hungry, very sore, and stiff. After his stretching and groaning routine was finished, he opened his eyes fully and sat up. There on the ledge of the outcropping he saw a familiar face.

"Good Morning, Lanagan. I brought you breakfast."

"Acorn! How are you, little buddy?"

The young squirrel removed a shoulder bag and reached a tiny hand inside.

"Mama wouldn't let me bring you any nuts," said the squirrel as he unwrapped a fig and handed it to Lanagan.

"Thanks, Acorn. I love figs."

"Good. I have five of them. Mama said I should go get more for you if you liked them."

Lanagan grabbed each fig delicately with his furry hand and savored each bite. He truly did love fresh figs.

"I heard that Olde Crow is off deciding what to do about your OFAD," commented Acorn.

"News travels pretty quickly around here, huh?"

"When something this exciting is going on, it does. We hardly ever get visitors and we've never had a dog here. Everyone's talking about you and Olde Crow."

"Do they think the bird will let me go?"

"They're not sure, but we all hope he does, Lanagan."

"I don't suppose anyone has heard how Olde Crow is progressing with his decision."

"Nope. When Olde Crow goes off on these wisdom quests, no one else knows anything until he gets back."

"Always the secretive one, is he?"

"Always. But, he's real smart and Mama says he's real fair too."

"Let's hope so, Acorn. Let's hope so."

The young squirrel darted off with a smile and a big wave, and Lanagan was actually sorry that his company had gone.

Throughout the day, he thought he heard whispering and other sounds of spying, but he was not sure. The idea of being watched and stared at was rather unsettling, but when he compared the spying to the tiger and crocodile fights, he became much less offended by the secretive peeping.

That night his dreams returned. He dreamed that he and William were at the lake; the day was just beautiful and William had pitched a tent under some pine trees. They had gone swimming that afternoon and William was getting the barbecue grill going. Peaches was even there. Murphy sat watching in amazement; watching the small drop of fire explode from the end of the tiny stick William held in his fingers. Murphy remembered fire; he remembered seeing it in the house; it was always a contained fire and William used to sit near it in the winter and drink coffee. One Christmas, William's father had started one of these fires in the morning and everyone thought it was so lovely when they came downstairs.

In the dream, Murphy was watching William start the fire at the campsite, and wondering if he could steal a hot dog from the plate sitting on the wooden table. Surely William had not counted them, and even if he did, certainly he would not itemize every one over the course of their two days there.

Or would he?

As often happens in dreams though, the dog was awakened in the middle of a great scene. He opened his eyes and could still smell the smoke from the campfire. He still tasted the flavor of the stolen hot dog.

He stretched but did not moan this day. He remained recumbent too; he thought that perhaps if he closed his eyes as tightly as he could and if he willed himself with enough effort, that maybe, just maybe, he would slip back into that dream world. But, alas, this day the sandman was not cooperative.

The big white dog finally stood and surveyed the morning. As was always the case in Everlife, the day was perfect. Since he had no idea whether Olde Crow would be back in a day or a month or a year, he figured he might as well start exploring and enjoying his temporary residence in this far section of Everlife.

His second day at Olde Crow's cave came and went, as did the third and forth. The dog remained at the mouth of the cave, moving little, eating even less, but thinking much. As dusk approached on the fifth day, he once again curled up into a large white ball and was just about to drift off to sleep when the cawing of a loud crow nearby awakened him. Knowing it could not be Olde Crow, he stretched and took his time getting up.

"I have a message from Olde Crow," said the black and purple bird. "He is on his way back and told me to find you. He will be here within the hour and since you are already here, I suggest you remain here until he returns."

"Did he happen to tell you what he decided to do?" asked Lanagan of the crow.

"I was simply told to relay a message."

Disappointed but understanding, Lanagan thanked the bird and it flew away.

This time, it was the dog that paced. He walked back and forth across the opening of Olde Crow's cave so many times that the sand and soil became packed. When he noticed something tiny and black in the distant sky approaching from the west, he knew it must be Olde Crow.

The old bird landed with the skill and grace of a raptor. After shaking his body and puffing out his feathers, he bent his wings at the midway point and poised them on his hips.

"I have given the matter much thought and prayer, Lanagan. After considering both the short and long term effects of reinitiating the OFAD, I have decided wholeheartedly to agree to their return."

The dog stood there with his mouth gaped. He could not believe what he had just heard.

"I get to go?" he asked.

"Yes, Lanagan. You have convinced me that this is the proper path to take. From now on, things are going to be much different around here."

"When can I leave? Can I leave from here? Do I have to go back to the other side of Everlife? How long can I stay? How will I get back?"

"You must return to the canine/feline area of Everlife. You must retrace your steps and travel through all the regions again. However this time your journey will be painless and you will receive assistance. By the time you see Cambium again, he will have been informed of my decision. I will leave the specifics up to him, as they are irrelevant to the larger picture. The crows from Black River will once again offer themselves as messengers, and I will relay that to Cambium in my message. The two of you may then do as you like."

Lanagan was speechless. He stood there staring at Olde Crow.

"Is there anything else you require?" asked the bird.

Blinking hard and trying to process everything he had just been told, the big white dog finally responded.

"No, no. There's nothing else, Olde Crow. I can't believe I'm actually going on an OFAD. Thank you so much. I don't know what to say."

"Your purple tag and your love have spoken volumes. I will see you again. Follow this path back down the mountain. Someone will be there to escort you out of Black River. Go in peace, Lanagan."

The dog bowed in gratitude and left Olde Crow's cave.

CHAPTER THIRTY

At the river's edge, the moles escorted Lanagan to a wooden bridge and when they reached the other side, Acorn and his mother guided him to the border of Black River. There he easily found his way back to the sandy beach. By now he was an old hand at the turtle/whale routine.

When he reached the northern mountain region, a large grizzly bear was waiting for him with a pail of honey.

"A peace offering?" said the bear.

"I'd love some, thanks," answered the dog.

After his snack, the genteel bear walked him through the forest for half a day and then through another underground shortcut. The dog had a sneaking suspicion who would be waiting for him at the jungle border.

His suspicions were right; it was the tiger.

"What? No peace offering?" asked Lanagan.

The tiger reached into a bush and grabbed the canvas saddlebag with his teeth, throwing it at the dog's feet.

"Just following orders, Pal," said the tiger. "Sorry I cut you so badly."

"I understand," said the dog assuredly. "Thanks for the backpack, but I don't think I'll be needing it anymore. Are you taking me through to the foggy divide?"

"If that's OK with you."

"Sure, let's go."

On the other side of Everlife, a shiny crow landed on one of Cambium's low branches, and the Tree instantly knew it would be bringing news about Lanagan. Half a dozen animals witnessed the crow's arrival and had crept in close to the Great Tree to eavesdrop.

"Cambium, I have word from Olde Crow," said the bird.

The Tree had not gone fully to sleep since Lanagan's departure, so with one brief crack of his eyelids, he was alert and ready to hear the news.

"Ah, yes, Deering. What can you tell me?" asked the Tree.

"Lanagan survived the journey. He's pretty beat up, but his injuries were not life threatening. He met with Olde Crow and the Chief has decided to allow him to go on an OFAD."

"Oh my, that is truly exciting news!"

"He is currently journeying back through the jungle zone just past the barrier. He will be back in less than an hour."

News of Lanagan's return spread like ants over a summer picnic. The four-walkers that had overheard the conversation ran to tell others, and before long, there was a throng of dogs and cats on this side of the foggy divide waiting for some kind of indication that the rumor they heard was true.

Flanders stood the closest to the divide, as he had before, as would be expected. No one was sure exactly where Lanagan would emerge from the mist, so they were spread out a quarter mile on either side of where he had walked through eleven days earlier.

When someone saw a shudder in the barrier, everyone stirred in anticipation. Then someone else thought they saw a slight color change several feet up from the ground. Both sightings proved to be false alarms.

The journey back through the jungle was long but easy for Lanagan, especially compared to the first leg of his journey. The tiger and the dog stood by the dense fog separator in silence.

"Well," said Lanagan, "thanks."

"Don't mention it. I guess I'll be seeing you again some time. Have you heard that Cambium and Olde Crow have been talking about establishing a more species diverse place here?"

"No, I hadn't heard. If it happens, I look forward to seeing you again, but on my turf next time, OK?"

The tiger nodded and the still scabbed and bloodied white dog started his way through the dense fog.

Miss Mallory was the first to see him begin to exit through the thick haze. Then Flanders saw something.

It started with a subtle color shift; a small, subdued white hue floating a short distance above the ground, still deep within the murky mist. Then the area of white increased and became more defined. Soon it took the form of a small cloud with legs, and by the time everyone was about to pass out because they had been too nervous to breathe, the distinct outline of a dog became clear enough to recognize.

Flanders rushed forward toward the fog but stopped before any contact was made with it. The black nose appeared first, then the white muzzle and face. The shoulders and arms came through next, followed by his torso and hindquarters. When Lanagan finally walked all the way through, no one moved or said a word.

He stopped and looked at Flanders, and then looked out into the crowd. Everyone stared. Some began backing away. He looked back at Flanders.

"What's going on?" Lanagan asked.

Even Flanders hesitated before answering.

"Lanagan. Is that you?"

"Of course it's me. Who do you think it is?"

"You look ... different, is all. You're in pretty rough shape, Buddy. You're bleeding. Do you realize that?"

"Oh," said Lanagan, looking down at his arms and around to see his sides and legs. "That's what happens when you're attacked by tigers and bears and crocodiles I guess."

Flanders turned around to face the crowd and yelled, "It's OK. It's him. He's gonna be OK."

At that point, the cheers finally erupted and Lanagan received the welcome home he so deserved.

Even Cambium was shocked by Lanagan's appearance. Passage Wall was designed to return the body to its ideal form during re-entry to Everlife, and Cambium had never seen wounds before.

"Are you in pain, Lanagan?"

"I'm doing a lot better now, thanks."

"Do you want me to restore you now?"

"No, that's OK. I'll just wait till I get back from my OFAD!" he said gleamingly.

"So I heard. When will you be leaving?"

"Olde Crow left that up to us to decide. He said he'd send word."

"He did indeed. So now it's up to you and me to work out the details, yes?"

"I think what he meant was that it was up to you, Cambium."

"Do not sell yourself short, Lanagan. You and I will together decide the fate of future OFADs. Agreed?"

"Agreed. When do we start?"

"Would you like to take time to rest?"

"No way! Compared to what I've been through the past week and a half, talking to you here is rest enough!"

"The old OFADs were each twenty-four hours and I think that would be a good place to start. The portal has already been modified for your special mission, so you may leave whenever you wish. When you return, you and I will discuss the specifics of future OFADs. Agreed?"

"Agreed. Most assuredly, agreed."

"Go in peace, Dear Lanagan. I will see you again tomorrow."

The big white dog, still carrying the physical reminders of the journey and the fights, thanked the Tree and ran to Flanders with the news. Together, they ran to Passage Wall.

A crowd followed them and murmured as they trotted. They still had no idea what an OFAD was or where Lanagan was going, but in twenty-four hours, everyone would know everything.

Lanagan stopped at one of the many green posts labeled "Departures" and placed his front paw on the transparent box. A thin red line of light scanned his hand and a voice came from the post saying, "Lanagan, you have been approved for a twenty-four hour OFAD. Please remove your collar and place it on the hook provided."

A hook appeared on the green post as the collar around Lanagan's neck simultaneously appeared. Bending his head forward, the collar slipped over his ears and a by standing great dane lifted the collar with his teeth and placed it over the peg.

"His ID tag is *purple*," exclaimed a westie.

"How could that be?" asked a small brown mixed breed.

"What Level is purple?" asked a greyhound.

The crowd noise grew louder and louder. Lanagan walked towards Passage Wall with Flanders, who wished him good luck one more time. A crow flew towards him and landed on his shoulder.

"I'll see you tomorrow Flanders," said Lanagan, and he turned from his friend and faced the wall. Taking a deep breath, he stepped forward and walked through with the crow.

CHAPTER THIRTY-ONE

When Lanagan reached the other side, he was free falling from the sky. He tumbled over and over again, spinning end over end. He tried to get his bearings but he could not. He was surrounded by nothing but air; air that rushed past him and caused his wings to whip about this way and that.

Wings?

Suddenly, everything made sense to him; he remembered. He thrust his new wings out from his body and he felt it ... flight. His body instantly leveled and straightened. His feet pulled themselves up into his downy abdomen and his tail feathers pushed backward in full extension. Lanagan was flying!

When the wonder and amazement settled into acceptance, he concentrated on the purpose of his mission. He remembered Cambium's instructions concerning the location of William's house.

To his surprise, the dog discovered that it truly was effortless to both fly and arrive at his desired destination. He discovered that a bird's thought processes are totally different than those of a cat or dog. He discovered that there was really nothing that could be considered "instinct." In reality, what actually happens to birds is simply that they embody the idea of being a bird.

It was early morning, shortly after sunrise. In the dawning light, Lanagan saw the house in the distance, albeit from a totally different perspective. Closer and closer he flew, until the letters and numbers on the license plate in the driveway became readable.

The crow landed in the maple tree in the front yard. It suddenly dawned on him that he did not know what day it was, or if William would be leaving for work and would be gone all day. He would just have to wait and see what happened; he hoped beyond all reason that Cambium had somehow considered the situation in advance.

Snow covered the ground and even capped the tops of the cedar fence posts. For many years, the fence had kept Murphy in the back yard, but now the slender slats kept nothing but memories within their borders.

The crow sat silently watching the house for two hours. No one passed by a window; no one opened a door.

It was then that Lanagan remembered what Cambium had told him about the original OFADs and their lack of success. He remembered the story of the crow modifications and realized that he was in one of the modified crow bodies right now. He decided it was time for stronger and more aggressive measures.

He had no idea how to caw, but he took a deep breath and exhaled with his beak open wide.

The sound that came out was so loud and piercing that his wings fluttered and he fell backwards out of the tree, and landed twelve feet below. He was as surprised as he was impressed by the sheer volume and tone of the caw.

He paused momentarily before taking a few steps on the frozen ground. He decided he preferred the vantage point of the tree limb, as well as the warmer surface. After a brief moment of consideration as to how to get back up on the limb, he remembered not to think and simply to do. So in an instant, the crow found himself back in the tree.

Now knowing what to expect from his voice, he proceeded more confidently with his caw. As suspected, the bold bellows from his mouth caused a stirring in the Colbert house, and at long last he saw William come to the upstairs window.

It was a moment of delightful anguish for Lanagan, but it was far too brief. William turned away as quickly as he had appeared.

The crow swallowed hard and tried to will away the dejection. He was beginning to understand why these OFAD journeys had been discontinued; the pain was indescribable.

After what seemed like hours of mournful silence, the garage door opened and William came outside, snow shovel in hand.

The crow moved his feet from side to side in a nervous dance and wondered if he should caw again. He wished he could somehow communicate with the man in the wool hat and mittens, but he knew his options were extremely limited. He feared that his actions would be misunderstood, so he just sat and watched.

When William finished clearing the driveway and the walkway, Lanagan let out a caw that nearly blew him off the branch again. He did not plan to do it, but it seemed to explode out of him. He supposed that his crow nature was more powerful than his will, after all.

The noise startled William too and he turned to look at the solitary crow in the leafless tree. Leaning on his shovel, William stared at the crow without speaking. For a moment, Lanagan thought the man understood.

"CAW" screeched the bird. "CAW, CAW."

William shifted his weight on the shovel and just stared.

"CAW, CAW, CAW" screeched Lanagan. "CAW, CAW, CAW."

William turned and went back to shoveling. After just another minute or two, the porch stairs and the walkway were finished and he went back inside the house.

Lanagan stood on the maple branch in dismay. Aside from his feeling of discouragement, he was also beginning to feel hungry. However, the idea of ingesting food common to the avian palette proved to be quite the appetite suppressant for the time being.

He was aware of his time constraints and the passing hours. He determined that it had to be a weekend because William did not leave the house. For this at least, he was grateful.

He wished that during his previous times with William, he could have been cognizant of his assignment, but he knew his wishing was a sea of regret that never ebbed.

Lanagan decided to take different OFAD positions in the yard. He flew to a fence post in the backyard, knowing that William often sat at the kitchen table having coffee and doing paper work. Unfortunately, William was neither at the table nor anywhere else in the kitchen.

The crow flew around to the front of the house again and stationed himself on a branch in a different tree. He was glad his eyesight as a crow was so keen and that he was able to see clearly from so far away.

There sat William, reclined in his easy chair, reading. Lanagan strained to read the title of the book but could not. William would periodically set down his glasses and have a sip of coffee from his large mug. And as unbelievable as it could be, Peaches was sleeping on his lap.

While Lanagan stood watching, something very profound occurred to him. When he was Murphy and living with William, he could often sense what William was saying to him, even though he did not fully understand all the words that were spoken. When he was with William, he could even sense his friend's thoughts and emotions, regardless of whether there was any conversation or not.

While standing there on the limb, Lanagan realized that upon his return to Everlife, his memories had been completed. All the words that had ever been spoken to him, and all the words that he had heard others speak when he was in the room—all these conversations came back to him. He remembered everything William had said to him; he remembered it all perfectly. Lanagan realized that his separation from William had made his memories more intense and deeper. He supposed that these recollections of words, events, and the time they had spent together had resulted in the incredible void he experienced when he returned to Everlife.

And now he regretted his inability to speak understandably. He wished he were in his other form so at least he could bark or wag his tail. There was nothing he could do to show his affection and Lanagan found this as equally devastating as the memories.

His thoughts returned to the recent conversation he had with Cambium. The Great Tree had warned him that he may feel worse when he completed his OFAD mission; that his regret might overshadow his pain. At the time, there was no way Lanagan could have predicted how he would feel; no one could. As he stood now in this tree watching his friend through the window, he realized fully that Cambium was correct.

The crow determined by his best estimate that he had about twelve hours left in his OFAD voyage. He also determined that continuing this mission would be emotionally unbearable. So, he decided to leave.

However, not quite this second. Lanagan would make one last contact with William. Or at least he would try.

Spreading his wings as wide as he could, he leapt from the branch and began flying around the outside of the house. The beat of his wings and the sensation of the wind rushing over his feathers was the most refreshing feeling he had had in the past twelve hours.

He circled the house again and again. Every time he passed by the window, he cawed as loudly as he could.

Peaches eventually got up and went to the window. The crow continued to circle the house and caw. William finally got up from his chair and went to the window. Lanagan flew to the front porch and landed on the railing.

"CAW, CAW, CAW," he screamed.

The front door opened and William stepped outside, holding his reading glasses in one hand. The crow stood there, five feet away from him, pleading with his small black eyes.

"CAW, CAW, CAW."

"What do you want?" asked William, pulling his heavy sweater over his chest.

The man and the crow looked at each other in silence. The crow tilted his head to one side. The silence continued.

Lanagan was tormented with frustration. He wanted to shout, "It's me! It's me!" but all that came out was a soft, muffled sound.

"Caw?"

Realizing the hopelessness of the situation, the crow took a few steps on the railing and then flew off the porch. William started to turn around to go back into the warm house, but something caught his eye.

Slipping his glasses over his nose, he walked to the banister and looked at the snow covered railing. There in the snow, were footprints.

Dog footprints.

The crow flew to the maple tree and turned around. William inhaled deeply and walked to the stairs. He took off his reading glasses and looked down at the snow-covered yard. There were more footprints.

He dropped his glasses into the snow and hesitantly stepped down the stairs, following the dog prints.

"CAW," said Lanagan one last time before flying away, his wings moving fervently up and down, up and down.

Hot tears began to stream down William's face as he followed the footprints to the base of the maple tree. There in the snow, he fell to his knees and wept.

CHAPTER THIRTY-TWO

Lanagan flew until he returned to the patch of sky where he had burst through a dozen hours earlier as a crow. He had no idea how he had navigated the return flight, he just flew where his wings took him.

He had never seen a bird exit the portal and had no idea what to expect. But since it happened so quickly, he really had no time to think.

His black beak and shiny black head suddenly flew into the soft, warm thickness of Passage Wall. His soaring came to an abrupt end and his body seemed to simply stop at once, as if he had flown into a cushioned net, only there was no rebound effect.

The bird floated through the portal and once it exited from the other side, it transformed into the familiar large white dog, this time void of cuts, scrapes, bruises, and bloodstains. A shiny crow stood on his back and flew away as soon as Lanagan took his first steps.

Unlike his other arrivals, no one was waiting for him at the wall. He walked over to the closest red Arrival Post and as he had done thousands of times before, he placed his hand on the translucent box for scanning.

"Welcome back, Lanagan. You have returned home early from your 24-hour OFAD mission. Please place your collar on your neck and report to Cambium." This was the first time he had ever been told to report to Cambium right away. This latest trip was certainly proving to be vastly different from all his others.

Lanagan walked past several other animals on his way to the Tree.

"Cambium, you asked to see me?"

The bark creaked and the eyes of the Tree opened.

"Ah yes, Lanagan. I see that you have returned early from your OFAD voyage. How did it go?"

"Not well, Cambium. Not well at all."

"Were you not able to see William Colbert?"

"Oh, yes. I was able to see him. But, it was definitely from a distance and very limited."

"Do you regret going, Lanagan?"

"In some ways I do. But in other ways I don't."

"Which ways outweigh the others?"

Thinking for a minute before answering, the dog replied, "I am glad I went, but when I was there, I wished I hadn't gone."

"I see. So ... are you telling me you would not want to go again?"

Lanagan got up and started pacing. Looking down while he walked, he replied, "I think you did the right thing when you discontinued the OFADs."

"It's interesting you say that Lanagan, because your OFAD has caused quite a stir. Ever since you've been gone, you've been the key topic of conversation and I can't tell you how many others have approached me, asking if they too could go on a 24 hour OFAD journey."

Stopping and looking up at the Tree, the dog spoke.

"Please forgive me for the mess I've caused. I was being selfish."

"Now, now," said Cambium, as he reached down with his limbed arm and gently patted the big white dog on the head. "Everything happens for a reason Lanagan, even here in Everlife. You must remember that your last assignment was very unique ... a Level VII assignment that ended up transforming your royal blue tag to a purple one. That has never happened before, remember that. We are all learning from your experience Lanagan, ever since its completion." After pausing and thinking for a moment, he added, "Actually, I have misspoken."

Lanagan tilted his head to the side, wondering how the Great Tree would reiterate.

"I am discovering that your assignment was not completed."

Lanagan immediately straightened his head and said in surprise, "What?"

"I have realized that none of them ever do. We were all under the impression that each assignment served a single purpose, taught a single lesson. I now believe that rather, each assignment leaves broader traces of the purpose, and deeper teachings of the lesson. Every animal that has ever crossed the path of a human ... each has changed the heart, changed the life, changed the journey ... of the other. There does not need to be a lesson or a teaching at every bend in the road, Lanagan ... there simply must be love. The animals were created to be the great balancer, to be the heart and the breath that keeps the human race on the path of love. In many ways animals are far superior to humans ... they do not know greed ... they do not know selfishness ... they do not know vengeance. However, domestic animals such as yourself do need the humans. If one considers this a fault, then this is surely your only one. The relationship between man and animal is perhaps the most perfect example of unconditional love. An animal seeks nothing, yet gives with every ounce of his being. The animal loves only for the sake of love itself. That, Lanagan, is love in its highest form."

"But what does it all mean, Cambium? Why are things the way they are? If love is such a wonderful thing, why do I hurt so badly?"

"Tell me this: If I erased the memory of your assignment with William Colbert, would you be happier?"

"No, Cambium! Please don't do it. I want to remember everything."

"Even the pain, Lanagan?"

After looking down at the grass and considering for a moment, he looked up at the consoling green eyes again and answered, "Yes, Cambium, even the pain."

"Why do you want to remember the pain?"

"The pain seems to be a reminder of the love," said Lanagan. And then after another moment, added, "Am I wrong to feel this way? Have I loved incorrectly? Is it possible to love the wrong way?"

"There is only one true form of love Lanagan, but there are many imposters. You must remember that all living things breathe with the same breath; they were all created with the same thought, with the same intention. Real love occurs between two hearts, regardless of whether those hearts are human or animal. To give love seeking nothing in return is never wrong."

"Do you think William is feeling this same pain? Did I cause it?"

"Love never causes pain, Lanagan. Loneliness does. Missing someone does. Empathy for another does. But, we must never confuse these feelings with those of love."

The big white dog looked at Cambium and felt the compassion and understanding in his eyes. The Tree smiled softly.

"Do people have souls?" asked the dog.

"Ah, Lanagan. Isn't that the age-old question? What do you think?"

"Well, if we came from the same creation ... and if we share the same breathe ... and if we are all capable of love ... I would assume that it is at least possible."

"All things are certainly possible. Quite possible indeed."

CHAPTER THIRTY-THREE

The animals in Everlife were becoming increasingly vocal about their desire to go on an OFAD mission and things had gotten to the point where Cambium needed to make a decision, one way or the other.

Lanagan was chasing Flanders in twelve inches of powdery snow when his ID tag started to flash.

"Looks like the big guy wants to see you," said Flanders.

"Have you ever noticed that he always calls when you're in the middle of something?" asked Lanagan.

It took about thirty minutes to walk from WinterQuad to the Meeting Place. Flanders walked with his friend until they were a hundred yards from the Tree.

"Are you going to wait for me?" asked Lanagan.

"Sure thing. Unless you're there for hours and I get hungry," smiled Flanders.

Lanagan approached the Tree and sat at attention at his roots.

"I'm here, Cambium."

The huge eyes opened and the Tree spoke.

"Thank you for coming, Lanagan. I need your assistance in resolving this OFAD business once and for all."

"You mean once and for all *again*."

"Yes, once and for all again. As you know, a few thousand animals have approached me, each wanting to go on an OFAD. I would like you to assist me in my decision making."

"Me? Why me?"

"Dear, Lanagan. You have the first purple tag in history. You recently returned from the first OFAD mission I have allowed in centuries, and you are the only animal in Everlife with your memory intact concerning that OFAD."

"Oh," said Lanagan, in understanding.

"There are a few options I have been considering. The most obvious is to prohibit all future OFADs."

"Again."

"Yes, again. But I am no longer inclined to repeat that decision. So, the remaining options all involve modifying future OFAD missions to make them more beneficial to everyone involved."

"Are you saying that it may be possible for me to go on another OFAD?"

"Yes, I'm saying that it may be possible. If it was, what changes would you like to see initiated?"

"Do they have to include crows?"

"Yes, I feel that is the best option. I have already negotiated with them and they have agreed to continue their involvement."

"So what other options are there?"

"We must decide on the total number of OFADs per animal and the frequency of the OFADs leaving Everlife. We must also decide on whether we want to continue the symbiotic nature of the OFAD with the crows or whether we simply want to send a crow and have them report to us upon their return."

"Are you saying that I could send a real crow to William, without going myself?"

"Yes."

"And the crow would come back to me and report what he saw?"

"Yes."

"How often could I do this?"

"How often would you want to?"

"Well, I might not even be here, right? I mean, I'll be going on assignments again and who knows how long I'll be gone."

"That is correct."

"So we'll have to schedule the OFADs for the times we're here … which means there really wouldn't be too many consecutively."

"That is correct."

"What about the assignment Level and the animals' qualifications? Would OFADs be restricted to Level VII animals?" asked Lanagan.

"That is how it has been in the past."

"What about the pain, Cambium?"

"What about it? I thought you wanted to keep it."

"I do. But, I don't want anyone else here to experience it. Is there a way you can let them keep their memories of love without the feelings of pain?"

"Dear One. Bless you for your compassion. Yes, there has always been a way to eliminate the pain ... there still is. No one feels it here except you. I think it has something to do with your purple tag."

Lanagan stared at the Tree in silence.

Cambium continued. "Whenever a four-walker —or a two-walker for that matter—passes through from the other life, they maintain their memories but never any pain."

"Are you sure?"

"Quite positive."

"Then why don't we remember our assignments after we get back to Everlife?"

"The portal currently erases the pain and sadness from every assignment as well as the memories from the lower Level assignments."

"And you have no idea why the portal didn't work on me?"

"I do not. I am so sorry, Lanagan. I know only as much as you do."

"So, I guess we should deal with the things we know, right?"

Smiling, the Tree agreed.

The dog got up and started pacing. He always did his best thinking when he paced. When he had gathered his thoughts fully, he continued.

"Cambium, I have an idea and I think it will work."

"Please share it with me."

"When someone feels genuine love for another soul it is a selfless love. There is no jealousy or anger or disappointment. In other words, because I love William Colbert, I only want what's best for him, even if that means he gets another dog to replace me."

"That is correct."

"So everyone here except me would not be upset if their former human got a replacement for them after they passed through."

"That is correct."

"Previously, when animals went on OFADs, they had completed Level VII assignments and although they felt no pain when they returned to Everlife, they did remember the assignment and they did miss their humans, right?

"Yes."

"I have an idea, Cambium. An idea that is radically different than the original OFAD but an idea that I think will prove to be beneficial to everyone."

"I'm all ears," said Cambium. Then smirking, he added, "so to speak."

"Every animal has to report to you when they return from an assignment, right?"

Cambium blinked his lids in acknowledgment.

"What if an OFAD was available to any dog or cat who felt genuine love for their person? When they report to you upon their return to Everlife, they could request that you send a crow to that person."

"Regardless of the assignment Level?"

"Regardless of the Level."

"A solitary crow, or a composite crow?" asked Cambium.

"Just a regular crow."

"And what would be the purpose of sending a crow?" asked Cambium.

"The crow will be a messenger. The crow will let the person or family know that their pet is thinking of them and still loves them."

"How will the humans know why the crow is there?"

"Oh, I think they'll figure it out eventually. Don't you?"

"I hope so."

"And we can add one more thing too. How about if any dog or cat in Everlife could approach you at any time and a request a crow be sent?"

"And the purpose of this would be?" asked Cambium.

"So the two-walkers will know they have not been forgotten."

"Will the crow report back to the requesting animal to tell them what they saw?" asked Cambium.

"Only if the animal specifically requests it."

"Well, I must admit that although your idea is not anything like I had in mind, it is most assuredly a finer idea than anything I had considered."

"I think it will work," smiled Lanagan.

"I think so too. Shall we call a meeting and tell everyone about the new OFAD policy?"

"Absolutely!"

Lanagan walked over to Flanders, whose ID tag just began flashing. Cambium had signaled all the animals by activating their tags. All over Everlife, ID tags flashed several times before remaining illuminated with their specific color. One by one, two by two, or group by group, dogs and cats came from the four Quads and from the other areas of the expanse.

"Children, friends," began Cambium, "I have called this meeting to discuss the initiation of my new OFAD policies."

The crowd cheered.

"As you know, someone among you has recently returned from a trial OFAD journey, and if this individual has no objections, I will ask him to come forward."

The multitude buzzed with curiosity and excitement. Many knew Lanagan personally but most did not. Many had heard of his purple tag or had witnessed his departure (or return) from Black River. They had heard of his crow assignment, but most had no idea what had happened. Very soon, anonymity would no longer be a part of Lanagan's life.

Animals whispered and pointed. Rows and aisles opened, and before long, the beautiful white dog once known as Murphy walked through the crowd and up to the front. Everyone clamored in conversation.

CHAPTER THIRTY-FOUR

It had been nine years since William's mother called him to wish him a Happy Birthday. He was now fifty-nine years old, and although he was instrumental in managing his father's company, he was confident that the corporation was in good hands with the young woman he had been training. He admitted only to himself and only on rare occasion that it would have been nice to have had a child to take over the family business when he retired. But he also recognized the strong possibility that if he had children, none of them may have chosen to pursue the family company anyway. So there were no regrets, which is as it should be.

Packing was more difficult than he ever would have imagined. His emotions flooded over him in a deluge of unrelenting memory. Some of the scenes were years in the making; others had come and gone in one glorious, life-changing moment.

The first items he packed were Murphy's bowls, his collar, and his leads. On top of them in the large box he stacked the toys—dozens of them, mostly gifts from Aunt Millie.

Ah, Aunt Millie. He carefully packed her coffee mugs and the special artist's rendering mug of her and Mom.

The photographs on the mantle were the most difficult items to pack, not because of their fragility but because of the faces carried within their frames. William held each of them with reverence, trying to recall the moments they captured. He missed his Father desperately; their talks, their fishing trips, the countless hours they spent at the office together. Maybe more than all those times, however, he missed the phone calls that came from out of the blue, with his Dad on the other end of the line telling his son he could sense something was troubling him.

William pondered how very unfortunate it was that life kept changing; that people we loved left us and disappeared forever. It was very difficult remembering to not pick up the phone to call someone you had routinely called for decades. It was very difficult to remember not to look for a birthday or Christmas gift for your family members who were no longer here. Yet it was so difficult to remember their voice, to remember their face clearly. How often had he sat alone at the kitchen table remembering the warmth of family laughter, the warmth of family love, and the warmth of a hand on his.

Why did the love in living seem to match proportionally to the loss at life's end?

Peaches watched as William packed each photo. Only one keepsake remained on the mantle now; the black and white photo of him and Murphy walking on that dirt road near his parent's farmhouse. Soon, William would be walking that road again, but this time he would be walking alone.

He held the treasured photograph and stared at the image of himself and the dog. A finger touched the glass over Murphy and remained there. Peaches meowed loudly and stood up, stretching his paws up William's leg.

Turning his gaze downwards, William then lowered the framed photo to show to the cat. Peaches looked at Murphy in obvious recognition and meowed again, this time very softly, as he too touched the glass over the image.

"Oh, Peaches," lamented William as he bent over to pick up the now eleven year old cat. "I wish you could tell me what you're thinking. What do you remember? Maybe you could help me make sense of all this. I know you miss him too and I know you still miss Mom terribly. I am so sorry that I'm all you have left in this world," he said as he rubbed his face against the cat's. "I hope I'm enough."

After packing his favorite photograph, William leaned back in his recliner and held Peaches to his chest.

The moving van arrived the following day to pack the rest of the house. William put the boxes of photographs and the boxes of other sentimental items in his vehicle to take to the farm himself. Backing out of the driveway for the last time was heart wrenching. The past was gone and there was no returning to it; the memories remained but only as shadows and echoes. William was tired and very, very lonely.

William put a harness around Peaches and hooked it to a lead he looped around one of the safety belts in the back seat. A litter box sat on the floor on one side and on the other sat bowls of food and water.

The first couple hours of the trip were difficult and filled William's mind with second thoughts. The little house outside of Canton symbolized a turning point in his life; it was a daily reminder of how life had changed for him after the fiasco with the patent so many years earlier. There were so many memories linked to that house; how could he just leave?

He felt he now understood how married couples felt after relocation out of state or after they outgrew their first house. So many people had expressed profound sadness when moving from one house to another, especially when children were involved. "That's where Matthew took his first step." "That's where we stood when I told you I was pregnant with Joanie." "That's the house we lived in when we had the twins." "That's where we celebrated our first Christmas together."

The latter comment was one to which he could so easily relate. Of course the memory he had was bittersweet. His first Christmas in the house was shared with Murphy and his parents, several months after Millie had passed. It was the beginning of many changes, the beginning of many endings. Yet when he looked back at it from the driver's seat heading back to Nebraska for good, the recollections of love did outweigh those of sadness.

After several more hours on the highway, William was ready to take a break. He came upon a filling station and pulled up towards the gas pumps, realizing suddenly that it was the same station he had pulled into eleven years ago, right before he met Murphy.

Coasting up to a vacant pump, his throat tightened and his eyes swelled with fresh tears. From the back seat, Peaches meowed.

William looked back and smiled at the beautiful orange and white cat. "How about we drive a little farther down the road? I don't particularly want to stop right here, OK, Boy?"

It was only ten minutes later that they came upon another gas station. Since this one held no memories in it's snare, William filled the tank and quickly went inside the convenience store for a cup of hot coffee. He decided to drive straight through, thinking it would be better for both of them to sleep in familiar surroundings, even if that rest did not come until after sunrise the following day.

Before returning to the highway, he unhooked Peaches from the belt in the back seat and placed him in the passenger seat in front.

They drove for another two hours before reaching another difficult landmark; the place where William's car had slid off the highway in the storm. My goodness, it seemed like a lifetime ago. In retrospect, it had been another life back then.

William pulled over to the shoulder of the road and shifted into park. The engine idled as his eyes stared off the side of the highway to the trees. The landscape had not changed over the years; the ground past the shoulder sloped down and you could not see where it ended. From the highway, all you could see were treetops and tree middles. Peaches looked out his window into the trees too, needing no explanation as to why they had stopped.

"This is where it all began," shared William anyway. "I wish I knew how it happened Peaches, but I don't. If I knew why, that would be even better, but I don't know that either. All I know is that on one cold, snowy day during a nasty snowstorm, your friend saved my life. Nothing after that was ever the same."

Peaches turned and looked directly at William.

"My Mother felt the same way about you, Boy. I wish you could have spent more time with her, she was such a special lady."

Peaches meowed.

"I miss her too. But, we have to go on, right? Isn't that what everyone says? You keep your memories but you have to move forward?"

William shifted back into drive and got back onto the highway.

They pulled up to the farmhouse the following morning. The windmill spun slowly in the breeze. Peaches was still asleep on the front seat when they arrived. William stared at the empty house for several minutes before stroking the cat on his back and waking him up with a whisper.

"You're home, Peaches. Wake up Buddy. You're gonna like what you see."

The cat yawned and stretched before peering over the dashboard. When he saw the house, he let out a loud meow of obvious recognition. William smiled and knew he had made the right move after all.

The movers arrived the following afternoon and William met them at the storage facility in town. He had decided several weeks ago to keep the house the way it had been for a while, and if he made any changes, he would do so gradually.

Peaches had been away for almost a decade but it took less than a day for him to fully recall every inch of the old house. By breakfast the following morning, he was sitting on the red vinyl stool next to the stove as William made coffee. After the pot was brewed and William brought a cup with him to the kitchen table, Peaches jumped to the counter and stood on the curtain rod, bringing it down with a clunk. Turning to look at William, Peaches expected reproach but saw only a smile and a look of complete understanding.

The first week was spent cleaning the barn. Peaches watched from the kitchen window, and even through the panes William could tell the cat was hollering and pleading to go outside. Knowing the guilt would be overpowering if Peaches ran away again, William debated for days whether to let the cat outside with him. Ultimately, he decided to do it. Had the cat had other company in the house, perhaps William would not have relented.

William first invested in a small collar and an ID tag, just in case.

Wearing his new collar, Peaches walked out the back door and a myriad of memories inundated his consciousness, the most prevalent being the one of his adventure many years ago. He stopped after only a few steps and looked up at William, who stood with his hands on his hips.

"After over a decade inside, three steps into the back yard is the best you can do? Oh, Peaches, you disappoint me."

The cat meowed and took a few more steps towards William, where he weaved in and out of his legs several times before being picked up and cuddled tenderly.

"Oh, Peaches. I do love you. I hope you're happy to be home again."

When the day's chores were finished, the two boys went inside for supper. William suggested he make a pot of tea to toast Aunt Millie, and surprisingly Peaches joined in the remembrance by dipping his furry hand into the cup and licking the light brown liquid from his paw. Millie had always liked her hot tea with cream and William made sure he always kept a fresh carton in the icebox, regardless of its frequency of use.

When William arrived at the homestead, he kept an appointment book to document his daily activities and putative schedule, as his father had done before him. And like his father, after a couple months of this nonsense, he too discarded the tiresome book to a desk drawer.

He slept in the guestroom where he and Murphy had slept when they visited. More often than not, his dreams carried him to a place of laughter and joy, contentment and love. Of course most of these dreams involved a big white dog.

William placed his photographs on the kitchen counter in-between the back door and the table. Since Peaches was still in the habit of 'opening' the curtains every morning, the framed pictures needed to sit a couple feet out from the wall, lest they hit the floor in the morning along with the curtains. When William sat at the table, he indefinitely found himself staring at those photographs of his family, which of course included his beloved dog.

Over one corner of the picture of a windblown Murphy in the snowstorm, William had hung the red "HERO" ribbon. It had faded over the years, and every month or so he would hang the red ribbon over a different frame. It seemed to grow more sentimental to him with each passing year.

He wondered what had become of those people saved by "his" dog that fateful day so very long ago. He wondered if they ever thought of Murphy during the course of their days or if they ever returned to the site on the highway where they had come so close to falling off the bridge. He wondered if any of those folks pondered the unsettling questions that had plagued William since that day: Why was I saved? What would have happened to my family had I been killed? Have I changed because of that event? Did the course of my life change because of that day? Have I made a difference in the lives of others? And of course the most prevalent question of them all: Did it all happen for a reason?

Sometimes William despised being a thinker. If his self-examination and hypothetical questions did not drive him to the brink of madness, at times he seemed to travel dangerously close to that border.

Murphy's leather collar sat reverently on the counter too, at the base of one of his photographs. His ID tag and his rabies tag hung from the metal ring, as well as the inscribed brass pendant Murphy had received outside the hospital eleven years previously. William held the tag and read the words etched so many years ago: "Best friend to William Colbert."

He added to his photograph collection occasionally with old photos of his parents or Millie, as well as recent photos of Peaches. The latest shot was that of the cat rubbing his cheek against the corner of a photo of Katie.

CHAPTER THIRTY-FIVE

William flew back to Ohio for meetings at ColPro every couple of months, sometimes more frequently. He was not ready to totally abandon the ship, like his father who never seemed to get bored at the farmhouse. On this upcoming trip to Canton, he would be meeting with the general manager he had been training for the past four years. It seemed the time was indeed approaching for William to hand over the reigns entirely.

Liz, the ever-faithful secretary that had served his father and him for forty years, had retired three years ago. Sitting at her desk was an equally efficient and conscientious assistant named Theresa. William hired her on the spot when she came to fill out the application for the position, apologizing for the small dog under her arm, saying it was too hot to leave him in her vehicle while she completed the forms. She had already proven to be as vital and valued as Liz had been for so long.

Everyone in the office adored William and it was with much sincerity that they welcomed him for these monthly meetings. Those who had been with the company for a long time remembered the days when he walked around with his faithful dog at his side. Many in the office had offered their boss a puppy over the years, many times actually, but William had always politely refused. Now they thought perhaps he was ready for another companion, so they conspired over the past several weeks and placed a deposit with a breeder towards the purchase of a samoyed puppy. William heard of the plan through an anonymous informant, and made it a point to mention in a recent memo that he and Peaches were not ready for a roommate.

He arrived at the office carrying a soft-sided carry kennel, in which of course was Peaches. No one else used William's old office and it remained untouched and unchanged for his short-term use when he was in town. There was one addition to the office, however: a litter box, which sat in the back corner of the room.

There were times when William still looked under his desk expecting to see Murphy there. Was it sanguine hope or simply the steadfast desperation of a lonely heart? Regardless, he often leaned back in his chair and rested his wanting gaze toward the emptiness under his desk wondering how he could possibly miss a dog so ardently.

A knock on his office door jarred his thoughts and he returned to the present moment.

"Come in," he answered.

A woman walked in smiling and confident as she approached his desk. He walked around to greet her, and instead of a traditional handshake they exchanged a friendly hug.

"Mr. Colbert, it's so good to see you."

"How is my understudy doing today?"

"Just great, thanks."

"Theresa tells me you brought someone with you today who will be sitting in on our meeting?"

"Only if it's OK with you."

"I trust your judgment. Who is this mystery person?"

"My Dad, Mr. Colbert."

"Your Dad? What a pleasant surprise. Where is he?"

"He's down the hall in my office. Do you want me to go get him?"

"Absolutely!"

The cheerful woman left his office and William walked back around his desk and stood facing the window. He looked outside and thought about all the changes he had seen over the years from this office. Buildings were torn down and others rebuilt. Streets were widened and trees had grown tall. People still walked the streets all day long and he still wondered where they were all going all the time.

A courteous knock on the already open office door alerted William that someone was entering. He turned around and in walked his young associate, hand in hand with her Dad, Rusty Morgan.

"It's so good to see you," said William as he walked over to Rusty who greeted him with an enormous bear hug.

"How's business?" asked Rusty.

"I don't know. I hope it's good enough to keep my paychecks coming," sneered William, smiling. "I suppose your daughter is planning on filling us in today."

Rusty turned to Donna, who assured him business was just fine.

"Phew, that's a relief," said Rusty to his daughter. "William and I have a lot of great plans for the money you're making for us."

Donna had her father's ever present smile and optimism, as well as Thomas Colbert's intuition and character. She refused to compromise her ideals or her goals and she was the perfect replacement for William in the company. He knew that when he finally retired completely, his father's corporation would be left in very qualified, capable hands.

Two days later, William and Peaches flew back home. As the plane taxied to the gate, William reflected on how incredibly wonderfully everything had turned out after all. The patent he had so fervently fought for—and lost—a dozen years ago, had ultimately been the means by which his life took on an entirely new course. And Rusty, the man who once had been his adversary, had become his closest friend. Hindsight was certainly a very ironic mentor.

Peaches was relieved to see William retrieve him in the baggage claim area and even happier to see the yellow farmhouse some time later. William too, felt the upwelling of repose when he pulled up to the fence.

CHAPTER THIRTY-SIX

In Everlife, things continued as they always had. Animals went away, animals returned. Debates raged and discussions continued. Cambium was asleep and three animals stood in the distance to the far right side of the Tree. One snickered and giggled as he tried to coerce the others into participating in his plan.

"I don't think he'll know we're there if we sneak up from the side," said the cocker spaniel.

"Oh, I don't know," said the bob-tailed cat. "We don't know for sure that he ever even goes to sleep. Just because his face is hidden doesn't mean his ears don't work."

"He doesn't have any ears," casually mentioned the border collie.

"You know, I never considered that," said the cat.

"I never did either," added the spaniel. "How does he hear if he doesn't have ears? Have you ever seen any ears come out of the bark when the rest of his face emerges?"

"Maybe he just has holes on the sides," suggested the cat.

"I've never seen any holes," said the border collie.

"Regardless," said the spaniel impatiently, "I say we should do it. The next Gathering is tomorrow morning ... who's with me?"

"I don't know," repeated the bob-tailed cat.

"Oh, come on. Don't be such a party pooper," said the spaniel.

"I'm in!" declared the border collie.

"Good!" said the spaniel, and the two dogs walked away whispering and giggling, leaving the cat behind.

The next morning, while the animals sat in front of the Tree waiting for the Gathering to begin, there was a tremendous amount of pointing and staring. Some of the animals trembled with fear, wondering how Cambium would respond.

Even Miss Mallory was afraid and did very little jumping around and even less talking. This was very strange indeed, especially for the normally prattling hen. When it was ultimately time for the meeting to begin, she hesitantly and in a low voice sputtered, "Uh … everyone's here, Cambium."

Loud creaking was heard across the plush meadow as two cracks appeared as eye slits in the massive trunk. Then the ample nose pushed out from the thick wood, then the mouth. Everyone stared in silence as the large green eyes appeared and looked out over the crowd.

A small dog in the front row covered his mouth with his paw. His body shook and convulsed. He finally fell to the ground and his hand dropped from his muzzle. His mouth opened and the laughter he had tried so hard to contain burst from his throat and he rolled in the grass uncontrollably.

His outburst spread like wildfire to the other animals in the front row, then to those in the second and third rows. Before long, most of the animals present at the Gathering were holding their stomachs and shrieking in pure delight. Dogs and cats rolled about and fell onto each other, collapsing to the ground. Looking out over the expanse, one could see tens of thousands of furry legs sticking up in the air, shaking in rhythmic time with the belly laughs from the animals on the ground.

Even Miss Mallory, who had a reputation for propriety and reticence, raised her red wings to her beak and laughed behind them.

"What is going on?" demanded Cambium.

The tiny hen shook her head back and forth, back and forth, unable to speak because of the laughter.

The Tree lifted a branched arm to his face. What was this stuck to his bark?

"Miss Mallory," croaked Cambium. "Fetch me a looking glass. Please."

The hen fluttered away and returned shortly thereafter with a mirror, which was lifted post haste by the Tree and held in front of his face. The majestic, noble Tree had long yellow hair flowing down from his brow on either side. Above his eyes was a pink hat with flowers around the rim. On the sides of his face where his ears should have been were bright pink and green earrings. A few feet under his mouth was a huge yellow bow.

He slowly and deliberately removed the blonde hair and bright accessories from his face and set them gently on the grass. When he had finished—and after another final look in the mirror—Cambium cleared his throat.

"I am certainly pleased to have provided so much entertainment this morning. Whom shall I thank for assisting me?"

The cocker spaniel stepped forward, still smirking and looking about to see if anyone was still giggling. The crowd grew quieter and eventually became totally silent.

"Ah ... Mingo," said Cambium. "I should have known."

"No harm intended, Miss," laughed the spaniel, his comment causing everyone to become quite giddy again.

The Tree held his arms out in front of him, gesturing for the crowd to be quiet. The animals obliged.

"I know, Mingo," said Cambium. "No offense taken." And again he cleared his throat.

"Well, you have all had a large helping of laughter this morning ... at my expense, I might add. Shall we move on to more pressing matters now?"

"Miss Malory. Will you please escort our returning friends so we may welcome and commend them?"

The red hen respectfully and dutifully untied the red velvet ribbon and a procession of dogs and cats paraded from their waiting area to the front of Cambium and into the aisles and crowd. Howls and loud meows rang from the multitude and pads stomped on the Earth in applause.

"Welcome back home one and all, welcome back. It is an honor to greet you all again and to thank you for the recent contributions you have made. The world is a different place because of your antecedent life, and the people you met along your journey have been changed as well. You have learned and you have discovered and you may have new questions to ponder. Use your tarrying time now to reflect and contemplate. Share your experiences and gained wisdom with others and glean from theirs. Use this time to prepare your hearts and minds for your next assignment and don't forget to *play!* We have three upcoming special events scheduled during your lacuna, I encourage you to sign up and participate in one or more of them."

Shall we begin?" asked Cambium.

And as had occurred once a month since the beginning of time, another Gathering began. A warm breeze suddenly came in from the west and Cambium's branches and leaves moved to and fro, to and fro. When the swaying ceased, tiny bright speckles appeared within the green leaves and continued to grow in both size and brilliance. Soon thousands of flat, shiny white crystal papers hung from the branches like flattened water drops from a rainbow.

His large hand-like branch reached upward and grabbed the first sheet.

"I have a Level V assignment for a canine. Species modification is acceptable. The assignment is long term and open to anyone qualified for Level V or higher."

Many other glistening sheets shook on the tree and Cambium reached up and grabbed them as they glided into his hands.

"It appears I have quite a few Level V assignments available today."

Flanders and Lanagan nodded to each other and walked together towards the front. Lanagan then stopped suddenly and Flanders turned to look at him. It was clear to Flanders that his friend was not ready for another assignment just yet, so the black dog smiled in understanding and continued forward alone. A hundred or more other dogs and cats sat with Flanders in front of Cambium.

"Thank you all for your interest in these positions, I will distribute them as I see fit."

He read each of them silently and then placed them in the mouths of the animals and they walked off toward the processing area to the applause of the crowd. One of the dogs holding an assignment sheet was Flanders.

Some of the departing animals were scheduled to leave that same day and others would be leaving sometime before the next Gathering. Unfortunately for Lanagan, Flanders was scheduled to leave the following day.

He met his friend near Passage Wall as Flanders was approaching a red Departure Post.

"Hey Buddy," said Flanders, "Are you gonna be OK?"

"Sure," said Lanagan, smiling. "I'm not quite ready to go again."

"Is your ID tag still purple?"

Lanagan lifted his neck and Flanders bent down to look. There beneath the layers of white was the glowing tag.

"How come yours isn't invisible?" asked Flanders.

"No one knows."

"Have you asked Cambium about it?"

"He's never seen a purple tag before, let alone one that stays visible all the time. He said the color of mine is even getting deeper."

"What do you think it means?"

Shaking his head, Lanagan replied that he had no idea.

CHAPTER THIRTY-SEVEN

Winter came wrathfully, with blizzard after blizzard and record low temperatures. William had heeded the Farmer's Almanac prediction for a nasty winter and stocked both the freezer and the pantry prior to the first major storm of the season. As often happened in the Midwest, this snowstorm had lasted for days and temperatures remained below zero.

William stared at the photographs lining the kitchen counter. He lifted one of them and looked at it tenderly. The face in the photograph stared back at him; the face of Murphy. Was it really possible that this photo had been taken twenty-five years ago?

The picture frames filled the entire counter now, even up to the wall next to the curtains. Peaches' collar and tag hung from the corner of a photo of him, and some of his favorite toys sat interspersed between the other pictures of the impressive cat.

William set the photo of Murphy back down on the counter and walked slowly down the hall to the closet, using his cane for support and balance. When he came back into the kitchen some time later, he was wearing lined gray wool slacks, a heavy winter coat, and snow boots.

Once again, he lifted the photograph and grabbed Murphy's collar from beneath it.

"Hey, Boy. Let's go for a walk," he said.

He grasped the collar firmly in his left hand and held his walking cane with his right. Carefully down the porch steps he walked; the windmill whining softly as it spun in the cold air. He slowly walked past the front yard and out onto the snow covered dirt road, the bottom of the cane disappearing in the deep snow with each step.

Visibility was poor and the barbed wire fencing that bordered the dirt road was ice-covered and invisible. If it were not for the old fence posts sticking through the snow, William would have no idea where the street was. He looked down at Murphy's collar; once, his dog walked beside him on this very road.

It became increasingly difficult to walk and soon it became difficult to breathe. The air was so cold and his feet were so heavy.

"Murphy," he whispered. "I miss you so much."

He took another step forward, his foot barely clearing the top of the new snow. When he lifted the walking stick to place it down ahead of him, his vision blurred and the fence posts bordering the old dirt road disappeared into nothingness. William fell into the snow, his hand still clutching Murphy's leather collar.

CHAPTER THIRTY-EIGHT

The large black dog set his paw on the transparent box and the red light scanned his pad. The voice from the post said, "Flanders, you are approved for departure for this Level V assignment. Please place your collar on the peg before proceeding to Passage Wall."

The dog bent his head forward and the translucent collar appeared, with a light blue tag attached. Lanagan grabbed the color with his teeth and flung it up onto the green peg.

"I'll see you when I get back," said Flanders, and he and Lanagan rubbed snouts and necks.

"I'll be here," said Lanagan, and he watched his friend turn and walk towards the wall.

Dogs and cats were departing as well as arriving all along the wall. A small calico cat emerged from the portal and transformed into a Pekinese. A beagle emerged from the wall and transformed into a Siamese cat.

Flanders turned around one last time before walking through, and Lanagan smiled a sad good-bye. Flanders faced forward again and his nose penetrated the viscous barrier.

Suddenly, the semi-fluid wall became solid and hard. All rippling ceased. The color changed from a milky blue translucency to a dark gray. Flanders' nose and face were pushed backwards and no one was allowed to enter or exit.

The portal had closed.

In an instant, the pale blue sky that had always enveloped this part of Everlife turned to a darker shade of blue, with streaks of lavender, purple, and bronze. Millions of shiny, metallic stars flew through the air, some with tails like comets. Bands and waves of multi-colored light flashed and flowed in the distance like the aurora borealis. Some of the animals were frightened; all were totally amazed and bewildered. The sky crackled and popped and sparks fell from above.

The animals stared in wonder. None had ever seen such a spectacle.

Soon, horizontal lightning pierced the sky. The colored lights grew brighter. Flanders and Lanagan had to shout to one another to be heard over the noise.

"Let's go ask Cambium what's going on," yelled Flanders.

Others nearby agreed with that idea and soon there were hundreds of animals running towards the Tree.

"What's going on?" Lanagan shouted up to Cambium.

"I have no idea," shouted Cambium.

Everyone continued looking up and all around. The sky remained a deep blue and purple backdrop and the streaks changed their contrasting colors and hues against it, modulating and pulsing with the sounds of the lightning bursts.

Then, just as suddenly as it had all begun, the colors and noises ebbed. The streaking bolts that filled the sky diminished into horizontal sparks and the dark red and orange splashes became pink and yellow washes of tint. Every head was turned upwards in anticipation of another extravagant display.

Suddenly, a breeze came in from the west, a warm delicate wind that seemed to push the indigo and violet from the sky. The animals turned toward the wind and watched the sky fill with low rolling billows of cloud-like mist that moved slowly toward them in puffs of pastel wisps.

The westward sky became effervescent with light. A smoky rose-colored wall appeared in the far distance. It glistened and sparkled with diamonds of white and pink light. The base was indistinct and it was impossible to tell where the wall began and where the flat ground ended. The faint pink melted into silver, which flowed into blue and purple, and then back to rose. Then, the fainter colors returned and gave way to other colors, each amazing and wondrous.

Shooting stars flew eastward and fell to the ground far behind the massive crowd. A rumbling began, initially so gentle that only a few noticed. Then many more of the animals looked down at their feet and around where they stood. The quaking then ceased.

The animals near the western side of the Meeting Place heard a sound coming from the billows and cocked their heads to listen more intently.

"Eeeeeeee" came the faint noise. "Eeeeeeee."

A few more animals heard it.

"Errrrrrr………..errrrrrrrr."

Soon, everyone was facing westward, listening for the sounds and watching the colored clouds pass over their heads. Then the sounds stopped and there was total silence.

Eventually another muffled noise came from the distance. Everyone began walking towards the mist like a hesitant and wary herd. Tens of thousands of dogs and cats moved almost as one enormous mass of ears and tails and furred hands and furred feet, all towards the pastel colored haze.

Suddenly the ground shook with the vigor and intensity of an Earthquake. Then the air echoed with the loudest, most earsplitting sounds ever heard in Everlife.

The animals froze and turned towards the deafening noise. The ground lifted and heaved, throwing some animals twenty or thirty feet in the air and sending others sprawling to the grass. Those farther from the seism steadied themselves to keep from falling.

The animals turned towards the source of the massive quaking and upheavals; all eyes turned towards Cambium.

The Tree leaned and stretched, leaned and stretched. He straightened for a moment or two and then once again leaned and stretched. His face grimaced with strain and exertion as he pulled with every fiber of strength he could summon. Some feared he would topple over. Again and again he leaned and stretched, leaned and stretched.

Green grass and dark, rich soil sprayed into the air as enormous roots snapped and released themselves from the depths. As each root tore from the ground, it lifted large sections of landscape with it, sending more animals flying. Those closest to the Tree had to cover their ears, as the snapping and cracking sounds were overwhelming.

Cambium leaned and extended, leaned and extended, and one by one he pulled his primary roots up from the depths. He discovered that the smaller ones were quite easily broken. Finally the Tree was loosed from his rhizome shackles and he took a step.

"I didn't know you could move," said Mingo in amazement.

"I didn't know either!" laughed Cambium, as he took another step, then another, toward the mist.

The animals began running alongside the Tree, whose long strides proved to be quite impressive. When Cambium was within one hundred yards of the rosy haze, he stopped and everyone else stopped with him. Raising his arms, he addressed the crowd.

"Inhabitants of Everlife. You are about to witness an event that I have only heard of in legend. Until this very moment, even I did not believe the story could be true. Now that I see the mist to the west, I understand."

He looked out at the multitude of animals and continued with a gentle smile.

"As you know, our land of Everlife is separate from the other land, which is inhabited by humans. Prior to today, I did not believe the story I was told many centuries ago. I had accepted it as fable, but now I know I was wrong."

"A soul has recently emerged from Passage Wall far, far from our portion of Everlife. However, this particular soul made a very unique request upon exiting the portal."

Once again, muffled sounds came through the mist, reverberating as they floated through the air. Everyone turned to watch, staring again in utter silence and amazement, even Cambium.

"Mmmmmerrrrr," came the low horn-like sound.

"Eeeeeeeee," it echoed.

The fog began changing color, turning from dusty rose to the palest blue imaginable. Every time a sound traveled through it, the mist would pulsate and billow.

"Mmmmmmmmerrrrr," came the call again and the mist swelled.

"Eeeeeeeee," rang the dull horn-like retort and the pale blue sky darkened slightly.

As always, Miss Mallory was the first to call attention to the shadow emerging from deep within the blue mist.

"Look, look," she cried. "Something is coming through."

"Or some*one*," added Cambium softly.

"Mmmmmmmmeeerrrrrrr," said the faint low voice.

"Phhhhhhhheeeeeee," added the echo.

Flanders was the first to understand. He turned to his friend, who apparently understood it all too.

"The voice is calling for *you*," said Flanders.

"Mmmmuuurrrrrrpphhhhhhyyyyyyy," came the voice again, this time more clearly.

The shadow grew more defined as it approached. The mist changed color again too, becoming bluer.

"Murrrrphyyyyyyy," said the shadow.

This time everyone else heard it too, including Cambium.

The animals near Lanagan stepped away from him, leaving him centered with Flanders inside a twenty-foot circle. Then the animals between the circle and the cloudy wall stepped back to form a wide aisle.

The blue fog grew brighter and darker and the shadowy figure became more clearly outlined. He was still deep within the fog, but everyone could tell that the approaching form was a two-walker, it was a man. He was well into his seventies and dressed in a winter coat and mittens. He walked very slowly with the aid of a wooden cane, and he was holding something in his hand.

The mist rolled gently, like wooly clouds that slowly changed their shape and form. Each cloud-like puff transposed with a deeper blue in its center, and the new color slowly worked its away outward. As the old man came closer to the edge of the fog, the middle of each cloud turned lavender and then purple.

He lifted his cane with each small step, putting it down again only a short distance ahead of where it had previously set. He stopped when he came close to the end of the misty wall and looked directly ahead at the solitary dog standing in the middle of the broad aisle. "Murphy," he said.

The dog tilted his head to the side. No one made a sound.

The old man lifted his walking cane from the ground and extended it forward into the divide. As each inch of it crossed the barrier, it dissolved into the air on the other side.

The man took a step through the wall with his snow-covered boot, and as his foot crossed into Everlife, the boot was transformed into a well-worn, maroon shoe with rawhide ties. The gray wool slacks melted instantly into faded blue denim.

Murphy turned to Cambium, who smiled tenderly.

The elderly man lifted his other foot and closed his eyes as he slowly stepped across the divide. His heel touched down on the other side and his body emerged, changing as it exited. To the amazement of everyone watching, his heavy winter jacket dissolved into the air like his boot and slacks had done, and was transformed to an old navy blue shirt.

The snowy hat faded into nothingness and the sparse gray hair bordering the aged baldhead turned dark and once again covered his scalp. The silver framed eyeglasses fell away and the old man's spotted and wrinkled skin firmed and was restored to a youthful texture and tone.

The visitor leaned forward, extending his left hand. Murphy's leather collar fell to the ground.

"Hey Boy," said the man.

Lanagan lunged forward, running as fast as he could, leaping into the arms of William Colbert.

The man fell backwards onto the plush grass and laughed heartily as the dog lapped his face and hands. Lanagan's tail wagged wildly.

When their greeting was finally completed and their penned up emotions were released, William got to his feet, and with Lanagan at his side, began to survey the region.

Every eye was fixed on the reunited friends and Lanagan gently grabbed William's hand between his teeth and escorted him to Cambium.

"You must be William Colbert. We have all heard so much about you. My name is Cambium and on behalf of all of us, I bid you welcome to Everlife."

Looking around and smiling, William replied, "So, I guess this place really does exist."

"It most certainly does, Mr. Colbert," said Cambium.

William bent down and hugged Lanagan around the neck.

"I waited a long time to see you again," said the man.

"Perhaps one day," said Cambium, "Lanagan will tell you all that he went through to see *you* again."

"Lanagan?" asked William.

"His given name," said the Tree. "The name he is known by here."

William looked at the dog and smiled. "So, it's *Lanagan* Murphy, is it Boy?"

The dog looked at Cambium and then back at William, and barked.

"It's OK, Lanagan," said the Tree. "You may speak to your friend."

"You mean you can *talk?*" asked William.

The white dog smiled and shook his head yes, still reluctant to finally speak to William.

"It's going to be so good to be able to really talk to you!" said William with a broad smile.

"And even better for me," spoke Lanagan, finally in reply.

"So what happens now?" asked William.

"I have no idea," replied Lanagan, who looked up at Cambium, hoping for an answer.

With as much empathy as the Tree could muster, Cambium offered a response.

"I am truly sorry Lanagan, but William cannot stay in this portion of Everlife."

Whispers and grumbles were muttered in every direction. Lanagan shook his head in absolute disbelief.

"WHAT? He can't stay here?" blurted Lanagan, still in shock.

William took a step closer to the dog and asked Cambium, "Then where can we go?"

"I am afraid I do not know," answered the Tree. "The two of you have certainly managed to disrupt the status quo and bend just about every rule ever set forth."

All the animals listened attentively, anxious for Cambium to continue.

"Things will never be the same," said the Tree, pointing a wooden finger at Lanagan, "because of *you.*"

The big white dog looked up at William, who returned his compassionate gaze.

A warm gentle breeze passed over the multitude of animals, as well as through Cambium's branches. A soft tweeting sounded through the balmy wind and everyone turned toward the west once again.

A small sparrow flew toward the massive Tree, and as it approached, a white tubular object was seen in its tiny beak. The bird came to land on a low limb and Cambium carefully reached a hand upward to remove the item from the bird's mouth.

A delicate piece of shiny purple ribbon held the rolled parchment. With amble fingers, the Tree untied the bow and opened the letter.

Whispers and murmurs of speculation resounded through the crowd once again. Dogs and cats leaned closer to one another sharing guesses as to what was written on the scroll. William sat down beside Lanagan on the thick grass and wrapped an arm around his shoulders. Those nearby stepped closer to the man and the white dog in a gesture of support.

Clearing his throat and lowering the vellum, Cambium raised his eyes and looked at Lanagan, and then at William. He finally spoke.

"As I suspected, William cannot remain in this portion of Everlife."

Once again, low talk spread throughout the expanse.

"However," he continued, "it appears that Lanagan may accompany his friend to the *other* portion of Everlife."

More prattle spread through the acreage, this time much louder. William smiled a wide, happy smile.

Flanders looked at Lanagan, then at William, and then at the great Tree.

"No, Cambium. I don't want him to leave." Looking back at his friend, Flanders pleaded, "Please, Lanagan. Don't go."

The flurry of emotions and confusion flooding Lanagan was overwhelming. He stepped away from William's embrace and walked closer to the Tree.

"If I go with William, will it be forever?" asked Lanagan.

"Yes. And no," answered Cambium. "It appears that the great divide between our section here and the other," he said, pointing westward towards the smoky mist, "has been altered ... forever."

"What does that mean?" asked the dog.

"It means that there is no longer a barrier separating the humans and the animals."

As the Tree spoke, the crowd once again whispered and muttered in low voices. Looking at Lanagan, Cambium continued.

"It means that you may go with William *and* that you may also return to us here whenever you like."

Flanders beamed. All the other animals grew louder and more excited.

"What about my future assignments?" asked Lanagan.

"There will be no more assignments for you."

Flanders looked at his friend and then back up to the Tree.

"But why?" asked Lanagan.

"That decision was not mine to make," replied Cambium. "I would presume however, that your purple tag and the recent request of William had something to do with it."

Lanagan took three steps backwards and returned to William's side.

"You must go with William now," said Cambium. "I do not know how or when you will return to us, but I am sure I speak for everyone here when I say we all will be anxious to see you again and hear about your journey."

Flanders stepped toward his friend and the two dogs stood face to face.

"Don't be gone too long," said Flanders.

"You'll never get rid of me," smiled Lanagan. "Anyway, you were just about to head off on your next assignment, remember?"

"Oh yeah," said Flanders. "I did forget. I'm going back as a puppy this time. Should be fun!"

"I'm sure it will be," said Lanagan, assuredly.

Flanders looked up at William. "Take good care of my friend," said the black dog.

"You know I will," smiled William.

The crowd of animals around the white dog stepped backwards and sideways to once again create a path for him. After a long and deliberate inhale, Lanagan turned towards the mist and slowly walked with William.

The Gathering Place was silent and everyone watched as the two friends walked into the distance, closer and closer to the foggy divider. Lanagan turned around several times to see Flanders at the far end of the path, sitting motionless as he watched his best friend leave him once again.

When William stopped suddenly and turned, some dogs and cats wondered if he had changed his mind about taking Lanagan with him. The man bent down and whispered to the dog, and then ran back up the aisle towards Cambium.

"Sir," began William, somewhat out of breath. "I was wondering if I may take someone else with Murphy and me."

"Someone *else?*"

"Yes, Sir. Is Peaches here?"

The crowd buzzed.

"Peaches?" replied Cambium to the man. Then, looking out into the crowd, the Tree bellowed, "Is there a Peaches here?"

William too, turned his gaze to the enormous crowd and looked for the cat. The crowd rustled and murmured.

"Peaches!" called Cambium again. "Is there anyone here once known as Peaches?"

Everyone desperately wanted to know who this mystery animal was. Some stood on tiptoes to survey the grounds. Dogs stretched their necks high and cats strained to see over the dogs. Off in the distance towards Passage Wall, the murmurs grew louder.

Soon a few chuckles could be heard amidst the muffled conversations. As had occurred a few minutes earlier, animals stepped backwards, forwards and sideways to create an aisle, which ran from Passage Wall all the way to where William Colbert stood. There at the far opposite end of the pathway, stood a rather embarrassed orange and white cat.

Snickers and giggles spread over the massive audience.

"Cimmaron? Cimmaron is Peaches?" whispered a Dalmatian.

"I can't believe it!" laughed a black and tan cat.

The jeers and laughter grew louder and Cambium decided to squelch the mob's verbal attacks before any fur flew, so to speak. The crowd calmed and Cimmaron held his head and his tail high as he walked towards Cambium.

William stooped down as the big male cat approached. "Hey, Boy. It's good to see you again," said William as the cat got closer. "Can you talk too?"

Rolling his eyes in true Cimmaron fashion, the cat replied, "Of course I can talk. And it's good to see you too, by the way."

William gently lifted the cat to his shoulder and leaned his head sideways to hug him. Then, turning to face the Tree again, William spoke.

"Cambium, Sir. May I bring Peaches with us? I know someone who would love to see him again."

"Your mother?" asked Cambium.

"Yes, my mother."

"Cimmaron, would you like to go with William and Lanagan?"

"Yes, I would," answered the cat, and then added as if an afterthought, "And the name is *Peaches*."

The big white dog walked towards William and the orange and white cat, and then the three of them walked together towards the mysterious mist, Peaches still over the man's shoulder. As they walked, all eyes—including Cambium's—watched in amazement and wonder.

Flanders was very accustomed to bidding his friend farewell, but also to eventually welcoming his friend home again. This time things were very different, and as it is with most people, Flanders felt very apprehensive and uncertain about how things would work out.

Lanagan began to step hesitantly and then stopped altogether.

"William. There's something I need to tell you," said the dog.

"Murph? What is it?"

"You may not want to take me with you after I tell you," lamented Lanagan.

The expression on William's face went from blissful to highly concerned within seconds.

The dog continued.

"Remember that time we went camping with Peaches out at the Lake?"

"Sure," said William.

"Remember that plate of hot dogs you left on the picnic table while the charcoals were heating?"

"Yes, I remember," answered William.

"Well ..." began the dog.

"You stole one," finished William.

Lanagan's eyes opened wide and he jaw dropped down in an expression of disbelief.

"How did you know?" asked the shocked dog.

"Because I counted them," smiled William.

"You *counted* them?" repeated Lanagan.

William laughed heartily. Peaches rolled his eyes.

"Can we get on with this?" asked the annoyed cat.

The three of them continued forward towards the mist. When they reached the divide, they all turned to take one more long look at the Gathering Place and at Cambium. Although Lanagan had been assured he could return here, both he and Cimmaron had their reservations and wondered what their lives would be like from this moment forward.

William was the first to step into the warm mist and as he did, the cat on his shoulder closed his eyes tightly. Lanagan stepped forward in anxious anticipation of seeing the other side. Within moments, the three of them vanished into the barrier, which once again returned to its previous murky, colorless wall of fog.

Simultaneously, the strange pinks, purples, and yellows disappeared from the sparkling sky of Everlife and the blue skies of old returned, laced with the traditional white puffy clouds. The areas of upturned soil, grass, and vegetation drifted, slid and fell back into place, and soon the Gathering Place was perfect again.

CHAPTER THIRTY-NINE

Rain fell on the windshield of the red truck as it drove down the dirt road. The man driving had been traveling for three days and it had been raining heavily during most of his trip. He was returning to his hometown and soon he would be there. Finally.

As he approached the outskirts of town, he noticed all the changes and all the construction that had taken place during his absence. The old filling station had been torn down and a new twenty-four hour convenience store with new gas pumps stood in its place. Shopping centers had been built all along the highway and even apartments and new office buildings had sprung up. It was amazing to see all the changes, and ironically, seeing them this first time was enough to begin to erase the mental images he had carried since childhood.

The wiper blades continued pushing water off the window as the truck drove through town. Thankfully, things looked more like they used to once he left the city limits. With a sense of relief as well as familiarity, the man began to see the landmark buildings and the farmhouses of his youth.

In the passenger seat to his right slept a little boy, now two months old. Unlike the red-headed driver, the youngster had dark hair and dark eyes. Every once in a while, the man would look over and smile as he watched the little one sleeping.

The truck slowed as the man looked ahead, expecting to see something recognizable from his past. Soon a large sand colored house with teal shutters appeared on the right, and the man lifted his foot from the gas pedal, allowing his truck to coast as it slowly crept by Millie Wilson's beautiful homestead.

Everything was exactly the same, except maybe the trees were larger. Everything on the property had been pruned and well taken care of over the years. The bushes surrounding the wrap-around porch had either been trimmed back every year or had been replaced, as they were identical to the shrubs that had been there over two decades ago. Recently planted flowers bordered the walkway and filled large clay pots. They looked exactly like those that grew here when the man was a boy.

A high chain link fence now enclosed the property to the east of the house, but aside from that, the house was exactly how he remembered it.

Except for the sign.

In the front yard, a large white wooden sign swung between two decorative posts. The black glossy letters had been painstakingly painted and although the words were simple ones, their meaning was profound.

MURPHY'S
Home for Abused and Unwanted
Animals
ALL ARE WELCOME

The red-headed man passed the house and saw some animals in the back yard: a horse, several dogs, and a llama. A few cats were walking around there too. Soon there would be many other animals.

The man smiled and reached his hand over to touch the dark haired boy. A small groaning whine came from the passenger seat.

"Go back to sleep. We're not quite there yet," whispered the man softly.

The red truck gained speed and reached a black-topped road again. Ten minutes later, it pulled into the driveway of another large farmhouse; this one not as luxurious as the other, but more familiar to the man.

Everything here was just as he had remembered it. A large but merely decorative windmill stood in the front yard. The man had been to this house on days when the blades spun fleetly and also when the windmill sat motionless, like today.

The house was pale yellow with white trim, and three steps led up to the front porch, where a wooden swing still hung. A white metal screen door hung where a wooden green once hung many years ago, and the only other difference he noticed were the new signposts in the front yard.

The two posts had been cemented in place and a 4" x 4" beam with heavy iron screw eyes imbedded in the underside awaited the hanging of the new sign. As in Millie's front yard, these posts were painted a glossy white.

He turned off the engine and the only sound remaining was the pelting of rain on the truck hood and windshield. Surprisingly, the little passenger to his right was still asleep.

He opened the driver's side door and got out onto the gravel driveway. He hastily walked around to the other side and opened the door. As he reached inside, the cold rain splashed on his neck and ran down his back. He would definitely be investing in a hooded raincoat at his earliest opportunity.

He carefully lifted the sleeping bundle, pulling a blanket over the little one's head as he drew him from the truck. Clutching the youngster to his chest, he walked up the porch steps and into the house as an older gentleman in a bright yellow rain slicker walked around the house from the back carrying a large white sign.

The worker held the new sign up beneath the heavy cross beam, aligning the left hook first and latching it, and then moving to the right hook and latching that one as well. The man stepped back to take a look at the new sign.

MURPHY'S
Free
Spay & Neuter Clinic

Satisfied with his work, the man walked up the porch stairs and shook his rain slicker the best he could before opening the screen door and stepping inside.

The front room had been converted to a waiting room and a woman in scrubs was hanging a large bronze plaque on the wall. The worker stopped to read it solemnly.

THIS FACILITY IS MADE POSSIBLE
By:
The William Colbert Family Trust
The Millicent Wilson Family Trust
The Eugene Morgan Family Trust

Another woman stood behind the reception desk, talking to the red-headed man.

"Roger, come meet our Veterinarian," she said to the worker.

The older man extended his rough hand through the sleeve of his yellow rain coat and the Dr. turned around to greet him.

"Roger Pearson," said the older man.

"John Grassmeyer, said the Veterinarian. "It's a pleasure to see you again."

Realizing that the worker did not remember him, the younger man spoke.

"I used to bang on your door selling a variety of wonderful chocolate and popcorn treats to help support my Cub Scout troop!"

"Johnny! I thought I recognized the name and the hair! You sure have grown up. Are your folks still living outside of town?"

"Yes Sir, they are."

"Is your wife from these parts too?"

"Oh, I don't have a wife," smiled Johnny shyly.

Shaking his head, the worker said, "I could have sworn I saw you carrying a baby in with you."

Smiling broadly, Johnny walked over to where he had set down his sleeping baby.

Johnny bent over to lift the little one to his chest. "He looks a lot more like his mother," he said, opening the blanket fully.

There, beneath the red plaid woven blanket, slept a two-month-old black puppy with long wavy hair.

It was Flanders.

ABOUT THE AUTHOR

Chris studied Wildlife Biology in undergraduate college and went on to receive her Doctorate in Chiropractic. She is the founder of "Paws To Love Me," a non profit organization dedicated to the neuter/spay of dogs and cats nationwide. She and her two teenage sons live in northwest Arkansas with a house full of rescued animals.